THE 81st SITE

THE 81st SITE

by Tony Kenrick

NEW AMERICAN LIBRARY

TIMES MIRROR

NAL BOOKS TRADEMARK REG. U.S. PAT. OFF. AND FOREIGN COUNTRIES
REGISTERED TRADEMARK—MARCA REGISTRADA
HECHO EN CRAWFORDSVILLE, INDIANA, U.S.A.

SIGNET, SIGNET CLASSICS, MENTOR, PLUME, MERIDIAN
and NAL BOOKS are published by The New American Library, Inc.,
1633 Broadway, New York, New York 10019

Designed by Julian Hamer

First Printing, May, 1980

Library of Congress Cataloging in Publication Data

   Kenrick, Tony, 1935-
      The 81st site.

      I. Title.
   PZ4.K368Ei 1980 [PR9619.3.K49] 823 79-25645
   ISBN 0-453-00379-6

1 2 3 4 5 6 7 8 9

PRINTED IN THE UNITED STATES OF AMERICA

DEDICATION

For Bill Hackney and Tom Latham, absent friends.

ACKNOWLEDGMENTS

My thanks to Gordon Williams,
Air Vice-Marshal Harry Southgate (ret),
Captain Don West, and Christopher Impey.

"All things will pass away.
Nothing remaining but death and the glory of deeds."

—Adolf Hitler
quoting from the Scandinavian *Eddas*

PART ONE
THE SEARCH

Lauter—April 1945

The bombers, Junker 88s, were parked in neat, orderly rows on an airstrip not far from the Austrian border. There was no tarmac, no concrete, just a flat grassy field, part of which had been covered with tarpaulins to keep out the weather. The field was dry enough now, had been for some time, but the planes hadn't moved from their positions for two weeks.

Under the wing of one of the bombers a cow grazed on the new grass, which had pushed up from underneath its blanket of snow, long since melted. A cow on a Luftwaffe airfield! Somebody would get in trouble. Probably.

A chilly spring breeze skitted over the field, humming through the aircraft's aerials and tugging at a piece of fuselage torn where a Mustang's 20-mm shell had ripped through it weeks ago. The bomber parked next to it had its starboard engine mounted on a mobile winch waiting to be refitted. Of the ninety-two aircraft on the field it was the only one which wasn't operational, although, had there been an alert, there was no way any of those planes could have taken off and flown for more than a few miles.

One hundred yards away, the men who normally would have been bustling around the aircraft, revving up engines, loading bomb bays, feeding in long spaghetti strings of machine-gun bullets were playing at being builders, working on a new messhall for Kampfgeschwader 56. The bomber squadron didn't need a new messhall, but they had the materials, and the men had to be kept busy. Only the aircrews escaped the chores. They were like passengers on a boring, bad-weather cruise, waiting out the clock till mealtimes. They lounged around their wooden barracks rereading the same old magazines, walking outdoors to look up at the same empty gray sky, or watching the slow progress being made on the new messhall.

3

When the officer in charge of the work called a halt for the mid-morning break, the men lined up for hot cocoa, then stood together in little clumps, warming their hands on the tin cups; backs turned to the silent airfield, "the Museum," as somebody had christened it.

The mood was surly; they resented the work they were doing, men who'd been trained to send bomb loads five hundred miles and back reduced to the role of common laborers.

In one of the groups, a stocky, thick-shouldered man swirled the cocoa in his cup and squinted at it sourly. "Look at this stuff," he invited anybody who cared to listen. "Thin as piss and just about as tasty." He looked up as he heard somebody running toward them and snorted through his broken nose. "Well, well, if it isn't Ober-gefreiter Lauter. Now my day is perfect." He tossed his cocoa onto the ground as the running man came up, out of breath from his long jog across the field. With his cheeks flushed, two red spots glowing in their hollows, he looked younger than his nineteen years. He had a slim, bony face, a slim, bony body that seemed to be the wrong shape for the baggy blue-gray uniform he wore.

"Hans," he said, excited. "It's true. The rumor. I just heard."

The man he'd spoken to, a big, hulking farm boy about his own age, frowned at his friend. "What rumor?"

"Not that shit about the fuel again," the broken-nosed man said tiredly.

Lauter ignored him and burbled on to his friend. "The colonel's orderly told me himself. It's all true."

Again the other man commented. "The only rumor I want to hear is true is the one about our glorious leader."

The excitement fled from Lauter's face as he rounded on the man. "I warned you yesterday, Wyss. Any further derogatory references to the Fuehrer and I'm reporting you to Oberleutnant Hoffman."

The other man looked as if he'd bitten into something hard. He made a noise that was supposed to be a laugh, then addressed the group in general. "You hear that? The kid's threatening me with the fucking SS." He turned back quickly. "Lauter, you were born stupid. If it turned out that that madman in Berlin really is dead Hoffman would—"

He didn't get a chance to finish saying that Hoffman would buy the whole squadron a drink because Lauter, fury pounding in his face, was rushing at him.

He got only a few feet. With a fast sideways lunge, his friend, much bigger and stronger, grabbed him, smothering him in his arms. "Willie! Forget it, Willie!"

Lauter struggled wildly. "Let me *go!*"

"Yeah, let him go," voices called. A fight would have relieved the tedium a bit, although it wouldn't have been much of a battle. But they were disappointed. The farm boy wrestled Lauter away from the crowd, bundled him round behind a hut.

Lauter couldn't do anything but protest.

"Forget it, Willie. Wyss will kick your head in."

"I don't care. He's a *traitor.*"

The big youth held him locked in his grip for a few moments then said, "I'm going to let you go now, Willie. All right? You okay now?"

He slowly released his friend but kept a restraining hand on him. Lauter was panting with anger, but the blind rage was ebbing.

"Did you hear what he called him, Hans? The Fuehrer. The greatest German who ever lived. . . ."

"He'll keep, Willie. Tell me the news. What did you hear?"

Lauter let out a long breath, recovering slowly. He straightened his uniform as his friend released him, and as the anger drained from his face, his earlier excitement surged back.

"It's fantastic, Hans. We're being transferred. All of us. Over the border into Austria."

"Why? What's in Austria?"

"The flying bombs. They've built launching sites there. Hundreds of them, all in secret. We're being transferred to operate them. The orders just came through."

Hans, doubtful, swept an arm at the airstrip. "But what about the planes?"

"We're abandoning them. All available fuel is to go for the flying bombs. The V-1s." Lauter's eyes were dancing as he raced on. "It's brilliant, Hans. It's the Fuehrer's masterstroke. Our squadron and several others airlifted to Wels on Thursday. A week to be trained in launching procedure, then the next day it starts, five hundred flying bombs an hour, twenty-four hours a day, day in and day out. London will be leveled, obliterated, and the English will have to sue for peace. And they'll force the Americans and the Russians to do the same."

"But Willie." The big man groped for a way to put it kindly. "It sounds wonderful, Willie, but it just doesn't sound possible."

"The Fuehrer makes everything possible," Lauter said tightly. Then, gushing again: "Think of it, Hans. No more waiting around like sitting ducks for the raiders. *We'll* be the raiders. The sky will be black with flying bombs. London will be reduced to rubble, and the war will be won with a single massive stroke."

Hans dropped his eyes to the ground, said uncertainly, "I don't know, Willie. You know what rumors are like."

"But this one's true. The colonel's orderly said—" Lauter stopped as his ears caught the scratchy sound amplified over loudspeakers. It was followed immediately by the blaring of a bugle. The first few notes had hardly sounded before Lauter was talking again, more excited than ever. "General Assembly. I told you, Hans. They're going to announce it now. Come on."

He grabbed his friend and they started off at a trot. All around them men spilled out of huts and converged on the airstrip that doubled as a parade ground. Two corporals were already there, setting up a raised wooden dais on the edge of a perimeter road that was nothing more than a track worn flat by heavy trucks. Boots thumped over grass as a gray sea of men swarmed into the area, jamming themselves into a tight box shape. There was a fast dress, and the lines concertinaed. The parade-ground sergeant shouted orders at them, smartened them up, then turned toward the sound of an approaching motorbike. It wheeled in, stopped exactly in front of the dais; the driver hopped off, ran round, and opened the tiny door of the sidecar, and the commanding officer stepped out and mounted the dais.

He returned the salute of the assembled officers grouped behind him, then turned as the parade-ground sergeant brought the men to attention, heels clicking like gunshots.

The colonel was a tall, straight-backed man, popular with the men because he'd flown one hell of a Heinkel 177 before he'd flown a desk. He nodded to the sergeant who saluted, stood the men at ease, then waited like everybody else. The colonel didn't say anything for a moment but briefly checked the sky, an old flier's habit, then brought his attention back to his command. When he began to speak, his voice was steady, almost conversational, but nobody had any trouble hearing him; the ever-present wind carried his words.

"No doubt all of you have heard a rumor lately to the effect that the Fuehrer is dead. I am happy to report that I have no official confirmation of this." He paused for a moment, wanting to give weight to his next sentence. "And unhappy to report that neither do I have any official denial."

In the middle of the third rank, Lauter shook his head. "He's not dead," he muttered. "The Fuehrer isn't dead."

His friend Hans flicked his eyes at him, then looked back at the man on the dais.

"However, there is another rumor you may or may not have heard about I have just received definite information."

Lauter nudged his friend, excited. "Here it is," he whispered.

"And," the colonel went on, "it is for this reason I have called this assembly." He stopped and looked over the sea of faces waiting for his news. With no expression in his voice, he gave it to them. "I am extremely sorry to tell you that at eight o'clock this morning the German forces in Europe began to surrender."

There was a moment of iron silence, then a murmured word: "Surrender." It drifted up from the ranks, the faces opening. It was a rumor that had been heard and discounted, and its sudden confirmation was a stunning surprise. The men looked at each other, looked back at their commanding officer.

"The Russians are in Berlin, the American and English spearhead has crossed the Rhine. The enemy is advancing almost unchecked on all fronts. We have no means of stopping them without air support, and no chance of that because our fuel and supplies are exhausted. Furthermore, with no news as to the fate of the Fuehrer we are, for all intents and purposes, leaderless."

When the colonel paused again the parade ground was so quiet that they could hear the sound of the windsock as it filled and snapped in the breeze. The colonel coughed behind his hand, cleared his throat, and continued in the same flat tone.

"Germany fought well and bravely." He nodded at them. "You fought well and bravely. But victory has been denied us." He let that sink in then said slowly, "Gentlemen, the war is over."

He stood very still for a moment looking at them, then turned, stepped off the dais, and headed for the waiting sidecar.

The parade-ground sergeant, as stunned as everybody else, forgot to order a salute and instead, dismissed the men, the edge gone from his voice.

Nobody moved very far. They milled around in small groups, the consequence of the news slowly dawning on them. Most of the men had been in uniform for the last five years, and their life had seemed a permanent one; the thought of a stupendous change, like going back home, going back to a normal life, was too hard to grasp immediately.

Hans was staring at Lauter, trying to get his mind around it. "It's over, Willie. I can't believe it."

Lauter was looking at him but not seeing anything; his eyes glazed as if he'd been struck. He shook his head, bewilderment stinging his words. "It isn't possible. We can't have lost. How could we have lost?"

"I'll see my parents again," Hans said. "My sister, my brother." The big youth reached a hand out to Lauter's shoulder, smiled, said quietly, "It's over, Willie. The war is over."

Lauter's eyes focused, glared at his friend. He began to shake his head, and kept on moving it in steady denial. "The war can never be over," he said. "Not for me. Never."

CHAPTER TWO

Pelham—London, December 17, 1978

Pelham had chosen Luigi's over Inigo Jones's because she struck him as the kind of girl who'd go for atmosphere over fine cooking and service. At lunch, anyway. She also struck him as the kind of girl who was used to going to smart restaurants and wouldn't be bowled over by the sight of a flaming chafing dish.

The lunch had gone even better than he'd expected, and he'd been pleasantly surprised to find that she had a brain to go with the long, slim body. He nodded toward the espresso she'd just finished.

"How about another liqueur? It's cheaper than another coffee."

She held up a hand. "Thanks, but as it is I'm going to have trouble typing this afternoon."

Pelham studied the tiny flame fluttering on his Sambuco and said, seriously, "I've been giving some thought to that. You know, my mother always said you should never jump into the typing pool straight after a meal. You can get writer's cramp."

The girl, whose name was Rossi, smiled and said, "I think she was right, but what can I do?"

"You can come to my place and lie down."

Rossi wagged a finger at him. "I was warned about you. The first day I got to United General the girls said to watch out for Jimmy Pelham." She spoke with a slight accent, a pretty one, Swiss.

Pelham said, "Did they tell you I'd take you to lunch the first chance I got, then try to get you into the sack?"

Pelham spoke with an accent, too, an American one.

"The sack? Isn't that what they call it when you're asked to leave?"

"Yep. It's also what they call bed."

"It sounds like one could get you the other."

"Answer my question," Pelham demanded. "Is that what the girls told you about me?"

"You deny it, of course. . . ."

"Absolutely not. Guilty as charged."

Rossi laughed. "And you still expect me to go home with you?"

"Well, look at it this way," Pelham said. "All the other girls did. You wouldn't want to get a reputation for being a snob, would you?"

Rossi started a reply, stopped, and raised her hands in a helpless little gesture. "Do you always proposition girls this way?"

"No, sometimes I just hit them with a club." Pelham counted out money for the check, then pushed his chair back. "Well, shall we go?"

"Where?"

"I already told you. My place."

"But . . . what about the office?"

"Forget it. There's no place to lie down there."

"No, I mean, I'll get into trouble for not going back."

"Don't worry about it. If anybody gets into trouble it'll be me." He started to get up. "Come on, let's go."

She was still having trouble with it as he led her out of the restaurant. "But what excuse do I give them?"

"Tell them you went to a matinee," Pelham said.

As she allowed herself to be helped into a cab she said, a little befuddled, "This would never happen in Switzerland."

"Aren't you glad you moved?" Pelham asked.

There was quite a bit more to-ing and fro-ing between them, but the net result was, twenty minutes later, they were getting out of their clothes at Pelham's flat.

Rossi surprised him: she was one of those tall girls for whom clothes disguise a voluptuous body, the type that needs a swimsuit to look her best. Or nothing at all. There was an elegant length to her: long, slim legs, flat tummy, but hips that angled out sharply, full breasts that, without a bra, jutted and hung. Her dark blonde hair crowded her shoulders, a soft curtain that enclosed a face made up of a compendium of nice things: a wide mouth, dark eyes that, Pelham thought, were her best feature, if you had to discount the body, which was something he wasn't willing to do.

There were no surprises in the way she made love; it reflected her personality exactly—intelligent, warm, and with a sense of humor. But Pelham also found her very, very exciting: the soft, cushiony drive of her tummy, and the way she locked those long legs around him, and the trick she had of lifting her hips to meet him—he thought he was going to disappear whole into a grainy, silky oblivion.

He also liked the way she got back at him when they'd finished and were lying still. She said, deadpan, "Funny, I don't feel any different. I always thought I'd feel differently."

He looked at her in surprise. "You're kidding." He started to say more and then spotted the tiny curl of a smile on her mouth, grabbed a pillow and belted her with it.

Half an hour later they left his flat to put in a token appearance at the office. But when Pelham got to his desk, the afternoon was ruined for him.

"See me soon as poss," the note read. It was signed, "Evans."

"Shit!" Pelham said. He balled the note up and tossed it away. He'd been certain he wouldn't be missed; something must have come up. He sat down in his chair, drummed his fingers on the desk thinking about some kind of defense, decided the hell with it, got up, and started down the hall toward the stairs.

There was no elevator in the building; it was too old and narrow to have one. It was a five-story Georgian building on Floral Street, its original red brick darkened to a muddy shade of brown. It seemed out of place now, an insurance office in Covent Garden, with its smart new restaurants and shops opening up everywhere. It was as if, like the fruit and vegetable market, the time had come for the underwriters and the publishers and the lawyers to move on, too; to pack up and make room for the newer, trendier businesses. Pelham's firm had tried to keep pace with the changing neighborhood by having the place refurbished. They'd hired a decorator whose usual clients were ad agencies, and he'd given the place the look of a 1930s ocean liner. It received raves in decor magazines as being in advance of its time, but as far as Pelham was concerned, it accurately reflected the kind of forty-year-old thinking that went on there; outdated, behind the times.

John Evans, Pelham's boss, was a humorless, dried-out-looking man who fitted the office perfectly. In Pelham's opinion the guy approached his work as if he were sitting for some kind of exam, and didn't think for a moment, as Pelham did, that you could do a good job without letting it take over your life.

Pelham nodded to his secretary, a dumpy, middle-aged woman

who gave him a tight look of disapproval as he went by her into Evans's office.

"Hi. You wanted to see me?" Pelham asked.

"I wanted to see you two hours ago," Evans replied in his high, starched voice.

"I'm sorry. Something came up."

"Shut the door please."

Pelham sighed. "Oh, come on. It doesn't have to be one of those, does it?"

Evans leaned primly forward on his desk, his thin face pinched in. "Look here, Pelham. If you're going to have it off with the secretaries, please do it on your own time."

It was a small office, it was no use Pelham denying anything; all he could do was try to make light of it.

"Hell, you're making it sound like I took her to Paris for a week. It was just for a couple of hours on a slow afternoon."

Evans snapped at him. "Slow or fast, you're being paid by this company. The least you can do is be at your desk. Good God, if you'd got sozzled in a pub, that would be one thing, but your little escapades keep another employee late."

"What do you mean, escapades?" It was the last thing he should have asked and he knew it. The other man jumped into the opening.

"I mean this isn't the first time, is it? Not by a long shot. This is an insurance office, Pelham, not a pleasure garden in Arabia. Perhaps you're used to spending your afternoon like some Arabian sheik. Perhaps that's how they do things in America, but it's not how we do things here."

Pelham hated the position he was in, being bawled out by a cipher like Evans. The guy was a zero. He'd even managed to somehow circumvent the decorator; his office looked about as colorful as a bank vault. He bit down on his anger and shot back at him: "You know that must make the tenth time you've compared the two countries. You don't like the United States, do you, Mr. Evans? And you don't like Americans."

"My complaint has nothing to do with where you come from."

"Oh, yes it does," Pelham said, louder than he meant to; he was getting mad. "Half the people in this country cross themselves when they hear an American accent. I've been here three years and most of the time I've met with nothing but rudeness. Christ knows how the English became famous for politeness. I've never met a more ill-mannered bunch in my life. Get on a bus or a train, or go into any store, and they walk right over you, push you aside like they were playing rugby, and if you complain to any of them, all you get is a scandalized look for speaking before you've been properly introduced. Just give them a newspaper to bury their heads in and the telly to bury their brains in and they're happy. But don't, for God's sake, try to talk to them."

Evans had the tiniest smirk on his mouth, as if he'd scored points by getting Pelham mad enough to raise his voice and carry on. He said very quietly, as if to emphasize civilized behavior versus the other kind, "If you don't like it here, Pelham, why—"

"Why don't I go home. I've heard that a few hundred times. Oscar Wilde, isn't it?"

Evans let that go by; he wasn't going to acknowledge the insult, and Pelham knew why: because the boss doesn't have to argue, he can always use his ultimate weapon: rank.

The man leaned back in his chair and said in the same icy tone, "It can't go on, you know. Either you're working for this firm or you're not. Either you make an attempt to fit in, or you don't. So what's it going to be?"

Pelham would have given a hundred pounds to be able to tell him what he'd like it to be but he couldn't; he couldn't afford to put himself out on the street a week before Christmas. The job market was extremely tight, he'd already checked. And if he quit or was fired now he'd stay fired for a long time. It killed him but he knew he was going to have to let this guy put his foot on his neck.

"Look," Pelham said. "If you want me to admit I made a mistake, okay, I made a mistake. But it still comes down to a couple of hours off on an afternoon when I knew I wasn't going to be wanted."

Evans leaned forward quickly, pouncing; Pelham had walked into it again. "You *were* wanted this afternoon."

"For what?"

"There was an explosion in some houses under our cover. We needed a report and you weren't here."

Pelham frowned. "Me? That's Carson's department, that kind of thing."

"Carson's gone on holiday, as you'd know if you had the slightest interest in this firm."

Pelham let the comment go. "I still don't see how I could've helped you. I've done some fire adjusting but I was never an investigator."

"I said nothing about investigation. All we want is a preliminary report. And I'm sure you don't mean to tell me you've never done a report on an explosion before."

Pelham shrugged. "If you have a fire you often get an explosion with it."

"Exactly," Evans said, another point scored.

"What's so special about this one?"

"The client who owns the properties. A man named Henshaw, Roy Henshaw. There's a question mark against him."

"You've had trouble with him before?"

Evans picked up a neatly sharpened pencil and tapped it against a perfectly even thumbnail. "Let us say we've had our suspicions. That's why, when this came up, we wanted to get somebody on the spot immediately." He glanced meaningfully out of the window. "Before it started to get dark."

"And you want me to take a look at this place now . . ."

"If you'd be so kind."

Pelham took a breath and counted to three to hold onto his job. "Where is it?"

"Hayes."

"The hell's that?"

His boss passed over a slip of paper with an address on it. "Take a train to Bromley South, then a cab from there."

"Bromley? That's miles away. It'll take me a couple of hours."

"Think of it as the hours you owe us," Evans said. He pulled some forms toward him and began signing them, as if Pelham had already left.

Pelham scrunched the piece of paper into his pocket, turned and marched out, very close to turning around and going right back in and getting himself fired. He kept a grip on himself, stopped by his office for his topcoat, then went out into the rush-hour traffic. Finding a cab was out of the question, so he was forced to endure the crush of the Underground. The trip to Victoria didn't do a thing to elevate his angry mood, and his arrival there didn't help any, either; he ran into a wall of people weighed down with shopping bags, and a zillion members of the briefcase brigade. He bought a ticket, found the right train, which was about to leave, squeezed through the infuriatingly narrow barrier they always refused to open any wider, and climbed into the first compartment he came to. The people inside moved grudgingly for him, as if, with the whistle already blown, he wasn't entitled to join the train. But Pelham was used to the sullenness of London train travelers; a year back he'd met a woman whose husband had left her with a Cortina, two kids, and a small house in Blackheath, and he'd moved in with her and commuted for the two months the affair had lasted. He'd hated taking the train every day, the zombie express, as he'd called it. Once, getting into a compartment, he'd accidentally poked a man with the umbrella he'd been carrying. He'd apologized to him, then apologized again, but the man had just looked at him as if he'd just arrived from Mars. The Great English Train Silence. You could even poke them with sticks and they wouldn't say anything.

He thought about his situation, holding on to a luggage rack and staring moodily at the lights on the river as the train rattled over the Vauxhall Bridge. The age-old question popped into his mind: if he didn't like it why didn't he go back to where he came from? The crazy thing was he did like it, or had liked it when he'd first arrived. But after three jobs, two of which he'd been thrown out of, London didn't appear to like him. And it wasn't getting much fonder of him; his days in his present job were clearly numbered. The hell of it was there was nothing else out there; around Christmas everybody sat tight. And he knew that things weren't exactly booming in New York, either, not for a guy with his meager qualifications: a thirty-eight-year-old middle management insurance man—dime-a-dozen stuff. What it came down to was pretty simple: he couldn't afford to lose this job, not with *his* bank balance. And that, he realized, put him squarely in the same boat as most of his fellow train passengers, who were probably trying to hold on to jobs they weren't crazy about either. He let his eyes sweep over them; some of the ones sitting down had surrendered to the soporific motion of the train, heads lolling, mouths open, while just about everybody else had found something fascinating in a newspaper. Pelham knew he was wrong to sneer, he was no better himself. He had to nine-to-five it too, and just because he went to the movies instead of watching the box, and slept with a different chick every week and ate in a lot of Italian restaurants didn't really place him in a higher category.

About the only thing he found to celebrate about his present position was that the train was an express and, fifteen minutes later, he was on Bromley South station joining the bottleneck filing up the stairs to the street. The cab rank was right outside, and he had to line up, which was another local custom he disliked. It was a national pastime to line up for things, and while he supposed it was a fair method of taking one's turn, he'd always found it demeaning, like shuffling forward for chow in the army. But the cabs came fast enough, which was a good thing because, as Pelham got into one, the rain that had been threatening all day finally arrived.

When he gave the driver the address the man said, "You'll be lucky to get near it, sir. Fire engines, police, crowds of people."

"Let's give it a try anyway," Pelham said.

The driver started down the ramp and waited there for a chance to join the traffic in the main road. He was an older man, the cheerful kind, and wanted to chat.

"Terrific explosion. I was stopped at a light in Shortlands Road and I could hear it from there, and that's a good five miles away."

Pelham asked him what it had sounded like.

"Like a clap of thunder, only longer. I don't think there's a window left in the entire street."

"What time did it happen?"

"Funny thing. I'd just looked at my watch and the next minute, boom. Twenty to four, it was. You could see the flames, too. At least until the fire brigade got there. Five dead so far. When those gas mains go . . ." The man sucked at his teeth. "Some of those fire inspectors spend too much time in the boozer, if you ask me."

He stopped talking and concentrated on easing his cab into the traffic. Pelham sat back and watched the high street unfold; it seemed to him to be a duplicate of any other he'd ever seen: the modern supermarket, he ancient greengrocers, the menswear store with dull, drab-colored suits, the TV rental store next to the Wimpey bar next to the Building Society office opposite its competitor, the branch bank across the road. A furniture store with English modern Danish in the window, a carpet store offering discounts on linoleum and hideously patterned broadloom. Was it really so different to suburban New York? Perhaps not in content, but in tone there was all the difference in the world.

He caught himself comparing the two cities again. He had to stop doing that and start accepting the fact that there was no nirvana; that there were pluses and minuses wherever you lived. It was just that lately the minus sign against London had become bigger and bigger.

The taxi climbed a small hill and the shops petered out, replaced, after a while, by some handsome period houses separated by low hedges. They traveled a mile, then took a fork road that led past some school playing fields, then bisected a scrubby common. On the other side houses began again, and Pelham could see the crowd up ahead, lights blinking on cars, fire engines, police everywhere. He asked the driver to come back for him in an hour's time, tucked up the collar of his topcoat, and got out into the slight drizzle. He moved through the crowd to where the police had set up temporary wooden barriers, then was stopped by what he saw.

The street was bordered on both sides by two-story stucco houses, almost identical in design, which could have been built at the turn of the century. They had high-pointed gables, a suggestion of gingerbread under the eaves, and new picture windows looking out on tiny front gardens. The houses, separated only by narrow side passages, had no garages, and many of the gardens had been filled in with multicolored crazy paving to make a parking spot for a car. Pelham had been expecting to see a ruin, but nothing like this: three houses were missing from the row on one side, missing completely like a gap in a picket fence. The houses on each side of the gap had lost their exterior walls, and their entire sides were exposed. They looked curiously neat, like doll houses, the downstairs living rooms and upstairs bedrooms and bathrooms differing only in the pattern of their wallpapers. But, in shocking contrast, the area where the wrecked houses had once stood was a crazy mélange of destruction. Thousands of bricks lay strewn around, not in large sections but individually, as if they'd never been mortared and built as walls. Pipes and steel girders and support frames were bent and severed, mixed in with furniture, blackened flooring, chunks of plaster, everything crushed or splintered, twisted or burnt out of shape.

Gray ghosts of smoke hung in the air and a frying, sizzling sound came from water dripping on still-hot metal. The smell of burnt rubber and plastic rode acridly over that of charred wood and scorched fabric.

The entire scene was lit by spotlights rigged up to a generator, and gave the wreckage a brilliant, shiny look. The houses directly opposite, lying in shadows, had had their fronts staved in by the blast, and Pelham counted five cars tumbled on their sides, looking like dead insects. He moved toward the wreckage until a policeman stopped him.

"It's okay," Pelham said. "I'm here on business."

The constable told him to check with Inspector somebody and pointed him out, one of a group of men who were poking around in the ruins, sifting through things. Near them some firemen with some kind of listening device were digging under the rubble.

The man Pelham went up to wore a stiff brown topcoat with a felt hat pulled down low on his head, giving him a slightly military look. Pelham identified himself. "I'm with United General. These properties belong to a client of ours."

"What's left of them," the inspector said. He didn't even look at Pelham's business card.

"How many dead?"

"Five. Still two people unaccounted for, but they may have been elsewhere."

"Let's hope so," Pelham said. "I'd like to look around if it's okay with you."

The policeman glanced at him briefly. "Look, but don't touch." He seemed annoyed about something.

Pelham thanked him and began to pick his way into the wreckage. He followed the path the firemen had made earlier, his shoes squelching in water as he went round the exposed side of one of the houses. Close up, the damage was even more appalling; most of what had been metal was either curled or warped or fused into unrecognizable shapes, and anything of wood looked like a burnt-out campfire, or was shredded and torn like matchwood. Water from the firehoses still dripped everywhere, and a chemical foam had dried on the rubble like salt left by a high tide. But there were still a few things that names could be given to: half a headboard, the blackened frame of an aluminum folding chair, a huge jagged piece of what once might have been a wash basin, a dented saucepan. Pelham carefully stepped up onto a small mountain of masonry where he could get a better view. When he'd first seen the wreckage he'd immediately had his suspicions about something and now, from his vantage point, his suspicions were confirmed. He clambered down again and continued his tour, working his way around to the rear of the ruined houses. A low, heavy wire fence had originally separated one of the houses from its neighbor, and on the side he was on several yards of it were still standing, although it had been blown over at a crazy angle. It was while he was trying to get by this that he saw it: something stuck in the webbing of the fence. It had been hurled sideways with such force that it had penetrated the wire and been held there.

It was probably its peculiar position that intrigued Pelham, and the fact that he couldn't figure out what in the world it could be. He took hold of it, put his foot against the sagging fence, and worked the object from side to side, finally tugging it loose. It was a bent metal frame about eighteen inches square in which were set four bands of what looked like louvers. At first Pelham thought it might be some of the innards from a washing machine, but he changed his mind when he saw the brand name etched into the frame; part of the brand name anyway—one corner of the frame was missing and the name was incomplete. Whatever it was it was ruined, and he tossed it down and went on with his examination.

By picking his way and being careful he was able to circle the area and get a look at the other side, but there was nothing over there except more of the same devastation. The firemen were wrapping up their equipment as he came back to where he'd started. The crowd had grown, swollen by people who'd probably driven miles when they'd heard the news. The inspector was still standing where Pelham had left him, a big, beefy man talking to him with a lot of arm movement. Pelham saw the policeman nod in his direction, and the other man jerk his head around as Pelham came toward him. He spoke loudly when Pelham was still twenty feet away, thrusting a belligerent finger at him. "You the johnny from the insurance?"

"That's right."

"What're you goin' to do about all this, then?" He encompassed the ruins with a sweep of his arm, glaring at Pelham as if it were all his fault.

The inspector made a grudging introduction. "This is Mr. Henshaw, the owner of the properties."

"Bloody right. Roy Henshaw, that's me. And I'm standin' here wantin' to know what happens now." He snorted out breath through a veined, bulgy nose, and bit down on stained teeth. He wore a loud plaid topcoat, a red silk tie, a flashy ring on both little fingers. Pelham was willing to bet he drove a twelve-cylinder Jaguar with fleecy leopard-skin seat covers.

"What you do is file a claim form," Pelham told him.

The man shot out a lumpy hand. "Give it over, then."

Pelham said tiredly, "I don't carry them with me. Contact the office. They'll send you one."

"Bleedin' right I'll contact the office. *Look* at this lot."

"You'll need a tenant list and an up-to-date inventory," Pelham said, preparing to leave.

"I knew you'd say that," Henshaw said. "I went right home and got 'em both, soon as I heard." He pulled stapled sheets of paper from his jacket, thrust them at Pelham, then jerked his thumb at the inspector. "He's got the tenant list."

Pelham asked if he could see it, and the policeman passed it over without a word. Pelham scanned it, then stopped when a name jumped out at him. There was a cross against it which meant that the person had been killed in the explosion.

"Bolan." He looked up. "Irish?"

The inspector, who'd kept himself on the fringe of the exchange, was suddenly interested. "Why do you ask?"

Pelham told him. "Because I don't think this was a gas main explosion."

"What?" Henshaw said.

"Why not?" the inspector asked. He was watching Pelham intently.

"Because the blast went sideways. If it had been a gas main the blast would have gone up, not out."

"Hey!" Henshaw pushed his face at Pelham and breathed scotch at him. "What the fuck are you sayin'?" His words went formal for a moment. "If you have any information about what it was destroyed my property, I got a right to know."

"My guess," Pelham said calmly, "is high explosives. I'd say that somebody in the center house, one of your tenants maybe, was fooling around with dynamite."

"*Dyn*amite?" Henshaw's head snapped back as he repeated the word and a look of fright flared in his eyes.

"What do you know about this guy Bolan?" Pelham asked.

"Rented the basement floor. Seemed a quiet sort of bloke."

"Where was he from?"

The big man's eyes crinkled. "The inspector just asked me that. What's all this about Bolan, then? And dynamite?"

"Was he Irish?"

"Irish, right. Brogue you coulda cut with a knife." Then Henshaw's face fell open as his slow mind made the connection. "IRA? Bolan was IRA?" Scandalized, he looked back and forth between Pelham and the inspector. "You sayin' the bastard blew it all up?"

Pelham shrugged lightly. "Somebody sure did. If it was Bolan he must have been planning on blowing up half of London."

Henshaw wheeled on the policeman. "How about it? Is the Yank right?"

The answer was officially neutral. "I can't comment until I have a complete report." But it was enough for Henshaw. The landlord's face seem to swell as if he were choking.

"The *bastard!*" he spat out. "The Irish pig *bastard!* I should never of let to him, never. I won't have no spades or pakis stinkin' up the street with their stinkin' curries, but I never drew the line at Irish like some. I'm too bleedin' kindhearted for my own good, that's my trouble, and see what it gets me. The fucker goes and blows up three of me houses."

The inspector's voice was weighted heavily with distaste. "I wouldn't go jumping to conclusions, if I were you. We have to complete a full investigation before we can attach blame. Until then I would advise you to remember the libel laws." He nodded stiffly at both of them and moved away.

Henshaw, watching him, very much aware of the higher class putdown, said, "Libel my arse." He swung back to Pelham. "I'm covered on every bleedin' thing in there. If a tenant wants to fuck around with a bomb it ain't my fault and it ain't God's. I get my money."

Pelham was slowly flipping through the inventory. "How current is this?"

"I brought it up to date a week ago."

"A week, huh? Good timing."

Henshaw's face went flat. In a pub fighter's gesture he slid his meaty palms down the sides of his topcoat. "What're you gettin' at? I bring it up to date once a month. Otherwise the bleeders steal me blind."

As if he hadn't heard him Pelham said, "I don't see the Arga stove listed here."

"The what?"

"The Arga stove."

When Henshaw laughed, the whiskey breath poured out thickly. "No, and you won't either." His face tightened again. "What, you mean one of them heavy iron buggers your grandmother used? Nothing in them properties was more than two years old. Fridges, cookers, boilers, the lot. Cost me a friggin' fortune." He snorted contempt. "Arga stove. Bullshit!"

Pelham folded the inventory and tucked it into his jacket. "I'll hold on to this, okay?" He started to move off. "File your claim, Mr. Henshaw, and we'll be in touch."

"You better be." The big man added an exclamation point with a jab of his finger, then when he saw that Pelham was walking back toward the wreckage, said, "Here. Where you goin'?"

Pelham didn't answer. He picked his way around the debris following the track he'd used before, walking around to where the low wire fence sagged against the side of the exposed house. He found the metal frame, the one he'd pulled out of the wire, and took another look at it. He saw, with intense satisfaction, that he hadn't been wrong: at the top of the frame were the letters ARG, the rest missing, where the corner had been torn off. He carried it back with him and found Henshaw still standing there watching him narrowly.

"What you got there, then?"

"Just a little souvenir."

"That's private property. *My* property."

"That's what I'm counting on," Pelham answered, walking by him.

Henshaw made no attempt to stop him, but shouted after him, "It won't do you no good."

Pelham kept moving to the ring of people who looked curiously at Pelham and the thing he was carrying. So did the constable Pelham had spoken to before.

"It's okay," Pelham said easily. "The inspector said I could take it."

The constable nodded and Pelham went by him, slipped through the crowd, and had to wait only a few minutes for the taxi.

It took him longer to get back to London than it had coming, but this time he enjoyed the trip.

CHAPTER THREE

Pelham—London, December 18, 1978

The laboratory that Pelham went to the next morning was situated off Theobalds Road in a curious area made up partly of fine town houses converted into offices, and partly by small factories and beans-on-toast cafés. Pelham had never been to the lab before, but he knew it was supposed to be the best in London, and that it did a lot of investigatory work for insurance firms, as well as certain jobs for the police and the military.

Sitting in the waiting room, he was warmed by the thought of Evans, back at the office, wondering where he was at nine forty-five in the morning. He was looking forward to walking in, cutting off the man's tirade, and handing him Henshaw's head on a platter. There was little doubt in Pelham's mind that the landlord was guilty as hell. He didn't think that he'd had anything to do with the explosion, only that he'd seized a chance to claim for merchandise and fittings that had never been in those houses. If Pelham could prove it, he could probably force Henshaw to drop all claims entirely, save the company a bundle, and emerge a hero. But it all depended on the lab's report, and they'd had the thing for the best part of an hour now.

He picked up a magazine from a table and flipped through it impatiently for a few minutes, tossed it down, and was getting to his feet as a door opened and a short bald man came in. He was wearing a dark blue lab jacket and carried in his hand the frame that Pelham had given him. He said, a little sheepishly, "I'm afraid we haven't made much progress. About the only thing I can tell you is that it's definitely not part of a stove. And it couldn't be the brand you mention anyway because the name is spelt A-G-A. It's pronounced as if there should be an R in it, but there isn't."

Pelham closed his eyes and winced. "Goddammit! You sure?"

"We've been on to some other stove manufacturers and described the object but they say there's nothing remotely like it in anything they make. Or ever has been." ·

"I was certain it was a vent of some kind," Pelham said. "And with that name on it . . ."

The lab man put the frame on the magazine table and held it upright. "It was a sensible guess. We checked our brands book and found a couple of firms with those three letters in their name, but none of them work in metal."

"Could it be part of some other appliance? An old refrigerator, maybe."

The other man looked unhappy. "Frankly, we're a bit stumped on this one. These metal flanges here suggest some kind of valve system; you can see how they're hinged. Of course, if the piece were intact, instead of being so damaged, its function would be easier to guess. But as it is I'm afraid we have no real idea what it's supposed to do, and therefore can't guess what it could have been part of." The lab man, seeing the effect his words were having on his client, tried to introduce a ray of sunshine. "However, there are one or two facts we've been able to ascertain. Whatever this thing is it was manufactured thirty or forty years ago at least. The metal tells us that. And see this blackened part across the center? That's new, so it's certain it was caused by the blast. The opinion is it was very close to the blast. Also, it was definitely intact at the time of the explosion."

"I see," Pelham said. He didn't sound thrilled.

"One other thing." The lab man turned the frame on its side. "There are some more initials, harder to see than the others. Did you notice them?" He was pointing to the other side of the torn corner.

Pelham squinched his eyes up and read them out. ". . . Erke. That mean anything to you?"

"We think it could be *werke*, German for works."

Pelham's head came up fast. "Then maybe it's part of an old refrigerator or something that was made in Germany years ago."

The other man began to wrap the frame in the brown paper Pelham had brought it in. It made a sad, dispirited sound. "It's possible, although I wouldn't hold out much hope. I doubt very much that it's part of a home appliance. However," he pushed the parcel across the table, "there is one other thing you could do. There's a man we sometimes use when we need an opinion on something foreign. He's German, incidentally, so he may be able to help you on this."

The man handed over a card that Pelham took, although he didn't want it; if the thing wasn't part of an appliance he wouldn't have a case.

He thanked the lab man, went out onto the sidewalk, and stood there, despondent. He looked at the card in his hand; an address on the Harrow Road. What was the point of going miles out of the way if the thing he was carrying was part of a duct from a German-made boiler, or something, which had been installed when Henshaw had been toddling round in diapers? Pelham swore; he was back to square one, an ace away from being thrown out on his ear.

He found himself walking toward a pub a few yards down the block. He pushed at the door, then pulled at it until he realized it was too early for it to be open. Sixty years back the government had restricted pub hours in order to get the munition workers back to the factories sober, and the same laws were still in force; another little irritant to living in this country. "They'll always be an England," Pelham said out loud, giving the door a final shove.

An empty cab was coming up the road and Pelham flagged it down, stepped up to the driver's window. He was about to say Covent Garden when he changed his mind. "What the hell," he said. "The Harrow Road."

"Aw, shit!" the driver said, a young man already fat. That was another thing that had changed in London, the rude cabbies who drove like bullets. Morosely, Pelham wondered if the reason he was taking such a thrashing was because the London he'd come back to live in, after a visit ten years before, was no longer there. Maybe that was why he was so out of it: London had simply changed the way everything changes, and the town he remembered no longer existed.

He was still brooding about it when the cab eventually made it to the address on the Harrow Road. The place turned out to be a foreign-car service garage, with its entrance around the corner on a side street. It was big and cavernous, full of expensive sports cars, mechanics buried in their open hoods. One of them was revving a Maserati, taking it all the way up and filling the garage with its roar. He wore greasy, double-breasted coveralls and a hat made of newspaper, and he sang along to the car's radio, which was blaring almost as loudly as the engine. It could have been a garage in France or Italy.

Pelham walked by a Porsche Turbo, all black including the chrome, and wondered where some people got the money. The mechanic working on it told him where he could find the boss, and Pelham went up a rickety iron stairway to an office overlooking the repair shop. The door was half open and he could see a desk covered with yellow dockets, the man behind it working an old-fashioned adding machine.

"Mr. Shotze?" Pelham asked.

The man peered at Pelham, mistaking him for a client, and tried to remember what car went with his face.

Pelham introduced himself, told him about the lab sending him over, and apologized for not calling ahead.

"Not at all," the man said. "I'll be happy to help if I can." He spoke perfect English with only a slight accent, but he was unmistakably German: gray hair clipped short, pale eyes, and strong, flat features. Pelham thought he might have been fifty-five or so. He stood the frame on the man's desk and began to unwrap it.

"I've got a toughie for you. I have something here but I don't know what it is or what it's from, and I'd like to. The lab figures it could have been made in Germany."

He stripped the rest of the brown paper away and lifted the frame out.

The German had no reaction for a moment, then slowly rose from his chair.

Pelham pointed his finger. "You can see a piece of a name here, ARG. There's also part of another word here, where the corner's torn. I originally thought ARG stood for Arga."

Shotze was staring at the frame, a strange expression on his face. He looked up and said, "Where did you get this?"

"That's a bit confidential. The point is, can you identify it? Is it anything you've ever seen before?"

"Yes it is," Shotze answered. "I just never thought I'd see one again."

"Is it part of a German refrigerator?" Pelham wasn't trying to influence the man, he just couldn't help asking.

"A refrigerator? No. But it was made in Germany. By the Argus Motorwerke. What you thought was Arga is Argus."

"Argus," Pelham repeated. "Okay, but you still haven't told me what it is."

"It's a valve box," Shotze said. He seemed mesmerized by the object.

"From a heating system?"

The German shook his head. "No, the Argus firm built things like submarine motors, torpedoes, and aircraft engines." He moved his hands over the metal flanges, hinging them back and forth. "What you have here is what's left of the flap valve inlet of an Argus pulse jet."

Pelham squinted at him; it didn't make sense. "That thing's from a jet engine?"

"A pulse jet, remember. Nothing like you're thinking of. These flanges here operate and close to admit air to the combustion chamber." Shotze nodded, confirmed his opinion. "It's from an Argus pulse jet, no question about it." He looked up. "You've found yourself a nice little war souvenir."

"What do you mean?"

The man gave a little shrug. "The Argus jet was only built for one thing, and never used for anything else. It was the propulsion unit for the Fieseler."

"The Fieseler?"

"The V-1. The flying bomb. It did a lot of damage to London. Carried something like a ton of high explosives. It made thousands of people homeless."

The phone rang and Shotze excused himself and picked it up. He didn't notice the look on his visitor's face.

The understanding shocked through Pelham, rocked him like a slap in the mouth. "My God," he said under his breath. "Somebody's trying to start up World War II again."

CHAPTER FOUR

Lauter—Munich, 1933-1955

Born as he was in the mid-twenties, Willie Lauter grew up at a time when the young in Germany were influenced by their elders to an extraordinary degree. But even so, the influence his father, Hervig Lauter, had over his son Willie was exceptional even for that era. Hervig Lauter had become famous in Fürstenfeldbruck, a small, semirural village on the outskirts of Munich, for his political foresight. In 1919 he'd been one of the twenty-five people who'd been privileged to hear the first speech ever delivered in public by Adolf Hitler. He'd also been one of the first to shake him by the hand and congratulate him on his thinking. By the time Willie Lauter was seven years old, the man his father had applauded that night in a Munich beer hall was chancellor of Germany, and Willie was brought up in a house devoted to this heaven-sent savior. His photograph and his flag adorned the walls. The saga of his brilliant rise from obscurity took the place of fairy tales. And the soft, sad Horst Wessel song was Willie's only lullaby. As Willie grew older, he continued to be a model German child. At age twelve his essay on National Socialism won a prize. At fourteen he was the leader of the village Hitler Youth, and went regularly to Munich or Nuremberg to attend the pulse-pounding rallies, and screamed himself hoarse when the Fuehrer assured them of triumph, should the Fatherland have to defend itself.

It was a great day when, in 1943, Willie was at last old enough to enlist in the Luftwaffe, and he went off to the war supremely confident of victory. The concept of there being any serious reversal to the Fuehrer's march to glory was ludicrous, and even when he saw the bombers he'd helped send off in the cold dawns returning shot to pieces, their numbers decimated, no replacements forthcoming, and the fuel starting to dry up, it still never occurred to him that it could be anything more than a temporary setback.

So when he'd heard the rumor about the squadron being transferred to Austria to launch the V-1s on London in a final victorious onslaught, he knew that this was what he'd been waiting for.

He'd had no way of dealing with the news that had arrived in its stead; there was no slot in his brain that would accept the idea of a German defeat.

When he'd been demobilized and had arrived back in Fürstenfeldbruck, the villagers were astounded by the change in him.

Hervig Lauter was a changed man, too; father and son both silent and morose. Each felt they'd let the other down; Hervig because the glorious dream he'd told his son about all these years had burst like a bubble. Willie because the magnificent military machine he'd been part of had been humbled.

Hervig became ill six months after the war ended, an illness that in an earlier day he could have easily shrugged off. But with his spirit broken, he faded away within a year. Helga Lauter, her husband dead and her son like a sleepwalker, couldn't seem to find her place in things and joined Hervig in the family plot less than twelve months later.

To Willie the death of his parents seemed a logical ending to the whole disaster, and he felt that his life was running down, too. Germany was devastated, any kind of food a luxury, the entire country creeping painfully along like a thing with a broken spine. Better to end its misery, better to end his own. He seriously contemplated killing himself, and would have but for the fact that he knew it would have been wrong. The Fuehrer had killed himself, but he'd died a soldier's death, taken his own life so as not to suffer the indignity of falling into enemy hands. But he, Willie Lauter, had no such excuse. In fact, the more he thought about it, the more he came to realize that his original reaction to the surrender was the correct one. He was still a soldier of the Third Reich, still able-bodied, still capable of carrying on the fight. The words of the Fuehrer came back to him, words the Fuehrer had pronounced during his last hours in the bunker. "Those who remain alive after the battles are over are inferior persons since the best have fallen."

It was true. Lauter was ashamed of being alive, and he became determined to put an end to his shame.

By continuing the struggle.

Slowly his sense of defeat and hopelessness was replaced by a slow-growing anger that Germany, the Fuehrer, his parents, his friends had been brought to such an ignoble end. And there wasn't the slightest doubt who was to blame. Not the Americans, not the Russians, but the English.

The Fuehrer had realized very early who the real enemy was; that's why he'd gone as a young man and lived for six months in Liverpool. He'd used the time to study the English, to get to know what made them tick. The Fuehrer had found them a stubborn and proud people, and their pride seemed to be centered on London, probably because it had been the capital of the world for hundreds of years. The Fuehrer had been right to try to destroy that pride and sap their will to fight. "It's their London that they love," he'd cried, defending his strategy of the Blitz. And it had almost worked, would have worked if they'd had the fighter strength to combat the RAF; would have worked if they'd had air cover to protect the V-1 and the V-2 sites.

So it became extremely clear to Lauter where his duty lay now: he had to find a way to finish the job the Fuehrer had started.

It seemed impossible, of course, one man continuing the war. But was anything really impossible if you wanted it badly enough? Wasn't it impossible that a postcard painter from a small village in Austria had, in only fourteen years, risen to be a conqueror greater than Caesar or Alexander? And yet that had happened, because the Fuehrer made it happen. And he, Willie Lauter, could do the same for his dream. All he had to do was pursue it with a similar single-mindedness and intensity, and let nothing ever sway him.

Nothing.

So Willie Lauter, filled with a glorious new purpose, began a new life at the age of twenty-five.

He sold his father's business, and the house, and moved into Munich to be close to people, sources, information. He got a job as a clerk in the headquarters of a firm that manufactured steel by-products and found an apartment in an old building on Luisenstrasse. From there he would walk to work each morning, to an office that quickly accepted him as a reliable, meticulous worker who rarely spoke and seemed to have no life outside of the business. He was a pale, slim young man, his straw-colored hair severely parted in the center, quite nice looking but seemingly impervious to shy glances from any of the young secretaries. One of the reasons Lauter had taken a job at that particular firm was because it was close to the public library. It was the newer books that interested him; he read everything pertaining to the war he could get his hands on, but found that such books were coming out only in a trickle, not surprising in a country that had been defeated.

On the other hand the English couldn't seem to read enough about their victory, and the shelves in the English-language section of the library were jammed. Even though the sight of all those bragging, chest-beating volumes filled Lauter with a cold rage, he knew that he needed them. So with a constant and steady application he taught himself English, a Germanic language, as he found out with bitter pride.

His life fell into an unswerving pattern: he'd go to the office, where he'd put in a solid morning's work, spend lunchtime at the library poring over histories of the war in both languages, return to the office for the afternoon, then go home to his apartment. After a quick dinner he'd lie on his bed and dream his dreams of revenge. At first his thoughts were wild fantasies; he'd imagine incredible things like traveling to Montevideo where there were hundreds of thousands of Germans, gathering around him a circle of like-thinking men, then somehow refloating the *Graf Spee*, scuttled in the River Plate in 1940, get it operational again and sail it, in a forty-knot dash, across the Atlantic right into the Thames estuary and level London with its fourteen-inch guns.

Or with fifty handpicked commando pilots take over a sleepy peacetime American air force base, load up fifty bombers, take off for London, and rain death and destruction down on the crowded lunchtime streets.

He tempered these fantasies by continuing to learn as much about the war and its conduct as he could, hoping that some hitherto unknown fact might spark his brain into developing a plan. He made an arrangement with a bookstore specializing in books in English: any volume that concerned the war was immediately sent to him. By keeping up his lessons, and constantly reading the new material, Lauter became proficient in English and no longer had to plod laboriously through the books with a German-English dictionary in hand.

It was such a rigid life he'd slipped into that time passed quickly and he was mildly surprised to find one day that he'd reached his twenty-ninth birthday. It seemed that the only thing he had to show to mark each year's passing was a larger collection of books, and a frown that had become deeper in his face. The disappointment and frustration of not being able to formulate a plan had taken its toll, and he'd become, as one person at his office had described him, a young-old man.

But Lauter never lost his dream; if anything, his dream of revenge burned brighter than ever as he saw that the German people had put the shame of defeat behind them, as if it were ancient history. He could understand perhaps, although not forgive, those who had been civilians acting in this way, but the millions of men who'd served under the Fuehrer, what possible excuse could they have? But his sense of outrage brought him no closer to any plan of action, and he was beginning to think that he was doomed to carry out his revenge solely inside his head until one evening a chance encounter changed everything.

Lauter had been on his way home from the office when he heard somebody call his name. He assumed it was somebody he worked with, because he had no friends, had no time to socialize, needing every minute to read and plan and scheme.

"Willie? Willie Lauter?"

Lauter didn't recognize the man.

"It's me. Kinderlen. Artur Kinderlen."

Lauter nodded, the name ringing a bell. Of course, Artur Kinderlen.

They'd been in the Luftwaffe together, in the same barracks during basic training.

"I almost went by you," the man said. "You've changed so much I wasn't sure it was you."

"You've changed, too," Lauter said, which wasn't true. Now that he was getting a good look at Kinderlen the man seemed almost exactly as he remembered him, and he remembered him as a neat, meticulous person who always had the shiniest shoes, the best pressed uniform, the best made bed in the barracks. He looked older now, of course, but still had the same strict neatness about him that showed in the perfectly fitting blue suit he wore, the tie and handkerchief just so.

"You live here in Munich?"

"Yes. And you?" Lauter asked.

"Frankfurt. I'm here on business."

There was a pause, then Kinderlen said, with a gusto he didn't really feel, "Well, this is wonderful running into you like this. You're not, by any chance, free for dinner are you? I'm catching a late train back. It'd be a nice way to fill in the time."

Lauter said lamely, "I'm not sure if, er—"

"Come along," Kinderlen said, taking his arm. "We've got a lot to catch up on. Do you like the Storchhaus? Excellent sauerbraten."

Lauter didn't want to go; there was a new book that might have arrived at his apartment he was anxious to see, but he allowed himself to be led. The book would still be there after dinner. Kinderlen, chatting amiably, steered him to a place Lauter had seen only from the outside, a quiet, dark-paneled restaurant where the waiters wore tails. When they were seated, Kinderlen ordered for them both, waved away Lauter's refusal of a drink, sat back, and looked at him.

"I can't get over it, Willie."

"Over what?"

"You're so different. I remember you bouncing around the barracks a ball of fire. I know that's some time ago but, well, you've changed."

"Germany changed," Lauter said flatly.

"Yes," the other man said, moving a fork an inch to his left. "Of course. But there's a new future ahead of us now."

A waiter arrived with steins of dark beer. When he'd gone, Lauter said, "It's not the future that was supposed to be."

Kinderlen picked up his beer, then put it down again. He said, not unkindly, "You were the most patriotic of all of us, Willie. I remember. But the war's over now."

"For some," Lauter replied.

His host frowned. "I don't understand."

"Very few of you do," Lauter muttered, and shook his napkin out.

There was an awkward moment that Kinderlen tried to cover by lifting his stein. "Health," he said.

Lauter repeated the word but only sipped at his drink.

Searching for safer ground, Kinderlen asked Lauter what had happened to him after the war, about his present job, and whether he was married. When that quickly dried up Kinderlen was starting to regret the dinner invitation; Willie Lauter had become a dull, morose person with no conversation, no personality. The arrival of some food saved any further struggle at conversation, which was something Lauter was happy about, too. He also regretted the invitation; Kinderlen was obviously one of those fools for whom the defeat in 1945 meant nothing more than an end to the hostilities, and a chance to get back home and start making money. Watching him eat his food, Lauter could plainly see that the man was prosperous, in his excellently cut suit and with that expensive gold watch on his wrist. He ate exactly the way he dressed: correctly, even nattily. He remembered Kinderlen more clearly now, when he'd been with him at flying school. A math brain, an astonishing ability at mental arithmetic, and in a class by himself at navigation.

"You became a pilot, I assume?" Laughter asked.

Kinderlen was grateful for the opening. "No, I didn't, as a matter of fact. I had it here," he pointed to his head, then placed a hand on his stomach, "but not down here. I just wasn't physically cut out to be a flier. So with my talent for figures they made me a quartermaster."

"That was a waste," Lauter said, and meant it. He forked up some food and chewed slowly; it was very good. It was a long time since he'd had cooking like it and he felt guilty. The wine in baskets, the chafing dishes aflame, the waiters moving silently, this was the Germany he despised, the Germany that had settled for defeat. He quietly put his knife and fork together and ate no more.

Kinderlen saw it, but made no comment. Instead he continued with his meal and asked where Lauter had been stationed. "On the Austrian border, eh? I was in Northern France myself. For the most part, anyway. With Flakregiment 155."

Lauter looked up quickly. "Colonel Wachtel's group?"

Kinderlen nodded. "Right. Did you know somebody there?"

"No. But I know that was the FZG group. The V-1s."

"We always just called them the Fieselers. Their original name."

Lauter glanced down at the thick slab of beef he'd hardly touched and for the first time reached for the glass of wine a waiter had poured. "There was a rumor," he began, hesitantly. "The last rumor I heard. It was just at the end. They said we were being transferred to secret sites in Austria to launch the V-1s in an all-out attack on London."

"From Austria?" His host sipped wine, dabbed at his mouth with a crisp napkin. "Impossible. Even the newer ones had a range of only four hundred kilometers. No, the only sites they ever built were in France. Plus a few around The Hague in Holland."

Lauter moved his head sadly. "Yes. I've since found that out. I've also read that if we'd had the fighters to stop the RAF and the Americans from bombing the sites it would have made a big difference. Perhaps all the difference the Fuehrer would have needed."

At the reference to Hitler Kinderlen moved food around on his plate and said, "Eat up, Willie. You've hardly touched anything."

Lauter didn't seem to hear him. "What do you think? Would it have turned the tide?"

Kinderlen almost sighed; it was a subject that held no interest for him.

"It would have prolonged the war, certainly, but I doubt it would have changed the result. They would still have bombed us into the ground." He put his fork down and touched his right arm. "I still have a piece of shrapnel from the last raid."

"Where were you exactly?"

"Loukeville, near Calais. They hit us so quickly. Typhoons. We had little warning. I wouldn't be alive at all except I was late getting to the shelter. It took a direct hit and everybody was killed."

"When was that?" Lauter couldn't seem to hear enough about it.

"September 1, '44. That was the last day the Fieselers were fired from French soil."

"You went to Holland with them?"

Kinderlen shook his head. "I was in the hospital. The day I finished some other duty and was supposed to rejoin them was the day Gruppen Nord and Sud surrendered to the Ninth Army."

"May 9," Lauter said heavily. "The day of infamy."

Kinderlen knew he should never have mentioned the fact and hurried on. "We gave them a run for their money, though. We never did get all eighty-one sites working at the same time, but I remember one day, June 15, 1944, it was, we fired three hundred and twenty-four missiles in a fourteen-hour period. But we were never able to sustain a rate of fire like that. Nowhere near it."

He hadn't meant to but Kinderlen had ended on a down note, and there followed a long stretch of silence.

They left soon after, and out on the sidewalk Kinderlen politely handed over his card.

"Next time you're in Frankfurt, Willie, call me. We'll have dinner again. It's been most pleasant."

They shook hands, Lauter mumbled his thanks, and Kinderlen gratefully said goodbye. Lauter walked back to his apartment wishing he hadn't run into the man; it had been an irritating dinner. He cheered slightly when he arrived home to find the book he'd been expecting waiting for him, an examination of Rommel's brilliant maneuver at El Mechili. He read a few chapters, then went to bed, falling asleep almost immediately.

At 4 A.M. he was wide awake again. Something Kinderlen had said was pinging on the edge of his subconscious. He got up, switched lights on, put on a dressing gown against the chill of the early morning, and thought back over the conversation.

It was a good twenty minutes before he got it.

A lot of the reading he'd done about the war related to the secret weapons that had been developed, and there was a figure he remembered concerning the V-1s that didn't seem to jibe with what Kinderlen had told him. He crossed to the shelving he'd had built from floor to ceiling and found the book he was after. He checked the index, flipped to the page, and there it was: the figure he thought he'd find. Either the book was wrong or Kinderlen was wrong.

He checked the publication date: 1948. A lot of books, published not long after the war, weren't quite correct on their facts; perhaps this was one. He put the book aside and started looking for another he knew he had on the same subject. In fact he had several on the subject.

He checked them all. And they all agreed.

He didn't allow himself to get excited, refused to even consider what it could mean if it turned out that Kinderlen was correct. Had it been anybody else he wouldn't have doubted the books for a moment, but Kinderlen had always had a phenomenal memory for facts and figures; "the Walking Almanac," they used to call him. And Lauter remembered the way he'd reeled off those dates in the restaurant at dinner. It was something that came naturally to the man.

There was only one way to find out for sure, and five hours later Lauter was standing on the steps of the public library as the doors opened. He worked quickly at the catalogs, experienced in this operation, filled out a request card and waited at a table in the vast reading room, trying to keep his mind a blank. It was only a five-minute wait, but it seemed like an hour before the books were brought. They were bound periodicals, two of them—one American, one English—intelligence reports that had been declassified for some time. They were a capsule history of the Allied invasion in Normandy in 1945, and had been written with precise military accuracy.

He found what he was after in the first one, then checked the second one.

He closed the books and knew that his hands were trembling, and that there was moisture inside his collar. But still he wouldn't let himself contemplate what it could mean; there was always the chance that Kinderlen was wrong.

He left the library, hurried to his office, surprising people by his late arrival; nobody could remember it ever happening before. He pulled Kinderlen's card from his pocket, picked up the phone, dialed the number, asked for Kinderlen, and had to repeat himself to straighten the tremor in his voice. When the man came on, he was surprised to be hearing from Lauter so soon. "Last night," Lauter said, jumping in without any preliminaries, "when we talked about the Fieselers, the launching sites in France . . ."

"What?"

"You remember our conversation, don't you?"

"Yes. But why the sudden interest?"

Lauter, unprepared, mumbled something about writing a book.

"I didn't know you wrote, Willie. Do you mean a history of the war?"

"Yes, exactly. And I wanted to confirm something you mentioned last night." He closed his eyes and kept them closed while he asked the question. "How many sites did you say were operational in France?"

The answer came back with no hesitation. "Eighty-one."

Lauter's hand tightened on the phone in a quick spasm. "You're absolutely certain? Eighty-one?"

"I'm positive."

"You . . . you couldn't be mistaken?"

Kinderlen had a lot of work to do, and he didn't need this conversation. And he didn't like having his memory questioned. He said, with more than a touch of exasperation, "I ought to know, Willie, because I was in charge of supply for all those sites. There were a hundred and eight sites built in France, but at the end of the war we had exactly eighty-one in operational readiness. I had to sign eighty-one bills of lading every time supplies went out."

"But the records," Lauter began. "They say that—"

Kinderlen cut him off abruptly. "Was there anything else, Willie?"

"No."

"Then I'm afraid I must go. Good luck with the book."

Lauter put the phone down as if it were made of crystal. He got shakily to his feet.

"Do you feel all right, Herr Lauter?" A secretary was hovering near, concerned by his blanched face.

"Yes, yes. Perfectly all right." He brushed by her, hurried out into the corridor and into the men's room. He dashed water on his face, gripped the cool-white porcelain of the wash basin and let the feeling flood through him: joy, astonishment, a crumbling disbelief. In the books at his apartment, in the ones at the library, in anything he'd ever read about the V-1s, all of them gave the same figure for the number of captured launching sites. Eighty.

So somewhere in Northern France, perhaps buried in a forest, hidden in some out-of-the-way wood, was an operational flying bomb site that had never been found. And if he could find it . . . that fantasy he'd had about stealing fifty American bombers and leveling London—he didn't need fifty bombers now. A single V-1 would do the job.

If it were carrying a nuclear warhead.

CHAPTER FIVE

Pelham—London, December 18-19, 1978

When Pelham left the German mechanic, still trying to get his mind around the implications of what the man had told him, his first inclination was to rush back to the office with the news. But he conquered his excitement and did the right thing: went back out to Hayes and talked to people who lived on the ruined block. He combed through the wreckage, again looking for another piece of the missile, but found nothing he couldn't identity. He took a mini-cab there and back this time—with what he'd found out Evans could hardly carp at the expense—and arrived back in London at around 4 p.m. As he'd expected, there was another terse note on his desk from Evans that he took great delight in balling up and tossing away. This was one meeting with his boss he was looking forward to.

The man greeted him exactly as Pelham knew he would.

"Where the hell have you been all day?"

"Around and about," Pelham said, sitting on the corner of a chair.

Evans's face got a little narrower but Pelham kept talking.

"I was out at Hayes talking to people, among other things. That explosion wasn't caused by a gas main."

"Then what did cause it?" Evans snapped.

"You're not going to believe it. A flying bomb. A V-1."

After a full five seconds Evans said, "Are you drunk?"

Pelham checked his watch. "No, but I intend to be."

"Look here, Pelham. I've taken about as—"

"I know it sounds crazy but I have definite evidence that those houses were blown up by a V-1. Where it came from, who fired it, and why are questions I couldn't even begin to answer, but—"

It was Pelham who was cut off this time, and very sharply.

"You're sacked, Pelham. Please clear your desk out immediately. I want you out of this firm in an hour's time."

Pelham came up out of the chair. "Sacked? You're kidding. I've just told you, I have the evidence."

"You regard this job as a joke," Evans said in his pinched-in voice, spitting the words out. "Either that or you're an idiot. And this firm is not in business to support fools."

There was quite a bit more said on both sides, all of it in raised voices, but five minutes later Pelham was back in his office, steaming mad and out of a job.

He moved around the room, opening and slamming drawers, took a couple of deep breaths and tried to fight his anger down. He picked up the phone, asked the switch girl for the number of the Ministry of Defense, hung up and dialed it.

There was no ringing tone, just silence. He hung up and dialed again, coming into the middle of a conversation between two women discussing their hair. Pelham slammed the phone down, said loudly, "If the weather or the people don't get you, the phone system will." He dialed once more, and this time the phone was answered on the first ring. He told the operator to connect him with a press officer, knowing it was always a good way of getting a foot inside the door of any big outfit.

"Army, Navy or Air Force, sir?"

"Air Force, I suppose."

A few moments later he was talking to a man who said his name was Strathallan. Pelham told him that he wanted to talk to somebody about an urgent matter and asked if he could come down right away. The man tried to put him off till tomorrow.

"Tomorrow it will be even more urgent," Pelham said.

The man relented and Pelham went straight downstairs and found a cab. It had to fight its way through the pre-Christmas traffic, taking an age to get down St. Martin's Lane and around Trafalgar Square. The huge Christmas tree was already lit up and shining brightly in the darkening evening, its colored lights stealing the show from Lord Nelson way up high on his pedestal, an English god.

The cab picked up speed on the long, wide sweep of Whitehall, and made a turn opposite a group of tourists gawking at the mounted Horse Guards. It stopped outside an immense, curving, soot-covered building that bulged outward as if something were pushing it from behind. The massive entrance was like a doorway of a temple, and there were two monolithic figures mounted above it that might have looked daringly modern once upon a time. High windows had lights behind them for nine or ten stories and, above them, a row of Ionic columns ran the entire width of the building. Twin cupolas, added perhaps as afterthoughts, topped everything off.

Pelham paid the driver, climbed the stairs, and went through the doors marked "Non Passholders." There were several uniformed security men in evidence and, at a central desk enclosed by clear glass, two women sat wearing blue cotton dusters. Pelham gave one of them his name and that of the man he'd come to see, then filled out a pass for himself while the woman used the phone. She told him that Mr. Strathallan would be with him in a minute. Pelham thanked her and nodded at the sign standing on an easel in the vestibule. It said, in permanent lettering, "Alert State." A hand-lettered word, "Black," had been slid in underneath it.

"Is that good or bad?" he asked the woman.

"Good," she smiled. "If it said 'Red' there'd be a problem. Some kind of trouble in the building."

Pelham took another look around; the two women were matronly types, and none of the guards looked to be armed. He knew that unlike the United States, where security was always bristlingly evident, England tended to keep it hidden.

A few minutes later, an athletic-looking young man came out into the reception area. "Mr. Pelham?"

"Hello there."

"Strathallan. Shall we go in here? I'll need your pass." He led the way into a glass-enclosed room located just inside the door.

The sign said, "Visitors." There was nobody else in there.

"Now," Strathallan said, "what can I do for you?"

Pelham fished out his wallet and identified himself. "I work for United General. You heard about the explosion down in Hayes yesterday?"

"Yes, I did. Quite a blast. Gas mains, wasn't it?"

"No. Explosives."

The young man's eyebrows lifted. "Really?"

"Mr. Strathallan, what's the pecking order in this place? I'd like to take this to the top if possible because what I've got is pretty heady stuff."

"You've been to the police?"

Pelham gave a fast shake of his head. "I think this is out of their league. I know what caused that explosion and it's a mind blower. That's why I'm here."

Strathallan said, "Yes," as if agreeing with him. "Well, I'm afraid you've come at a bad time, Mr. Pelham. Christmas week and all that. You should really talk to my superior, the Director of Public Relations, but I'm afraid he's gone for the day."

He stood there as if that was all the explanation needed; as if he expected Pelham to say he'd come back some other time.

"Then let me talk to his boss."

"That would be difficult. You see, we have to go through correct channels."

Pelham, annoyed at the bland reception he was getting, and still smarting from his confrontation with Evans, got mad.

"Screw going through correct channels. I'm not talking about piloting a boat. I've got something that's so hot you're not going to believe it. I've got to talk to somebody now. Not tomorrow, not next New Year's Eve, *now*."

Strathallan, shaken verbally by the lapels, blinked at Pelham for a second, then excused himself, left the room, made a fast phone call, and returned.

"Come along then," he said.

Pelham accompanied him down a corridor and into an elevator.

"Who am I going to see?"

"I called the Undersecretary of State's office. His secretary was just leaving but he's agreed to see you."

They got off at a high floor and went down a long carpeted hallway. Strathallan knocked at a door marked with just a number, opened it, and ushered Pelham in ahead of him. The office was large, comfortable in an efficient kind of way but without much personality. The man who was walking around from behind his desk looked like the headmaster of a fair to middling private school: fortyish, balding, heavy black-rimmed glasses on a no-nonsense face. He had a fixed, thin-lipped smile on his mouth as Strathallan made the introductions.

The man's name was Radford.

"Please sit down, Mr. Pelham."

Pelham took a chair, noticing that Radford remained standing. He got the impression that Radford wasn't too crazy about the young man bringing in somebody so late. On the sofa was a topcoat and a briefcase all ready to go.

"Thanks for seeing me, Mr. Radford. I hope I'm not keeping you."

"Perfectly all right," the man replied. He resumed his seat.

"You're Canadian, Mr. Pelham?"

"American."

"Oh." It was said without any particular color, but there was no mistaking the tone. Pelham thought that the man might as well have added, "Too bad." It looked like it was Yankee Go Home time again.

Radford said through his tight smile, "Mr. Strathallan tells me you have some earthshaking news for us."

Again it was said politely enough, but it was clear the guy didn't believe he was going to hear anything fascinating. Buddy, Pelham thought, hold on to your hat.

"I'm with United General."

"So I understand."

"Okay, then Mr. Strathallan probably told you I'm investigating that explosion down in Hayes. It wasn't a gas main. One of the tenants was Irish and the police think it was an IRA bomb factory."

"But you don't think so," Radford said. The inference was that one American insurance man would of course know better than all the experts at Scotland Yard.

"That's right," Pelham answered, doing a good job of keeping his cool. "For a couple of reasons. The main one being something I found in the wreckage."

He went on to describe the frame, told Radford what he thought it had been and how he'd taken it to the German mechanic.

"The guy recognized it right away. It was part of the thing that blew up those houses."

"Which was . . . ?" Radford asked, still making a show of politeness.

Pelham tried to think how he could soften it, make it sound any less crazy than it was. There didn't seem to be a way.

"A flying bomb."

"Pardon?"

"A V-1. A buzz bomb."

Radford's eyes darted to Strathallan, whose face had colored.

The young man murmured something and quietly left the room.

Radford looked up at the molding on the ceiling. He said, "A V-1, eh? Good heavens. Well, I'm certainly glad you brought this to our attention, Mr. Pelham. My goodness, yes. A V-1." He started to rise, the smile back on his face. "We'll get onto it first thing. Meanwhile—"

Pelham jumped up. "Wait a second. I'm not a nut who's wandered in off the street." He fumbled in his jacket, threw his identification down on the man's desk. "Go ahead, call my office. My job was to check out that explosion, ask them. Now I know it sounds insane, so I can understand you thinking you're dealing with a weirdo, but facts are facts, Mr. Radford, and it's a fact that those houses were blown away by a flying bomb."

Radford picked up the plastic card, examined it; name, address, Pelham's photograph, and the logotype of his company. It was clearly genuine.

"All right," Radford said. "It appears you are not crazy, Mr. Pelham, but perhaps just a victim of an outstandingly vivid imagination."

"Imagination? I didn't imagine a valve box from a V-1's power plant, Mr. Radford. I found it in that wreckage."

"And from that you deduce that a V-1 hit those houses? You're not making sense. Thousands of V-1s landed on London during the war. Many people kept souvenirs. I know a man who has the glass from a German submarine periscope. If his house blew up, and you found the glass, would you conclude that his house had been torpedoed?"

It was a good blow, and it stung. Pelham's voice got a trifle louder. "That's not fair. You're talking about something that's impossible, and I'm talking about something that's very possible."

Radford squinted at him in disbelief. "A World War II buzz bomb hitting London today is possible? Where's it been for the last thirty-three years, flying around running out of fuel?"

"I don't have the first idea where it's been," Pelham said hotly. "And I don't know where it's come from or who sent it. All I know is it arrived."

"Rubbish! Absolute cock!"

"Is it?" Pelham shot back. "Well you just listen to this, sport." He grabbed angrily for a notebook inside his jacket. "I went back out to Hayes today, knocking on doors, asking questions, asking people if they'd heard anything before the explosion. This is what some of them said." Pelham flicked to a page, began to read. " 'A loud noise, like the old taxis used to make.' " He flipped over another page. " 'I heard a helicopter overhead then I heard it stop. I thought it had crashed when the explosion came.' " He raked through the notebook a third time. " 'I heard a noise like a motorboat.' " Pelham jerked his head up. "I also talked to another guy, an older man who was a little deaf. He hadn't heard anything but he told me something that really pinned my ears back. He'd been an air-raid warden during the war and when I asked him what the V-1s sounded like, do you know what he said?" Pelham consulted his book. " 'They made a chugging, burbling sound like an old car going uphill.' " He snapped the book closed, slapped it against his open palm. "Now is it starting to sound a little less crazy to you?"

Radford made a scornful sound in his throat. "Why? Because a couple of people heard traffic noises? None of those people *saw* anything, did they?"

"They were all inside."

"What time was this?"

"The explosion? Three-fifty."

"It would have been getting dark. If you'd checked with your air-raid warden, Mr. Pelham, he might have told you that the V-1s were also called fire arses. And for a very good reason. They spurted flames from their jets that you could see at high noon, let alone a December evening."

"It was rainy and cloudy. Nobody would've had a chance to see it. And," Pelham hurried on, "the fact still remains that at least three people in the vicinity heard a chugging noise before the explosion, one of them certain that it came from above."

"That person thought it was a helicopter," Radford replied quickly. "Why the hell," he said, getting up, "shouldn't it have been a helicopter? Answer me that."

"Because it was a goddamn flying bomb, that's why. A flying bomb that wiped out three houses."

Radford pressed a button on his desk then moved toward the sofa. He said coldly, "I'm afraid you'll have to excuse me, Mr. Pelham. I'm late for an appointment."

Pelham, not quite believing it, watched the man getting ready to leave. "You mean that's it? You're not even going to check into it?"

"Mr. Pelham," Radford said crisply. "I don't mean to be rude and I don't mean to draw too close a parallel, but a few months ago somebody came to us claiming he had definite proof that the moon was a Soviet spaceship. We didn't check into that one, either."

"Whoa! Hold up, now." Pelham was steaming. "I've spent half my entire life in the insurance business and—"

"I'm sure your record is exemplary, Mr. Pelham. However, in this instance you appear to have struck out, as you people say." He made it sound like a racial slur, but Pelham was stopped from any reply by the appearance of a security man at the door.

"The guard will show you the way out," Radford said.

Pelham, his head shaking, said, "I don't believe this. I just do not believe it. At least take a look at the evidence I found. At least send somebody out there to ask questions."

Radford picked up his briefcase; it made an irritated sound as he snapped it closed. "Look, this matter should never have got as far as my office in the first place. I've been very patient with you, but enough is enough." He nodded to the guard.

"Come along, sir," the guard said. He took a step toward Pelham, a big man, broad through the chest.

Pelham's voice rose. "For God's sake, Radford."

He didn't get any further; the guard grasped him under the arm and propelled him toward the door.

"Radford!" Pelham shouted.

The guard was polite, almost amiable as he bundled him out into the hallway. "The lift is this way, sir."

Pelham dug his heels in, wrenched his arm free. "Okay! All right!"

He shook himself, straightened his topcoat, glared past the man at the office door, which closed firmly. "Boy," Pelham said bitterly, "you've got some real winners around here, you know that?"

"Yes sir," the guard replied, a smile glued to his face.

"The lift's this way, sir," he said again. He shepherded Pelham down the hall and into a waiting elevator.

Pelham, fuming, spoke through his teeth. "Hey, tell me something. Why are the English so fucking English all the time?"

"I couldn't say, sir," the guard replied, benign as ever.

Just as the elevator doors opened the guard said, "Who has your pass, sir?"

"Who the hell cares?" Pelham answered and strode ahead making for the entrance. But when he reached it another security man stepped in front of him.

"May I have your pass, sir?"

"I don't have the damn thing."

"I'm sorry, sir, but you can't leave unless you surrender it."

Pelham gaped at him. "You mean you even need a pass to get thrown out? Jesus, what a country."

"I have his pass," somebody said. It was a large, plump man who came hurrying up. "Mr. Pelham, my name is Jakes. I wonder, could you spare me a moment?"

Pelham threw up his arms. "Why not? I'm a prisoner anyway."

"My office is on this floor. Shall we?"

He didn't say anything as Pelham followed him back up the corridor and into an office. It was similar to Radford's but smaller, standard metal office furniture, contract carpeting on the floor. Pelham ignored the man's invitation to sit down. "What's all this about? You going to give me a ticket for having bad manners?"

The plump man took a chair, smiling. "John Radford does have his rough edges, doesn't he?"

"Most of them around the brain," Pelham said. He meant it; he was still very angry at Radford's reaction, and a bit confounded by it, too.

"You should never have seen him. Young Strathallan hasn't been with us long. He should have brought you to see me first."

"Uh huh. This is the nut department, right?"

The other man chuckled; he seemed the type to whom laughing would come easily. He had a rotund, Santa Claus figure with curly ginger hair and a cherubic face that sported a classic RAF mustache. He wore a dark suit with a tightly knotted striped tie, but he looked relaxed in his clothes; a comfortable, pudgy man.

"I'm what you might call a troubleshooter. I field all the toughies that don't come under any general classification. Strathallan told me about your theory regarding that explosion in Hayes, but I'd like to hear it from you."

"Why? You don't believe it, do you?"

The man lifted his hands in a little gesture of apology. "Well, no, I can't say that I do. But the world has become a strange place. People are doing outrageous things these days. I try to keep an open mind."

Pelham, mollified by the man's understanding manner, lowered himself into a chair. "What did you say your name was again?"

"Jakes. Brian Jakes."

Pelham said, "Let me ask you something, Brian. What is it with your countrymen? How come half of them are humorless, uptight stuff shirts like Radford upstairs, and the other half"—he gestured toward the man—"are normal, polite human beings."

Jakes moved his chubby shoulders. "They're shy, I suppose. A bit wary of letting their hair down unless they know you pretty well, so they adopt a stern attitude. Hide behind it. At least that's what I've always thought."

Pelham wasn't convinced. Was that the problem with stiffs like Radford, and Evans? They were shy? They certainly didn't act shy.

Jakes leaned forward, folded his arms on his desk. "Tell me about that explosion and what you found."

Pelham did; told him everything in far greater detail than he'd told Radford. Then he added a thought on the end.

"Explosions are funny things. They'll often pulverize everything for yards around and leave something at the center of the blast relatively untouched. It was just a fluke that the valve box was still intact. The rest of the buzz bomb must be spread all over the entire neighborhood in burnt-up little pieces."

"Apart from the thing you found," Jakes said, "what else makes you think it was a V-1?"

"Because it's the only explanation."

"But what about the theory the police have, the Irishman?"

"It doesn't hold up," Pelham said, "and they must know it. That guy rented the basement flat. And that blast didn't come from the basement. Its shape was all wrong. It came from above." To further prove his point Pelham read from the notebook, read out the reports of the people he'd interviewed.

Jakes listened thoughtfully, then picked up a phone, dialed a three-digit number, asked a question, got an answer, then hung up. He looked at Pelham like a doctor with bad news. "There *was* a helicopter in the area yesterday. An RAF Whirlwind. They're big, and I'm afraid a chugging sound is exactly the sound they make."

"Whereabouts? What time?"

"Near Croydon. About three-forty."

"But Croydon's a couple of miles away. And the blast was at three-fifty, ten minutes later."

"That's true," Jakes allowed. "But it's been my experience that there's nothing more unreliable than a reliable witness. People are basically very unobservant. The people you spoke to said they heard those noises immediately before the explosion. Immediately could be five minutes, ten minutes before. And as for the distance, a big helicopter makes a heck of a noise, and if the wind's in the right direction a mile or two isn't that far off."

He read the look on Pelham's face and held up a pudgy hand. "I'm not saying it was definitely the helicopter they heard, only that it could have been. But that's not what bothers me."

"What is it then?"

"A couple of things. Let us say, for argument's sake, that it was a flying bomb that blitzed those houses. The first thing I wonder is, where did it come from?"

Pelham shrugged. "I don't know. Where did they come from during the war?"

"Northern France."

"So maybe it came from the same place."

"All right," Jakes said, reasonably. "Let's say it did. Now, how did it get here undetected?"

"Because the weather was lousy. Overcast and rainy. It was hidden up there in the clouds."

Jakes conceded the point, but not totally. "I'll buy that on one level. People have lost interest in the sky anyway. But I wasn't talking about a visual sighting, I'm talking about radar. The traffic over the English Channel is extremely heavy, one of the world's major air corridors. There's almost as much radar surveillance as there is around Moscow or Washington. You've got military and civil air controllers, both English and French, who have a blip on their radar screens for everything that's flying. Now"—Jakes raised a finger to give his words emphasis—"out at West Drayton if a CAA controller has a blip on his screen he can't account for, and the RAF

controller working beside him can't account for it either, they get a
Phantom interceptor into the air before you can say Jack Robinson.
And I know for a fact that there was no scramble yesterday, no
report of anything on the screens that shouldn't have been there."

Pelham shifted in his chair, moved his feet. "Maybe it didn't show
up on the radar because it flew under it."

"That's not as easy as it once was. There's something called 'Look
Down Radar' now. Perhaps you've heard of it. Regular radar covers
horizontally; Look Down covers vertically, right down to sea level.
There's just no way you can get beneath it."

While Pelham was chewing that over, Jakes continued.

"There's something else that bothers me. If it was a V-1, where
did they find it? And who are 'they'? If they're terrorists of some
kind, why haven't they claimed responsibility to dramatize their
cause? And if it wasn't fired to get their names in the paper, why
was it fired? Why would anybody use a hopelessly out-of-date
weapon like that?"

Pelham opened his mouth, then closed it again; these were all
damn good questions, and ones he couldn't answer. He sighed, the
fire gone out of him. Jakes had very politely, and very expertly,
taken his theory and punched great big holes in it.

"I guess I'm beat," he said. He got tiredly to his feet; Jakes rose,
too.

They didn't say much walking down the corridor toward the
entrance; Pelham looked slack, deflated, and Jakes, aware that his
arguments were the reason why, felt the embarrassment of the easy
winner.

He surrendered Pelham's pass to a security guard, and gave Pelham his card. "Call me sometime," he said. "We'll have a drink."

Pelham shook his hand and tried for a grin. "Brian, thanks for the
kind treatment."

"Not at all."

Pelham walked through the door into the cold wind gusting off
the river a hundred yards away. He stuck his hands into the pockets
of his topcoat, his mood matching the gray, drizzly evening, and
began walking toward Whitehall. It occurred to him that his exit
was a lot different than his entrance: in like a tiger, out like a lamb.
So much for rushing back to the office with a Ministry of Defense
medal pinned to his lapel and watching Evans grovel in apology. He

knew he'd done it again: gone off half cocked and got unreasonably angry at people, the two things he seemed to have been doing all his life. Somebody had once told him that he should adopt a more Zen-like approach to living. How? Go sit on a mountaintop in India and think things through? He couldn't afford the fare to India. He had a severance check coming and nothing else looming on the horizon.

He stopped when he reached Whitehall, watching the rush-hour buses shooting by full of people going home from jobs, jobs that, unlike him, they'd be going to next day.

What an insane thing to get fired over anyway, three suburban houses that had been mysteriously blown up. Maybe a crazy Irishman had done it, or maybe they'd been ray gunned by Martians in a flying saucer—whatever had happened to them he no longer cared. He was out of it now, out of the whole cockamamie thing.

He walked back to Trafalgar Square to a pub he knew but changed his mind and didn't go in. Getting sloshed and mooning about being canned wouldn't help any more than it had the other times it happened to him. Besides, there were better ways of losing yourself, and the one he was thinking of couldn't be done on his own.

CHAPTER SIX

Lauter—Munich/Rouen, 1955-1978

The day after Lauter called Kinderlen from Munich, he surprised and annoyed the man by turning up unannounced at his office in Frankfurt. He apologized for bothering him again, explaining that the telephone line had been bad, and because he wanted the book he was planning to be quite accurate, would he mind if he asked him the same question once more: was he absolutely certain there had been eighty-one sites and not eighty as all the books claimed. As patiently as he could Kinderlen told him to forget about what the books claimed.

"If the books say eighty then the authors were working from old records."

"Then what happened to the new records? The up-to-date ones?"

Kinderlen raised his hands. "Destroyed in a raid, probably. And even if they weren't you have to remember that toward the end of the war there wasn't much time for accurate statistics. Every clerk who wasn't absolutely essential was pulled out from behind his desk, given a rifle and sent to the front."

Lauter knew that was true, which further strengthened the chance of Kinderlen being right. Still, he had to be sure, he had to be positive, and Kinderlen saw the look of lingering doubt on his face.

"Look," he said with a sigh, "the records, the main ones, the ones they brought up to date whenever they got the chance were kept at the regiment's headquarters in Saleux. Now I know better than anybody how understaffed they were because I was on the line to them twice a day. The place was a madhouse. It doesn't surprise me one bit that the records weren't all that they should have been."

"Yes," Lauter persisted, "but some of the books I'm talking about didn't get their figures from records. They obtained them verbally from people like yourself."

"No, no. Not people like myself. The English, the Americans never asked the noncoms, only the officers because officers are supposed to know. But you were in the war, Willie, so let me ask you this: whose opinion did you always trust, the man who had to supervise the job or the man who actually had to do the job?"

It was an excellent argument, and coupled with Kinderlen's famous memory for detail, a very convincing one.

The possibility of a site still existing, half buried and forgotten in some tiny wood in Northern France was further supported over the next six weeks by the books Lauter sent for. He learned that the later launching sites had been cleverly disguised, and built with German labor, not French labor, so as to keep the location a secret.

Lauter also learned the names of sixty-six towns and villages where a site had been built, which left him fourteen of the officially recorded ones to find out. He accomplished it by going to Berlin where the war records were kept. It took some doing because much of this material wasn't being made available to the general public, but by passing himself off as a war historian, Lauter was able to gain access to some of the less restricted archives and returned to Munich with all eighty names.

His next move was to run a classified ad in the leading newspapers in the major cities. It said, "War historian seeks full or partial list of French locations in which V-1 launching sites were situated. Remuneration guaranteed on verification."

The results were disappointing. He got many replies but they were mainly from people who'd simply gone to the library and found the twenty or so names in the books available. One or two more enterprising people had obviously gained access to the same records he'd found in Berlin, and sent him the same eighty-name list. There were also a number of letters from ex-Luftwaffe personnel, boring reminiscences for the most part about time spent at a site Lauter already knew about. These were a waste of time anyway because, as Lauter strongly suspected, the eighty-first site had more than likely never been used.

He wasn't really surprised at his failure to find the missing name; great discoveries had never been made easily, but only after a tremendous amount of painstaking endeavor. So Lauter set out to do what he'd known he'd have to do: look for the site himself. He knew full well it might take him years to find it, and that his sole basis for believing it was there at all was the memory of one man. But as long as there was a good chance of Kinderlen being correct, Lauter knew he had to make the search; because he was still a soldier of the Third Reich, still able to serve his Fuehrer. And if his search did prove successful, how gloriously he'd be able to serve his Fuehrer then! London laid waste. Just like Hiroshima and Nagasaki had been.

He began his search by enrolling in a language school to learn French, and so intensely did he throw himself into it, studying till 3 or 4 A.M. every night, that three months was all it took him to become fluent.

His next step was the move to France.

He chose Rouen mainly because it was geographically suitable as a base, but also because quite a few German firms had branch offices there. The first one he applied to snapped him up: excellent references, fluent French, twenty-nine years of age and in fine health, a quiet, respectful demeanor—he was just the kind of man they were looking for.

He arrived in Rouen on a cold March evening and found an apartment the next day. It was in a tall, shuttered house in the old part of the city on the right bank, an area full of twisting streets and two-hundred-year-old houses whose foundations had been used since medieval days. It wasn't far from the famous Gothic cathedral the English and American bombers had destroyed.

The apartment suited him: a living/dining room, with a tiny kitchen at one end hidden by a drawn curtain, an equally tiny bathroom which before the war had been a walk-in closet, and a bedroom. The bedroom was small as well, but Lauter wasn't planning to sleep in it: this was going to be his operations room, his war room.

It was the only room he spent any money on. He got his landlady to exchange the bed for a sofa, which he planned to sleep on in the living room, then he went out and bought a wooden draftsman's table, some metal shelving, and some large sheets of corkboard. He bought pens, pencils, notebooks, a ruler, a compass. He bought an atlas of Europe, a map of central London, a map of Southern England, a map of Northern France. And he bought two Michelin maps showing all of Normandy, Picardy, and the Artois, road maps with a scale of two kilometers to one centimeter.

When his books arrived from Munich several days later, he'd

settled nicely into his new job, and had got his room just about the way he wanted it. The books went straight into the shelving he'd put up on the wall opposite the one he'd nailed the corkboard to. Beneath the corkboard he'd placed the drafting table to which he'd pinned the Michelin maps, butting them together. Then with his books on hand for reference, and the other things he'd bought beside him, he was ready to begin.

He knew the limits of the area in which the sites had been placed; it had to be within two hundred fifty kilometers of London, the greatest range the V-1s had had till the new models had been introduced in the last months of the war. But, according to Kinderlen, these had only ever been fired from Holland. The vast majority of the sites had been situated between Calais to the north, and Dieppe to the south, close to the coast. But many also had been built as far inland as Arras, one hundred kilometers from the coast on a line with London. So plotting the area for his search was an easy matter. He opened the atlas of Europe to a page that showed Southern England, the Channel, and Northern France. He picked up the compass, fitted a short pencil into its holder, stretched it over the kilometer scale, and measured off two hundred fifty kilometers. He put the sharp metal compass point on the square dot that marked London and with a twist of his fingers moved the compass in an arc. Then, doing it freehand, and with intense, painstaking care, he transposed the arc onto the big-scale Michelin maps. When he finished, he saw, for the first time close up, the task that faced him.

The area had to be the best part of eighty-five hundred square kilometers, over five thousand square miles, a vast sea of green woods and forests. The fact that the site was lost meant that it had to be hidden; it wouldn't be enough to just visit all those woods and forests; he'd have to explore every corner of them, every yard.

He ran his eyes slowly over the area: thousands and thousands of tiny villages, and at least half of them in, around, or verging on a green-shaded part. It would take him half a lifetime to cover them all. Nevertheless, as long as there was a chance that his action might result in the continuation, perhaps realization, of the aims of the Fuehrer, he had an obligation to pursue it. He picked up a ruler and a pencil, made some measurements, calculated some figures, then began to divide the area into small squares. He gave each an alphabetical and numerical connotation, from A1 to Z26, then AA27 to

JJ38. The next question was, where should he start? Were any of those squares likely to prove more fruitful than any of the others? Without a doubt the site would have been among the last to be built, but according to all the books, they hadn't been built in any geographical order. So the site was just as likely to be in square number B2 as it was in G6 or EE9.

He decided to start with the squares closest to him and gradually fan out.

Next morning he bought two more Michelin maps, which he marked in exactly the same way as the ones pinned to his table, and his only major purchase: a small, two-stroke motorbike. The following Saturday, March 26, 1956, a cold, forbidding day, he began his search.

Lauter had to ride only a few kilometers out of the city to reach the first of the green areas in the square he'd chosen. Following his map, he turned off the main road at a village called St. Martin-de Boscherville, then took a narrow D road over the Seine to a section of land shaped like a thumb, the river looping round it. Le Grand Bois, it was called. The wood was bordered by three tiny villages connected to each other by another narrow road. It certainly looked promising; none of the sites had been built far from a road, and few had been located in any really deep forests; a leafy shelter was all they required. And an access road.

The first village, Ambourville, was no more than a handful of houses perched on the edge of the river. He rode through it and continued for half a kilometer going very slowly, looking for evidence of a track leading into the wood. It didn't have to be much; wide enough to take a truck, that's all.

He found one—running off to his right. He could see at once that it was artificially made; the trees had been cut down in a spot where the wood thinned, not recently but not a hundred years ago either. He turned his motorbike into it and the wood swallowed him up. It was dark and colder than ever, the trees dripping moisture, his rear wheel starting to spin on the uncertain ground. He parked the bike and continued on foot through the tall silent pines that were slim and branchless for thirty feet, then sprouted into greeny-brown cathedrals. There was dead silence except for the squish of his shoes in the moist carpet of pine needles, and now and then the rustle of a bird somewhere. The track continued for one hundred feet, then began to narrow to a width no truck carrying steel and cement would ever have been able to negotiate. It ended in a small clearing, little circles of fire-blackened stones here and there: a summer picnic spot, damp, deserted, sad looking.

Lauter trekked back to his motorbike and continued on down the road that linked the villages. The wood was solid for two kilometers, then broke for a small collection of old houses, which the sign on the road said was les Nouettes.

There was nobody in sight, and there seemed to be no reason for the village to exist. Its name was repeated on another sign not fifty feet from the last house, this time with a red diagonal stripe through it, as if the village had been cancelled years ago.

Lauter went on to the next village, almost a duplicate of les Nouettes, following the road that encircled the wood, eventually landing back where he'd started. He spotted several more tracks into the trees, but they were no more than paths cleared, perhaps for a horse and cart.

He stopped, opened his saddlebag, took out the Michelin map and a notebook and pen. He opened the book to the first page—light blue lines on crisp white paper, pristine in its newness—and recorded the date, the name of the wood, le Grand Bois, and its map location. Then he wrote: "One entrance road approx. ½ kil. from St. M. de Boscherville. Ended picnic area. No other vis. entrances." He marked the wood on the map with a tick, and checked the next green area. It wasn't far.

He went back to the D road and followed it north to Duclair, where he crossed the river again and traveled a little way down its right bank, turning off where a sign pointed to Yainville. It turned out to be another collection of gray stone houses on the perimeter of a wood called the Forêt de Jumièges. Lauter found two roads running into it that looked promising. However, the first one led to some kind of garbage dump; the second, on the other side of the wood, started off well but then, for no reason, petered out into a muddy walking trail. There were no other entrances of any size, so he recorded what he'd done, put a tick on the green area on his map, and ate the sandwich he'd made himself for lunch.

He studied the map again, then recrossed the river heading for a wood that was far larger than the other two, the Forêt de Brotonne.

It was riddled with roads leading into it, many of them strong possibilities. He'd only half finished exploring them when the sun ended its short day and the trees began to lose their definition as murky, deep shadows spread out beneath them.

He rode back to his apartment, made himself a simple meal, then quickly went to his workroom. He tore the wrapping from a large diary he'd bought and entered in the day's record, copying it scrupulously from his notebook. Then he did the same with the maps on the drafting table, marking the areas he'd explored. He sat looking at it, excitement building inside him. He knew it would be a piece of colossal luck, a freak thing if he were to find the site in only the third place he'd looked, but there was something about the forest he was searching, something that told him he was near. He'd felt an atmosphere, an aura that hadn't been present in the other two places, a premonition almost.

He slept fitfully, impatient for the morning, and was off on his motorbike shortly after the day dawned cold and gray again.

He picked up his search where he'd left off the day before, in an area on the north side of the forest. He carried a blueprint in his mind of what he was looking for, apart from the access road: there'd be four or five buildings, one very long, the others much smaller, and a space for the launching ramp, a path that didn't have to be any more than fifteen feet wide, provided it was long and straight and pointing in the direction of London. The trick would come in recognizing the site in its half-buried or overgrown state. But by the time he'd finished exploring the rest of the wood, the light beginning to fade, he'd seen nothing remotely like what he was after, and he realized that his earlier feeling had been nothing more than excitement at being on active duty again.

Later, back at his apartment, a bowl of hot soup chasing the chill from his body, he was glad that he hadn't found the site. It would have been too easy finding it the first time out; it would have diminished the glory of his quest.

But Lauter needn't have worried about finding the site too soon, or too easily.

The weeks became months, and the months became a year, and it seemed to Lauter, looking at the areas he'd covered on the map and the ones he still had to go, that he'd hardly even started.

* * *

Lauter's life had settled into a solid routine; his job continued to be bland and undemanding of any extra time and his fellow workers regarded him as the archetypal German: quiet, correct, efficient, drab.

He invariably arrived five minutes before he was supposed to and worked steadily through to lunch, an apple and some cheese usually, which he ate at his desk. Then he'd walk around the Old Town lost in his dream. At the close of business he'd stroll to a brasserie where, in good weather, he'd sit outside and watch the painfully slow progress being made on the restoration of the cathedral. It seemed to him to be an analogy of his own situation: the cathedral was Germany, destroyed, humbled by the English, but faith, which had built it initially, was rebuilding it, restoring its former glory brick by brick. He was embarked on a similar task, and just as the Rouen cathedral would be successfully completed one day, so would his endeavor. Time and faith were all that was needed, and he had plenty of both.

After dinner he'd walk back to his apartment, change into pajamas and dressing gown, and unlock the door of his workroom. He'd had a stout lock fitted shortly after he'd moved in, and he kept the key in his pocket at all times. There he'd plan the coming weekend's itinerary, checking his books for any mention of the area in general. His bookshelf had grown, mainly with books from England. The English still poured out books about the war, revealing things about the top-secret German projects that were still classified in his own country, or simply never mentioned. They were necessary, those books, although he hated reading their mocking, gloating words, and he took huge satisfaction in knowing that none of the books were complete; after he'd found the site there'd be a whole new chapter to be added to the history of the war.

The proud fools thought it was over.

But nothing he had ever read brought him any closer to his goal; none of the new books ever mentioned a village in connection with the V-1s that he didn't already know about.

The little room had changed somewhat in a year. There were heavy curtains at the window, more shelving on the near wall, and a high-intensity lamp bolted to the map table. He'd also added two shelves along the bottom of the corkboard that was now festooned with newspaper clippings, photocopied book pages and drawings.

And photographs, too: shots of flattened houses, a bus depot torn and twisted, a ruined factory. And many photographs of what had caused the damage. There was a side-on view of a V-1 rising in the air, skimming some treetops; another, in a long shot, diving toward some London rooftops. One buzz bomb lay on a beach where it had crash-landed; another, wingless, was being rolled onto a huge trolley by Luftwaffe personnel. The same fat torpedo shape was evident in all the photographs, the jet engine like a tapering stovepipe mounted at the rear of the missile and extending beyond it for a few feet.

And there was a photograph set off by itself, as if it were enjoying pride of place, a shot that had a thirties quality to it. It was simple enough: two middle-aged men, intellectual looking, scientists perhaps, awkwardly facing the camera in a manner that suggested shyness at having to pose. Across the bottom of the print Lauter had scrawled four numerals, quickly and with a flourish, as if he'd written a triumphant finis to something.

But it was the photos lined up along the two new shelves that were the most arresting. Eighteen in all, sixteen of them of Adolf Hitler. A few showed him smiling and relaxed, pinning a medal on a pilot, or receiving flowers from a member of the League of German Maidens. One showed him as the new chancellor wearing a frock coat and carrying a silk topper. But in most of the rest the camera had caught him in the middle of fiery oration, his fist raised, or leaning forward, hands gripping a lectern, or with one arm slashing across his body as he drove home a point.

All the photos were beautifully displayed in velvet-backed silver frames that Lauter had found in a pawnshop. The pawnshops of Rouen still contained many such things, little luxuries that people had sold during the war. Lauter had snapped them up for a song and thrown away the wooden frames he'd been using, and not a day went by that he didn't admire the collection. He'd found another way of improving it even more, and quite by accident. He'd been in the room one night studying yet again the pattern of the eighty site locations when the lights had gone out, a short power failure that happened now and then in Rouen. He'd bought two plumber's candles the week before, which he fetched and set up on saucers. It had been too difficult to read the tiny print on the maps, but the candle-light had flickered and danced on the silver frames, and the effect on the photographs had been magical. So he'd bought long, tapering table candles, gone back to the pawnshop and found two silver candlesticks, and set them up on each side of the photographs.

From then on each night, after he'd finished his reading and his map study, he'd light the candles and turn off the lamp, and sit in spellbound reverence. The fluttering, bouncing candle glow seemed to animate the photographs, moving the Fuehrer's arms and face and eyes so that Lauter could almost imagine him alive, almost hear the stirring words pouring from his mouth.

He'd watch for an hour or longer before going to bed, and always woke the following morning feeling spiritually refreshed and all the more convinced of the correctness of his pursuit, and its inevitable successful conclusion.

Only once did he falter in his resolve.

It was toward the end of his fourth year in Rouen when he'd been riding back to the city after searching, fruitlessly, an area around Doullens. There were still patches of snow braiding the road edges, and a freezing wind from the northeast leaned heavily on his back. Coming around a curve, he'd jammed on his brakes, skidded, and fallen, as something, a cat perhaps, had flashed out in from of him. He hadn't been injured—some abrasions down his right side—but he'd been winded and badly shaken up. The chain had broken on the bike, and he'd had to push it two kilometers to the next village to get it fixed. He'd got back to his apartment exhausted, bruised, chilled through, and completely dispirited. It seemed hopeless, futile. He hadn't covered a fifth of the map, he still had thousands of areas left to explore. And for what? A site that, even if it could be found, was probably useless beyond any repair, the missiles rusted, the machinery crippled with age. The whole thing was impossible.

Listlessly, in the pit of depression, he'd eaten some food, which warmed him up, then taken a hot bath, which had eased his aches, put on pajamas and slippers, and let himself into his workroom. He'd lit the candles right away, needing the comfort it always brought him, and in the magical, flickering glow he'd begun to feel ashamed. How could he even think about quitting? That's what those generals who'd had the nerve to call themselves Germans had done in 1945—given up, surrendered because they'd had no backbone, no faith. Because they'd forgotten whom they were serving.

The light danced on the photographs and the Fuehrer seemed to be glaring at him in reproach, his eyes boring into him, scolding, accusing. Only cowards give up, those eyes seemed to say; the brave, the truly dutiful, scorn adversity, fight back harder than ever.

In future years Lauter looked back on that day as his time of trial, almost as if the Fuehrer had been testing him. He came out of it more determined than ever to pursue his mission, and to never again doubt it.

He continued his search with renewed vigor.

He sold the motorbike and bought a Volkswagen camper so he could sleep in the back and save the money he'd been spending on hotels. Once a year he ran the "war historian" ad in the German newspapers, but stopped eventually when the replies, from the same people and a few new ones, were no different than they'd ever been.

By the fall of 1964, almost nine years after he'd begun to look, he filled in square number P18, and saw that he'd covered approximately half the search area. By now the records of each day's exploration filled nine of the diaries, one for each year, and he'd gone through almost fifty notebooks. He'd learned a lot in the time and had a better idea of what a site looked like, having explored six of them that were still in existence. They were in ruins, for the most part, dark, smelly places that children played in through the day and were lovers' haunts at night. He'd found quite a few old blockhouses, too, and other kinds of fortifications.

Once or twice he'd spotted something in the deep shade of summer, or buried under a ton of leaves in the fall, which had sent his heart thumping, but they'd been very brief, those moments of excitement, and the site stayed stubbornly hidden.

A summer passed. Then another. And another.

Then another.

The day finally came when Lauter had filled in seventy-five percent of the search area, but he noted it without emotion. Even though he was running out of territory and had nothing to show for the long years spent looking, he refused to despair. The site was there, and he'd find it; it was as simple as that. The fact that it was in the last section of the area was just unfortunate. He had no trouble adopting this attitude because mentally he was tougher than he'd ever been. He'd changed physically, too, although not in a way he would have wished.

He was faintly shocked to discover one day, going through some papers, a photograph of himself taken in Munich on his twenty-ninth birthday. He was also surprised to realize that that was thirteen years ago. He was forty-two. He went to a mirror and for once took a good look at the face he shaved every morning.

The young man in the photograph could have been his nephew. His face had the same cumulative look as the young man's, but the features were blunted now, fleshed out, the corners rounded. His cheekbones no longer protruded, and the line of his jaw was softer, fuller. His hair had undergone an autumnal change, going from straw yellow to drab brown, and thinning. And too many years of quick, out-of-the-can meals and lack of any real exercise had thickened his body, rumpling his shirt over his belt. He now looked, Lauter realized, like a typical German burgher, and nothing like the slim, upright soldier he'd always seen himself as. But his appearance was of no real importance to him; what did it matter what he looked like as long as he had a pair of keen eyes with which to find the site?

But he didn't find the site. And it wasn't because he hurried or tried to take any shortcuts now that the area was narrowed down. He was as ploddingly methodical as he'd ever been.

But the site refused to reveal itself, and on his next birthday he was still looking.

He was still looking on his forty-fourth birthday.

And he was still looking two years and five months later, on a day with wide blue skies and a smell of hay on the breeze, when he searched the Forêt de Nieppe near St. Omer, the last wood in the last square on his maps, and found nothing.

Lauter drove back to Rouen faster than normal, concentrating on the road and the traffic and blocking the outrageous thought that kept trying to burst into his head. He refused to think about anything but changing gear, slowing, speeding up, negotiating bends, and he chose not to notice the sick churning in his stomach, or the way he couldn't seem to stop blinking. When he reached his apartment he went straight into his workroom, lit the candles, sank exhausted into the chair, and sat there taking deep, shuddering breaths, his head bowed on his chest. Recovering gradually, he lifted his face and watched the candles playing hide-and-seek in the filigree of the silver frames, soothed by the gentle fluttering and the mystical thing it did to the photographs. He switched his gaze a fraction and began to soak up the strength that emanated from the Fuehrer's eyes, felt it coursing warmly through his body, reviving him, cleansing him, draining away the torrent of despair that had threatened to drown him.

He stayed in the room for a long time, then, recovered, at peace with himself, went to bed and slept soundly.

The next morning he did something he'd never done before: called the office and lied, telling them that he had the flu and wouldn't be in for a few days. Then he went back into his workroom and started.

He was convinced the answer lay in the diaries, certain he'd find recorded in one of them a clue as to how he'd come to miss the site. Because that's what he was sure had happened. Somewhere over the years he'd been careless, hadn't checked an area out completely, hadn't been as observant as he should have, had been shoddy in his procedure. Perhaps the cold had tempted him to hurry one day, or it had been roasting hot and the mosquitoes had been bad.

One by one he took down the diaries and began to read through them. He was surprised to find how quickly the entries had become terse and abbreviated, the handwriting developing into a fast, angled scrawl. He wondered if, unconsciously, he'd adopted a code against the chance of the diaries being discovered. It was the first time he'd ever read back through them. There'd never been any reason to before, it was always the next entry he'd been interested in.

Lauter wondered as he leafed through the first three diaries if that had been when he'd missed the site, the early years, through overeagerness, perhaps. In the Forêt de Maulévier, or le Bois-le-Vicomte? Some place practically on his doorstep? That would indeed be cruel.

Or the long middle years. Had he grown complacent? Too settled into a routine that had taken the edge off his concentration? Or the closing years. Was it possible that, running out of areas, he'd hurried past the site one day, too anxious to notice it?

He read through the diaries, studying them like a biblical scholar rocking over the Testaments. He kept it up for four days straight, reading the history of the major part of his adult life, checking back and forth between the diaries and the maps, navigating his way over the years, trying to spot where he'd gone wrong.

He found dozens of entries that were possibilities, dozens of locations he might have covered more thoroughly, places that either the weather or watchdogs or intransigent farmers had made difficult or impossible to search correctly. And there were other places, too, a lot of them. Private property, mainly, where trespassers were not encouraged, and he was forced to put a question mark against them.

On the fourth day, Lauter finished reviewing the last diary, then went through them all one by one, copying down every entry he'd marked as being suspect. He was shocked to find that there were over a hundred, and that they were spread all over both maps, the length and breadth of the entire search area.

What it meant was that all the time he'd spent searching had really been just a weeding-out period so that the real search could begin. It was a staggering thought, and it was only because the Fuehrer was there right in front of him, watching him, depending on him that Lauter was able to find the strength to accept it.

He returned to his office on a Friday.

The following day he set out once more, this time with brand-new maps and a brand-new notebook. And brand-new hopes.

Lauter was prepared to devote the rest of his life to the search if need be. But he didn't have to. Because on October 10, 1978, five and a half years later, which was twenty-three years, seven months, and four days after coming to Rouen, he found what he'd been looking for.

CHAPTER SEVEN

Pelham—London, December 19-20, 1978

Rossi lived on Cathcart Road, not far from the Little Boltons and the big white mansions the Arabs had been buying up. She had the basement flat of a handsome Georgian house with a bright red door, and Pelham was impressed.

He was further impressed when she answered his ring wearing a short terry toweling bathrobe.

"Hi," he said. "I called you at the office but you'd already left."

The girl ran a hand through her hair. "I was just about to take a shower."

"You going out? You have a date?"

"No."

"Then let's have dinner."

She inclined her head, smiled. "I'd like that. Come in while I get ready."

The flat was small, but she'd done nice things with it; smart and understated, Pelham thought, like the girl herself. She told him there was some liquor in the kitchen if he wanted a drink, then left him.

Pelham moved into the kitchen, admired all the utensils, and made himself a gin and tonic. He drank half of it, then went over to the bathroom door. The sound of a shower running came from behind it.

"Rossi?" he called.

"Ye-es?"

The door wasn't locked, so he opened it a fraction. "I wouldn't mind a shower myself. I had what you might call a hard day at the office."

"I'll be through in a minute," she said over the sound of the water.

She rubbed a soapy cloth over her forehead, taking a long time with it, then lifted her face up to the shower head. She blinked, knuckled her eyes, turned around, and got a surprise. Pelham, naked, his drink still in his hand, was getting into the shower with her.

He said, reasonably, "Seems silly to waste water." He finished his drink, put it down on the floor, and took the soap from her. "Tweed," he said. "That's my brand, too."

She burst out laughing. "Do you know what you are?"

"What am I?"

"I think the expression is 'forward.'"

"Well that's always been my motto anyway," Pelham said. "Turn around and I'll soap your back."

He moved the soap over her shoulders, then down over her flanks and the fine curve of her spine, slowing as he reached the firm smoothness of her bottom.

"You said my back."

"I got bored with your back." Pelham lathered his hands, dropped the soap into its dish, stretched his arms around her, and began to soap her thighs, moving his hands up over the soft swell of her tummy and up onto her breasts.

She moved against him. "Nice," she murmured.

"It could get better," he said.

She reached her hand back for him, bent forward slightly, and guided him as he took hold of her wide, bony hips, and they moved slowly against each other, settling into a steady, easy rhythm, the water falling on them like a gentle rain.

Then the rhythm quickened and they locked together briefly in a shuddering embrace.

"Wow," Pelham said, breathing hard as they slowly broke apart. "After that I need a shower."

"All right," she said. She stepped nimbly out of the tub, turned off the hot water, turned the cold full on.

Pelham leaped out, threw a towel at the laughing girl, started laughing himself. "Hey," he said, "do you know what we just made in there?"

"What?"

"The beast with a back and a front."

Their mood continued through dinner; they felt easy, comfortable with each other.

It was only after they'd got back from the restaurant and made love again, in bed this time, that Pelham reverted to his earlier depression.

They lay half under the covers, the only break in the darkness was a ribbon of streetlight touching a corner of the room. Now and then the sound of tires squishing through puddles came to them faintly, breaking a silence that was bothering the girl. She looked at Pelham who lay with one arm around her, the other tucked behind his head, staring at a ceiling he couldn't see. She studied his face: it wasn't a specially unique face but, Rossi thought, it was one that worked. His nose made a strong statement, which was seconded by the firm line of his cheekbones. The eyes were good, deep set and with a brightness to them in spite of their gray-green color. And there was a pronounced Celtic stubbornness in the shape of the underlip. A good-looking man, Rossi decided, but a strangely moody one.

"What's wrong?" she asked.

"Huh?"

"Do you have, what I believe is called, the post-coital blues?"

"What makes you say that?"

"You're holding my nipple like a cigarette."

Pelham shifted his arm. "Sorry."

A few moments went by, then she asked, "Is it me?"

Pelham sighed. "No, it's me. I got the bullet today."

"The bullet?"

"The prong. The old bounceroo."

Rossi said, "I'm sorry, it took all my time learning regular English. I still don't know all the slang words."

"I lost my job."

She put a quick hand on his arm. "Because of us? Yesterday afternoon?"

"No, no. I just got chewed out for that. What got me fired was a report I turned in." He told her about the trip to Hayes and the blown-up houses. "My boss, Evans, didn't like my theory of what had caused the blast."

"What did you tell him it was?"

"Oh, nothing much. Just a World War II flying bomb."

Rossi knew from his tone of voice, by the disgusted way he said it, that he really had told Evans that.

She sat up in the bed and said, trying to sound consoling, "I'm afraid a lot of people just can't take a joke."

"I wasn't joking. I really did think it was a flying bomb."

He explained why, telling her about what he'd found and how the people he'd interviewed had described the sound they'd heard overhead. "But then I spoke to a guy at the Defense Department who told me a few things I didn't know, things I should have checked on before I mouthed off to everybody. So they fired me for being dumb. And," Pelham concluded heavily, "I have to admit they have a point."

Rossi leaned her forehead against his cheek. "No they don't. They were very unfair. Based on the evidence you made a logical conclusion. They did make a noise like those people described."

Pelham pulled his face away, looked at her. "How do you know that?"

"My uncle was in England through the war. At Croydon airport."

"There's an airport at Croydon?"

"It's been closed for years, but it used to be the main London airport, like Heathrow is today. So he became pretty familiar with flying bombs. *Vergeltungswaffe*, it was called in German. Revenge Weapon. It was shortened to V-1."

"They tried to knock out the airport, huh?"

"No, it wasn't that," Rossi said. "Apparently they weren't very accurate and a lot of them fell short of London and landed on Croydon."

Pelham sat up, too, his melancholy gone. He was looking very, very interested. "I didn't know that."

"My uncle never stopped talking about how one of them nearly killed him." Rossi smothered a laugh. "He was living in a boardinghouse, in Croydon. Everybody was out so he sneaked down to the landlady's kitchen and made himself a sandwich. He was sitting there eating when he heard a flying bomb coming over. He heard it cut out, so he dived underneath the table, and a few moments later the house blew up. Fell down all around him. When they dug him out he was still eating his sandwich. The kitchen table saved his life."

Very carefully Pelham said, "Let me get this straight. He knew it was going to drop because he heard the motor cut out?"

"Oh, yes. He used to say that you were never in danger as long as you could hear them."

When Pelham said nothing she mistook the fixed look on his face for worry, and commiserated with him again. "It's so unfair, Jimmy, losing your job." She hesitated a moment and then said, "What are you going to do now?"

"Get it back again," Pelham replied.

Thirty minutes after Brian Jakes got back from lunch the following day he was showing Pelham into his office for the second time in twenty-four hours. Jakes hadn't expressed surprise at Pelham's coming to see him again so soon, assuming that he had a good reason, and when he'd sat him down in his room he heard it.

"Brian, I let you talk me out of believing that a V-1 zapped those houses and I shouldn't have."

"Oh? You have some new information?" There wasn't a hint of anything in the question except polite interest.

"Yeah. Last night I found out a couple of things I didn't know, and today I found out a whole lot more. I just had lunch with an air correspondent who works on Fleet Street. He's very fond of the grape so I kept buying and he kept talking, and from what he told me I think I know why Radford tossed me out of here yesterday."

Pelham's rapid burst was in sharp contrast to Jakes's slow, considered reply. "Start with what you found out last night."

"Two things. One, Croydon, less than two miles from where those houses went up in Hayes, took a hell of a shellacking in the war from V-1s. Why? Because as I found out at lunch it's a fact that most of the V-1s fired at London fell short, south of the Thames anyway. And a good proportion of those blew hell out of the southwestern suburbs, places like Croydon, Mersham, Chislehurst. And Hayes, Brian, Hayes."

"Yes, I know that."

"You do? Then you've got to admit it makes my argument for a V-1 stronger."

"I realized that yesterday," Jakes admitted. "What's the second thing you discovered?"

Pelham edged forward on his chair; he was barely sitting on it. "That was the real clincher. I found out that people learned to duck when they heard a buzz bomb stop, when they heard the engine quit, because that meant it was coming down. Correct?"

Jakes confirmed it. "The buzz bombs had that reputation, yes."

"Now," Pelham pulled out his notebook. "Remember me reading this out yesterday? The guy who thought he'd heard a helicopter? I'll read it again. 'I heard a helicopter overhead, then I heard it stop. I thought it had crashed when the explosion came.'"

Pelham snapped the book closed in triumph. "He heard an engine stop, Brian, then the explosion. Only it wasn't a helicopter's engine he heard stopping."

Jakes picked up a pen from his desk and tapped it against his teeth. He said, after a moment, "That's true, of course. No helicopter crashed. However, we still can't say with any certainty that a buzz bomb did. Because," he hurried on, cutting off Pelham before he could jump in, "the same arguments I advanced yesterday still remain."

"There are answers to them, Brian. There have to be. Something blew up those houses, and if it's too outlandish to blame a buzz bomb, it's too easy to blame some poor guy just because he was Irish."

"I'll grant you that. I checked with the police officially. As far as they know, that dead Irishman had no connections with the IRA." Then Jakes said, "What did you mean about knowing why Radford had you thrown out?"

As if he'd been waiting outside for his cue, the door opened and Radford walked into the room. He recognized Pelham but didn't acknowledge him. He said, in his crisp manner, "When you get a moment, Jakes, pop up and see me, would you?"

Pelham sprang out of his chair. "Mr. Radford. Remember me? Jim Pelham?"

Radford gave him a slight inclination of his head and then said to Jakes, "If you could be through in five minutes I'd appreciate it." He started to leave but Pelham's voice stopped him.

"Just a moment, Mr. Radford. About yesterday afternoon . . . I found out today why you threw me out."

Radford, already irritated by Pelham's presence, fired back an answer. "I had you thrown out because you were rude and talking nonsense."

"I didn't start the rudeness."

"Mr. Pelham." It was Jakes trying to smooth things over. "I think it would be better—"

"Just a second, Brian. I want to get this said." Pelham swung back to Radford. "Sure you thought I was talking nonsense, but it still made you think. I sinned yesterday because I introduced an idea that scared hell out of you. You don't believe a buzz bomb hit those houses because you can't afford to believe it. Because that would mean this country is vulnerable to attack from the south."

"Ridiculous!" Radford snapped.

"Is it, Mr. Radford? Isn't it true that this country's defenses are set up to parry a blow from Moscow? To stop an attack that's most likely to come from the east, or over the pole from the north? They're the areas the Early Warning System monitors, aren't they? Everything's designed to counter a five-thousand-mile-an-hour missile looping down from a couple of hundred miles up, and coming in from either of those directions. But what if something came from the south, from a friendly neighbor like France? It's five thousand miles, Moscow to London, less than a hundred from Northern France. And what if it was something like a V-1 limping along at four hundred miles an hour and flying level most of the way at two or three thousand feet? Who's going to mistake it for the latest Soviet superweapon? You'd be in trouble, wouldn't you, Mr. Radford? Because even at four hundred miles an hour it'd be across the Channel before you could turn around. Face it, Mr. Radford, somebody fired a V-1 at us. Why, I don't know. But you won't even admit the possibility because if you do you have to admit that they beat the radar. You'd have to admit that there's a picket missing from your fence."

Radford, his lips tight against his teeth, said, "That's the most asinine thing I've ever heard in my life." He stabbed a finger at Pelham, flicked his eyes to Jakes. "I want this man out of the building immediately. And under no circumstances is he to be admitted again." He wheeled around and marched out of the room.

There was a long silent moment before Pelham said, "I guess that's progress. Yesterday I was just tossed out. Today I'm barred for life."

Jakes pressed at his mustache as if it had come unstuck. He looked embarrassed. "Well, you weren't very diplomatic, were you?"

Pelham made a face. "It's never been my strong suit."

"Come on." Jakes got wearily out of his chair. "I have to chuck you out."

Walking down the corridor Pelham said, "You haven't said what you think about my theory."

"Very shaky. It's all based on one boozy lunch with a newspaperman who sounds like less than an expert."

"That's your official answer. What's your unofficial opinion?"

"About the same," Jakes replied, but he didn't look at Pelham when he said it.

He handed in Pelham's pass, walked through the door with him, and stood with him at the top of the steps. He said, "Do you know what also bothers me about your ideas of buzz bomb? Two things. Firstly, with a weapon that old they couldn't be sure it would even get off the ground, let alone fly a hundred miles. And secondly, they weren't very efficient when they did work properly. I think that each one that hit in an urban area killed an average of seven people. So I have to ask myself why anyone would use something like that. When the Germans fired thousands it made some sense. But just one by itself makes no sense at all."

"Brian, none of it makes much sense, at least not at the moment. But it's going to."

"How do you know that?"

"Because," Pelham said, "I'm going to make it make sense."

CHAPTER EIGHT

Lauter—Rouen, October 10, 1978

It was a Sunday. Lauter had slept well in the back of the Volkswagen camper, which he'd parked the night before in a little wood a few miles from Dieppe. After a cup of coffee made over his butane stove, he'd reached the village he'd been aiming for around 9 A.M., and from there had taken a winding dirt road which paralleled the coast. He was close enough to the cliffs to be able to see the gray smudge of the channel. The road snaked toward a thick clump of pines, and a few minutes later he stopped when he spotted an old, unreadable farm sign at a side road which vanished into the trees. He checked the notes he'd copied from one of the diaries and saw that he'd visited this place nine years before.

According to his records the road had been flooded by the torrential rains that year and he hadn't been able to drive in. And he couldn't explore on foot because there'd been a mean-looking bull inside the fence, which had charged the moment he'd put a hand on the gate. It was only a small farm, and the tree area was small, too, so he'd passed it up. And he shouldn't have.

There was no sign of any bull now, no cattle, nothing moving at all. He slipped the catch on the gate and entered. The dirt road, muddy and puddled from an earlier rain, curled for a few hundred feet, then disappeared into the pines. Lauter followed it in. It was a drab-colored morning with a cold stillness in the air that got colder as the pines tented overhead, water dripping from them.

He walked through the gloomy silence for a while till he came to a path that crossed the road at right angles. It opened onto a view of furrowed fields; beyond them had to be cliffs and the sea. But it was the little building at the other end of the path that caught his attention. It looked a bit like a sentry box except it was larger and lower, and was situated where the path began in a clearing.

He'd already noticed that the path pointed toward the northwest, toward London, but he'd come across too many straight, narrow paths that pointed the same way to get excited. Except he'd never seen one with a small building like that built to one side. And that *was* exciting.

He hurried toward it, his eyes straining to see what lay beyond at the back of the clearing. As he drew level he would have given the little building a lot more than just a quick glance if it hadn't been for what he'd spotted: even in the murky light he could see it plainly, bulking long and low, and set back under the trees. With his heart thumping he trotted toward it, trying to smother his excitement, remembering how he'd found something similar once that had turned out to be old, abandoned chicken houses.

But even as he reminded himself of this, he could see that the mound was the wrong shape to be a disused farm building: it looked to be about one hundred fifty feet long and less than five feet high. He reached the perimeter of the clearing, kept going into the wood, his boots crunching on broken branches, slogging through a damp, ankle-deep mulch of dead leaves and bracken.

He halted in front of the mound, his breath coming in short, little stabs. It was definitely man-made; it stopped and started too abruptly not to be. He clambered up it, slipping and sliding on the soggy carpet of pine needles, stood on top, and looked around.

Something flip-flopped inside him when he saw the other mounds; three of them, smaller and with different dimensions, exactly as it should have been.

It was a site, no question about it. The mound he was standing on would be the assembly building, the one on the left would be for fuel storage, the one on the right would house the wings and other components, the square-shaped one would be the anti-magnetic compass building, and the little sentry house was the firing hut. It was certainly an unrecorded site, but was it *the* site, the eighty-first site, the one that had been operational?

Lauter scrambled down, trotted through the wood into the clearing, his lungs starting to burn. He was certain that twelve inches beneath the rocky path he was running on was the concrete base of the launching ramp. But he didn't stop to check; a ramp was no good, nothing was any good, if there weren't any missiles inside the long building.

He turned onto the road and ran along it to the front gate, his head carried on one side, pain beginning in his arms and legs. He reached the van, leaned against it trying to recover, got in, and drove it back the way he'd come. He took it past the little building, stopped in the clearing, jumped out, opened the rear doors, and grabbed hold of the tools he always kept in readiness: a small pickax and a collapsible shovel. His mind was tumbling over rationalizing his conclusion: the road was certainly wide enough to take a heavy truck, and with those trees for cover it was a perfect place to build a site—close enough to a supply road yet far enough away from the village to keep it all a secret. And another thing: it couldn't be more than two hundred kilometers to London, easy range; and being right on the Channel, any misfires would have fallen harmlessly into the sea.

He hurried back into the trees, climbed on top of the mound, and measured off half its length. In front of him the trees had been thinned for a track that he knew had to lead to the door of the building. He clambered down, dropped the pickax, and began to shovel away the layers of leaves and broken rotting branches. They were wet and heavy, compressed into place by time and the weather, almost a part of the forest floor. He threw the shovel aside, grabbed up the pickax, and began to take large chunks of black earth away from the side of the mound. He stopped, panting, his breath making little gray ghosts in the cold air. He wiped his wrist across his forehead, started in with the pickax again, gouging out shrubs and grassy roots and wet, textured layers of pine needles, the morning beginning to fill with the thick, moist, fecund smell of new earth.

He swung the pickax, swung it again, felt the point tugging on something. It wasn't a root, it was fiber of some kind, dark black fiber. He scraped the dirt away, uncovered it, and saw what it was: netting. Exactly the thing you'd use to keep an earth cover over a cement building.

He attacked the mound harder than ever, working at the hole he'd made. The netting, rotted through, crumbled immediately. He went through earth, leaves, roots again, then stopped, tried to swallow between gulps of air, his arms aching, his skin clammy under his clothes. He swung the pickax once, twice. The third time there was an impact he could feel all the way to his shoulders and with it came the dull clang of metal on metal. He snatched up the shovel, spaded earth away, and saw the grainy glint of rusted steel.

It took him a half hour to clear the door down to the heavy padlock, and another half hour to clear down to the bottom of the door. He had to stop to rest, the thumping in his chest almost hard enough to hurt, the soft skin on his palms chafed away, already blistered and broken.

The padlock was made of brass as thick as his finger and secured a massive bolt that stretched across the tight join of what had to be double doors. The huge brackets, riveted into place, could have come from a medieval castle.

Taking a fresh grip on the pickax, he hefted it, swung it, and drove it with all his strength into the hasp that held the lock, smashing at the metal again and again. The padlock held but the hasp loosened, and was finally torn away, taking a jagged piece of the bracket with it. Lauter pushed at the left side door, shoved at it, kicked at it. It moved back an inch, two inches, then stopped there as solid as a rock.

He waited till his chest had stopped heaving, then made his way back to the van, dug out the jack and a toolbox, got a flashlight, and carried everything back with him. The jack was a light, simple arrangement, and it was an easy matter to wind the support bar all the way down, turn the jack on its side, and position it between the two doors. When he slowly began to crank the handle, the support bar rose up its steel column, contacted the left side door two inches away, and strained against it, and after a moment's stubbornness, pushed it back on its old hinges.

Gripped by a choking, suffocating kind of thrill, he found that part of him didn't want to go through the doors, afraid that if there was nothing but emptiness inside, he'd be too crushed to continue the search. Another part propelled him forward to a possible triumphant conclusion of the first stage of his master plan.

He squeezed his body through the opening and stepped inside. The first thing that struck him, while he fumbled with the flashlight, was the smell. It seemed to be in two layers: the dank, dark smell of a long-locked basement, and riding slightly above it another smell, dry and tomblike, a smell of age and preservation, of dusty, unexplored attics.

The flashlight beam stabbed into life, lit up a long, tunnellike interior, traveled over the concrete floor and stopped at the coffin-shaped crates stacked against the rear wall.

It was a sight Lauter had seen before in a thousand dreams: the crates, ten of them, thirty feet long, four feet high, stacked in a double layer, untouched, pristine, waiting for him.

Like a sleepwalker, he moved toward them, ran a hand over their rough, boxwood sides. The wood was warped by age, the nails starting out of their holes. A tin strip wrapped around the crates bound them in the middle and at both ends. He put the toolbox down, selected a pair of wire cutters, and went to work on the crate nearest him.

The tin strips severed easily, fell away. He put down the wire cutters, took up a large screwdriver, and began to pry away a boxwood strip near the end of the crate. The nails offered little resistance, slipping out quickly from the dry wood, and as a tarry, oily smell drifted out, the flashlight beam reflected dully on its source: black tarpaulin cloth.

Lauter pried loose another slat, saw that he'd guessed correctly, that this was the rear of the missile; the bulge he was looking at had to be made by the tail plane. He reached for the wire cutters again, took a handful of the tarpaulin, and cut into it in a long, even slice.

He knew what he was doing; in his mind's eye he could see the drawing on his corkboard in his workroom. The schematic drawing of a V-1 cut from an American aviation magazine. There was an access plate slightly forward of the tail plane, and Lauter was right on top of it. The flashlight shone on heavy khaki-colored steel, and a smooth metal plate about eighteen inches across. He went to work on the screws that held it closed.

Perspiration rolled down and stung his eyes. He blinked it away; in a minute he'd know. That the site had missiles had been obvious the moment he'd seen the crates, but in what condition? Were they going to be usable after all this time, or had their innards been irreparably eaten away by rust?

There were five screws, in tight, but each responded to pressure from the large screwdriver. Lauter drew four of them, carefully placing them in his pocket, then paused, staring at the plate in the flashlight beam. He was like a man who'd broken into a pyramid and was on the verge of entering the treasure chamber. Surrounded by pitch-black silence, he loosened the final screw and swung the plate away.

What he saw snatched his breath: the gyros, the auto pilot, all the delicate control mechanisms were not only bone dry, but layered with a thin coat of grease that, although hard and stiff, was still protective.

He moved the plate back, replaced the screws, and boarded up the crate again, hardly aware that he was doing it. It was fantastic; far better than he'd ever dared hope for. He swung the flashlight to his left, running the beam along the floor and around the walls and ceiling; reinforced concrete three feet thick, and heavy steel doors that fitted perfectly, that's what had done it. There was no seepage, no cracks for the rain to enter, and the tightly wrapped tarpaulins had kept the humidity at bay, preserving the missiles almost in their original state.

Moving down the floor, Lauter found ten more crates stacked up, and could tell by their size and shape that these contained the propulsion units, the jet engines. And because he knew that, for security reasons, the missile had always been the last things supplied, it followed that everything else—the wings, the ramp stanchions, the steam generator, the launch piston—would be in one of the other buildings.

He followed the beam back to the doors, squeezed through them into the cold morning light. Hooking the pickax into the broken hasp, he pulled the door closed and began to cover up the doors, shoveling back the earth he'd removed, piled up leaves, branches, smoothing it all into place. He stepped back to look at the result and was struck again by the site's wonderful disguise. It was, as he'd known it would have to be, a modified site and, without doubt, one of the last to be completed. Built as it was, half underground with its layer of forest floor covering it, it would have been totally hidden from even the sharpest aerial photography. Hidden from the villagers, too. It would have been a simple matter for the Luftwaffe to close off the winding road and spread the rumor that what was being built was another defense post against the coming invasion. Then had come the chaos of the retreat, the panic of the Normandy

beachhead, a clerical oversight by an army struggling for its life. . . .
The site had never officially existed for very long, and being so
cleverly disguised on this tiny, out-of-the-way farm, it wasn't hard
to see how it had stayed undisturbed all these years.

But it wouldn't be staying undisturbed for much longer.

Lauter turned and visualized the launching ramp stretching away
down the path, steam blasting from the catapult, the winged bomb
rushing into the air. And it was then that understanding really struck
him for the first time; grabbed him, weakened his knees. He became
aware of somebody's voice, discovered it was his own.

"*Ich hab's! Ich hab's!*" He didn't seem to be able to stop saying
the words, "I've found it! I've found it!"

Lauter walked to the farmhouse, a low gray stone building with
several smaller structures tacked on to it. Smoke twisted from somewhere behind it and hung limply in the still air.

He went around to the back into a big, untidy yard. Old fruit
boxes were stacked haphazardly in one corner, and in another, an
ancient piece of farm machinery lay crippled under a blanket of
rust. A long rickety chicken house ran down one side, a sagging
wooden and wire affair, with a corrugated uralite roof, and opposite
it, smoke billowed from a low brick incinerator into which a man
was feeding a pile of garbage.

He turned at Lauter's approach, watching him cross the yard, an
old man in faded blue overalls buttoned over a torn sweater, a dark,
work-worn face, stubby, wrinkled hands.

"You lost?" he asked. His voice had a raspy, irritable quality.

Lauter walked up to him. "No. I wanted to talk to you about this
farm."

Suspicion flared in the old man's face. His rheumy eyes flicked
over Lauter, noting the hair plastered to his forehead, the dirt on his
clothes, and no coat on such a cold day. He threw out an arm in an
encompassing gesture. "What's to talk about? Seven days a week I
grub out a miserable living."

"You used to have a bull, didn't you?"

"It wasn't mine. I'd just rent it for the cows. But I got rid of them
five years ago. Too old to get up on freezing mornings for the likes
of them."

Lauter could see that the old man didn't know what to make of him but was playing it safe, thinking that he just might be from the tax department. He tried to be a little more affable.

"I suppose chickens are easier than cows."

The farmer grunted, still pleading poverty. "Nothing's easy when you farm. You break your back, and for what? A few sous a day."

"Still," Lauter said, "a farm like this must be worth something. You'd get a good price for it, I'm sure."

Instead of answering the old man picked up the ax he'd been using and went back to work on a log. He brought the ax chomping down into the wood twice, and severed it on the third swing.

Lauter, waiting till he'd finished, pressed on. "How much would you say it's worth?"

"This place? Very little. Who'd be fool enough to want it?"

"I would," Lauter said flatly.

It stopped the old man, but only for a moment. He picked up the split wood and added it to the fire inside the incinerator, then forked in some trash.

Lauter didn't want to ask about the buildings right after he'd shown interest in the farm, but he was bursting with the question.

"I noticed some mounds in the trees not far from the entrance. Know anything about them?"

Flames licked up the blackened bricks of the incinerator, then smoke billowed out and hung in the breezeless air.

"Blockhouses. The Bosche built them in the war."

It was a matter-of-fact answer, no concealment there. And no insult either; Lauter had been worried that the old man might know he was German, but his accent had become very slight. People often thought he was Belgian.

"They seem different somehow," Lauter said, venturing onto thin ice because he had to. "I wonder what's inside."

The farmer, busy with the pitchfork again, still found time to shrug. "The same as what's in any blockhouse. Shit and old newspapers."

"You never had a look?"

The old man said irritably, "I know what shit looks like."

Lauter watched him work for a while, sensed that he was nervous, waiting for him to produce identification and ask official questions. Lauter made an attempt to relax him.

"The Bosche must have been all over this area. You were lucky the house wasn't bombed."

The farmer stepped back from the incinerator, looked at the farmhouse with distaste. "It would've improved it. When the bombers started to come over I left. Stayed with my daughter in Provence. The fields were in ruins when I got back, and they've never really recovered."

Lauter asked the question quickly. "How much would you take for the farm?"

"What?"

"I want to buy this farm."

The old man slid his eyes away more cautious than ever, now that the talk had turned to money. "Not for sale," he said.

"I'll give you a good price. You can name it."

The farmer squinted at him. "Why would you want it? You don't look like you could live off the land."

"For my son," Lauter answered.

"You wouldn't be doing him a favor. The place has gone to seed."

"A hundred and fifty thousand. I'll give you a hundred and fifty thousand francs."

"It's not for sale."

"Two hundred thousand francs. I can bring it tomorrow. Cash. I've got it in Rouen."

It was true. Living so frugally, Lauter had been able to salt away most of his salary ever since he'd come to France. He'd known he'd be needing every penny someday.

The old man was shaking his head, still being cautious. "What would I do with money like that? I've never seen twenty thousand in one place."

"Whatever you want. Go back to Provence. Live in the sun with your daughter."

The old man sniffed. "That one. She's too busy running a shop in Aix. I wouldn't be welcome."

"Then you could live somewhere else. You could retire."

"Only rich people retire."

"You'd have more than enough to live on. And comfortably."

The old man, silent, began to feed the incinerator again, and Lauter spoke to his back. "You could leave all this. You said yourself it's backbreaking work."

"Maybe it is," the farmer muttered, "but it's all I've ever done, and all I know how to do."

Lauter saw that it would be pointless talking any further. The old man was stubborn, uneducated, cemented in his ways; hating the land yet tied to it. Retirement, even with money, would be foreign to his thinking; a man worked till he died.

Realizing this, Lauter knew what he had to do.

The ax lay on the ground, the dull morning light reflecting in its sharp-edged head.

He took a few precautions first, disguising them well.

"If you can't use the money, perhaps another member of your family . . ."

"I have nobody. Just my daughter. And her I never see."

"A friend, then."

"My friends are dead," the farmer answered. "Like I will be soon."

Lauter, his mind racing ahead, missed the irony of the prediction. "But there must be somebody you're fond of, somebody who comes to visit you perhaps?"

"Nobody comes. Only Leclerc to buy the eggs. And cheats me every time."

"It's not right to live so much on your own," Lauter said. "Suppose you got sick?"

The old man drove his pitchfork into some garbage. "I don't have time to get sick." He shook the load, getting the balance right, and was in the middle of hefting it when Lauter, moving normally, picked up the ax and hit the farmer with the flat end of its head. It caught him at the nape of the neck and made a brittle, crunching sound. The old man tumbled forward onto the pile of trash and lay there with his head at a crazy angle. Lauter tossed the ax aside, bent down, and grasped the man under the arms, dragged the thin body to the incinerator and tipped it in. He picked up the pitchfork and shoveled refuse on top.

The flames leaped up, and there was a smell of burning wool and cloth, then, after a while, a harsh, high smell of something else.

Lauter, feeding wood into the incinerator, felt nothing. The old man had been an obstacle, like the padlock on the building had been an obstacle. It was regrettable that he'd been forced to smash them both.

But his mind was full of other things. The first part of his plan was now complete, the second part would take a lot less time, six months or less with luck. It depended on how long it took him to find the expert help he needed: the engineer and the pilot.

But one thing was certain: he wouldn't find them in France.

After twenty-three years, he was going home to Germany.

PART TWO

THE PREPARATION

CHAPTER NINE

Lauter—Munich,
October 20-December 1, 1978

There was no trouble with the farm; the man who came to buy the eggs wasn't surprised to hear that the farmer, whose name turned out to be Chennard, had gone to stay with his daughter in Provence —he knew about the daughter and that she was often unwell. Lauter told him that he was a neighbor of hers and as the old man had trouble reading letters, and as Lauter had been coming north anyway, he'd brought the news of the woman's illness.

After that it was simply a matter of Lauter's hiring a local to look after the place, which he did, making sure that the man was the stolid, incurious type who wouldn't go poking around. He also used the few days he spent at the farm to open up the rest of the site, and found things to be exactly as he supposed. Then he proceeded to wind up his affairs in Rouen, or at least suspend them temporarily. He left most of his balance intact in the bank, paid six months' rent in advance on his apartment, which he was maintaining, and arranged to garage the Volkswagen camper. His office had acceded to his request for a transfer back to Munich, and he returned to that city a week later.

He found a furnished apartment in a slightly seedy area, taking it because it was inexpensive and immediately available, then embarked on the next step of his plan: contacting the people he was going to need.

He knew that these people would, of course, have to feel the same way as he did but he had no real idea of how to go about finding them. The only visible political groups were the antithesis of what he was seeking: the ruling government party and its opposition, both dedicated to continuing the shameful alliance with the victors; the liberals, who were thinly disguised Communists; and the Neo-Fascists whose tenets were a mockery of National Socialism.

He thought about the problem for some time, then arrived at a very simple solution. He had to wait only a few days to try it out, once it had occurred to him. On November 8 he went to a place, in the old section of the city, which had once been a beer hall, a very famous beer hall—for Lauter a national landmark. The original building was gone now, replaced by a new one that had a modern restaurant on its street floor, one of a chain of fast-food outlets where the waitresses wore old-style Bavarian dress, and gigantic menus, decorated with a cartoon pig eating a sausage, dangled from the ceiling. It made Lauter sick to his stomach to see the change, but he forced himself to go in.

He chose a table with a view of the door, ordered the simplest thing he could find, and ate while he watched who came in.

At the end of an hour and a half Lauter was beginning to think he was wasting his time, but ten minutes later a man came through the door who immediately caught his attention. He was a short, plump little man who looked hesitant, unsure of his surroundings, and, Lauter noted with interest, the man appeared to regard the place with intense dislike. Lauter watched him move into the restaurant, noting that he limped heavily on his left foot. He chose an empty table and sat looking around him uncomfortably. He seemed flustered when a waitress arrived to take his order, and the way she had to point at the menu, and the way he merely glanced at it, it was obvious that he wasn't there because he was hungry.

Lauter was pretty sure the man wasn't a tourist, which might have explained his behavior; he looked like any of the meaty faced, pale-haired Germans Lauter worked with, and he was dressed in the same kind of conservative suit and tie that most of the city's office workers wore. Also, Lauter thought the man looked to be about his own age, another good pointer. After watching him toy with his food, Lauter got up and crossed to the man's table.

"May I join you?"

The plump man hadn't seen Lauter coming and was surprised. "Pardon?"

Lauter said quietly, "I think we might both be here for the same reason."

The reply was nervous, defensive. "I'm here to have dinner."

Lauter sat down. He said, low enough not to be overheard, "Let me tell you why I'm here. I came to celebrate the memory of what happened on this spot fifty-five years ago tonight, in 1923. The start of the November Putsch, the first real demonstration of his power."

"What putsch? Whose power?" The man made a poor attempt at acting dumb.

"The greatest German who ever lived," Lauter said. "My father shook his hand."

The man couldn't hide his reaction to that, didn't try to. "A great honor," he breathed, and his eyes shone behind his thick-lensed glasses. The glasses were round like the rest of him—round face, round little body, round skull peeking through sparse, stringy hair. His fingers, nervously playing with a stein of untouched beer, were like little cocktail sausages, the nails scrubbed and perfectly manicured. In spite of his out-of-shape body, there was a general impression of neatness about him, of personal correctness.

"My name is Lauter."

"Hoff," the man replied. Then he said, hesitantly, "Your father was . . . active?"

"His party number was 512."

Hoff reacted to that, too. He said, with surprised admiration, more to himself than to Lauter, "Just ten more."

It was all the proof Lauter needed; only somebody who felt as he did would know that the Fuehrer's party card had been number 502. No more tests would be necessary.

"You live in Munich, Herr Hoff?"

"Yes."

"I've just returned. I've been living in France for a long time."

Hoff frowned as if he'd detected a serious flaw. "I can understand leaving Germany and its," he gestured about him, "ruined memories, but France . . ."

"It was unavoidable," Lauter answered. "You see, I have a plan."

Hoff looked at him, expecting him to elaborate, but instead Lauter seemed to strike off in another direction. "I was in the Luftwaffe. KG 56. You?"

Hoff looked down at his plate. "I did not serve," he said, and there was a word of disappointment and shame in the statement.

Lauter remembered the man's limp, and understood a lot about him. He leaned toward him, said very low, "If you'd still like to, it's not too late."

Hoff, mystified, said, "What are you talking about?"

Lauter slowed his words, spacing them out. "I've found a way to continue the fight." Then he said to the man's blank face, "I don't live far from here. I'd like to tell you about it."

Hoff hesitated, but as Lauter got up, he got up, too.

They paid their bills, slipped into their coats, went outside, and got a cab.

Neither man spoke during the ride, or when they were mounting the stairs to Lauter's apartment, or till after they'd sat down facing each other in the only two armchairs. Then Lauter began speaking and Hoff listened, mesmerized as Lauter told him how he'd learned about the missing site, and how he'd searched for it and found it. "Twenty-three years," Hoff said, and again Lauter heard the note of awed admiration in his voice. The more Lauter saw of Hoff the better he liked his choice; the man was clearly the kind who not only respected leadership but needed it, needed the strength in others he did not possess himself. Lauter was glad to see it; in this endeavor, absolute loyalty and obedience were paramount.

Lauter got up, moved across the room to a desk that he unlocked, slid his hand under the paper lining of a drawer, and brought out an envelope. Inside it were photographs of the site that he'd taken with a Polaroid camera, so that no photographic lab would get a look at the prints.

He showed them to Hoff, the mounds shot from different angles, one of the photos showing the exposed doors of the main building.

"It's fantastic," Hoff said. "Fantastic." He swallowing with excitement, his voice gone husky. "But can it work? How do we operate the missiles?"

"We'll get an engineer or a technician to show us. We'll also need the services of a pilot," Lauter added, then explained his idea of getting through the English radar system.

Hoff's head moved in wonder. "How were you able to think of such a thing?"

"Because I saw this," Lauter said, "in a book." He pulled another Polaroid print from the envelope, a photo he'd taken of a picture he'd pinned to his workroom wall in Rouen. It showed, from an underneath angle, the profile of a Spitfire and a V-1 flying wing tip to wing tip. "The technical aspects of radar are publicly available,"

Lauter went on, "so by doing some research I knew what I had in mind was possible."

Hoff, nodding over the print, said in a whisper, "You have done a wonderful thing, Herr Lauter. A marvelous thing. You are to be congratulated. Applauded." The print trembled in his fingers. "I can't believe it, a chance to fight." His eyes came up quickly, a fast flash of embarrassment as he amended his words. "A chance to continue the fight."

"This time," Lauter said, watching Hoff closely, "to the conclusion that was denied us before."

Hoff tried but didn't understand, and his plump face showed it.

But instead of explaining, Lauter reached into the envelope for the last print and handed it over. It was a photograph of another of the pictures on Lauter's corkboard wall: the two middle-aged intellectuals gazing uncomfortably at the camera.

Hoff read out the number scrawled across it, then said, puzzled, "I'm sorry, but I don't recognize them."

Lauter told him who the two men were and what they'd done, and how that event led directly to what they were going to do with the V-1.

When Hoff heard the news his eyes and his mouth formed little circles of astonishment, and he couldn't seem to speak for a moment. When he did, fright wobbled his voice. "A nuclear bomb? It can't be possible . . ."

"I believe it to be entirely possible," Lauter said firmly, his pale eyes drilling into Hoff. "If we get the right kind of help."

"The right help," Hoff repeated. "Yes, of course." He was still stunned; a fine bead of moisture had started on his upper lip. "When . . . how long before . . ."

"The target date is December twenty-fourth."

"Christmas Eve. Why?"

"Because I feel that such a momentous event should take place on an appropriate date," Lauter answered, and gave his reasons for choosing the date.

"I see," Hoff said. "Yes. Most appropriate."

"I take it you are with me on this?"

Very slowly, and after a long moment, Hoff nodded his head.

"Then may I ask you if you know of any group or organization we might safely approach for help? Without revealing why we need help, of course. No one must ever know about this except the people we engage. You do understand that, don't you, Herr Hoff?"

Lauter weighed the last sentence, fixing Hoff with his flat, straight gaze.

Hoff had begun to recover and had mentally stiffened himself for the awesome responsibility he was being charged with. He found his voice and replied—it was the most outrageous, the most breathtaking, the most thrilling thing he'd ever heard of in his entire life.

"I understand completely, Herr Lauter. The need for secrecy is, of course, essential. And I believe I do know somebody who can help us."

When he said the last word Hoff felt a charge of pleasure surge through him. "Us," he and Herr Lauter; this remarkable man who had devoted his life to regaining Germany's honor had chosen him as his lieutenant. Pride swelled his words as he went on to explain. "There is a man named Planckendorf. Have you heard of him?"

Lauter reminded him that he'd been out of touch with Germany for two decades, so Hoff told him about Planckendorf. He'd been an officer in Vampyr, the clandestine group formed in 1945 to carry on a guerilla war after the surrender. The organization had collapsed, but its officers had formed another group dedicated to helping former members of the Reich. "I'm sure I could contact him," Hoff said. "They are entirely discreet, and I understand that their fee is relatively modest."

Lauter pursed his lips. "They are in business then?"

"Oh, no. They are true Germans like us who remember the glories of the past. Most of the money, so I'm told, goes to support former officers living in exile. South America."

"I dislike the idea of supporting cowards."

"As do I, Herr Lauter." Hoff waited, willing to go along with anything Lauter suggested. But Lauter allowed that, while it was unfortunate that his money would be put to such an objectionable use, it would have to be regarded as an unavoidable evil. He suggested that Hoff try to locate the pilot for a start, and Hoff said he'd begin his inquiries first thing in the morning. They talked for another hour, Lauter questioning Hoff about his background and present situation, then Hoff said goodbye, walking home through the streets of Munich on a little cushion of air, his life changed forever.

Hoff threw himself into his new role with intense purpose and succeeded with the help of an acquaintance, a former SS officer, in contacting Planckendorf a few days later.

That was on a Monday. The following Thursday a man named Uher called Hoff, said he was a pilot, and mentioned Planckendorf.

Hoff gave him Lauter's address and arranged to meet him there that evening.

The meeting was set for 9 P.M., but the man arrived forty minutes late without offering either an excuse or an apology. It was instantly apparent to Lauter and Hoff that he wasn't the type that went in for apologies. His manner reminded Lauter of the arrogant pilot officers he'd served under, haughty individuals who'd been very conscious of their elite position as bomber crew captains.

"Uher," he announced crisply, then sauntered into the room, making no attempt to disguise his opinion of the small apartment in that drab section of the city, or of the apartment's two inhabitants.

"You are Hoff?" he asked, with the same faint expression of disdain.

"Lauter. This is Herr Hoff. Please sit down."

The pilot had a face composed of firm, straight lines, firmness in his body, too, an athlete's flat stomach, and wide shoulders. His hair was silver, probably colored that way to cover the gray, Lauter thought, and had been blown dry and sprayed to hold its shape.

"Planckendorf said you had a job for me," Uher said, a busy man getting straight to the point.

"It's possible," Lauter answered. "I would like to ask a few questions first."

Uher preempted him, perhaps guessing from past experience what they'd be. "My name is Karl Uher. I am fifty-one years of age and presently licensed to fly a single-engined aircraft anywhere in the world. I own my own plane and I'll fly it anywhere, anytime, and for anybody who cares to hire me as long as the money's right. Now what do you have for me?"

"A few more questions, if you don't mind."

The two men locked eyes for a moment and Uher apparently recognized a personality in Lauter that was a lot stronger than he'd suspected on first meeting him. He checked a flashing digital watch then said, still trying to keep the initiative, "I'd appreciate it if you could make it fast."

"You are ex-Luftwaffe, I take it?"

"Nine J.G. Two."

"And after the surrender?"

Lauter's use of that word, rather than war, told Uher a lot.

"I was with Lufthansa till one of their officious inspectors went through my flight bag one day and found a souvenir of Turkey."

"And since then?"

Uher made a gesture of nonconcern. "Wherever the money was. I flew for Biafra in their little skirmish with Nigeria, then for Nigeria when they offered me more. I flew for the Somalis, and in Rhodesia. In between there was always work for a good pilot with his own plane who knew how to hedge-hop under radar."

"What kind of plane do you own?"

"A Focke-Wulf 190."

That stopped Lauter for a moment. The aptness, the correctness of it—it was perfect, absolutely perfect.

"You said you flew under radar. Whereabouts was that?"

"Everywhere. Even Australia. I had a regular run flying little packages in from Timor to the Northern Territory." Uher sniggered. "They tried to catch me with a troop transport."

"And England? Have you ever flown from France to London?"

Uher looked at Lauter hard. "If the job involves dodging the English radar you can forget it. A seagull couldn't fly under those defenses."

"I think I have a way to defeat the radar."

"Oh?" Uher said, speaking as he would to a child. "You're a pilot? Or were you?"

"Ground crew. Bombers."

"Bombers. That must have been exciting." Uher glanced at Hoff, hoping for an audience, but Hoff's mouth was set in a thin line of distaste.

Lauter ignored the pilot's derision. "Perhaps, Herr Uher, I should tell you exactly what we intend to do, then see if you're interested in joining us."

"If the money's right, I'm interested. Beating the radar, that's something else."

"First let me make something clear," Lauter said. "This job; there will be people killed."

"English, I take it."

"Does that bother you?"

Uher moved his mouth in a sour little grin. "Not in the slightest. Smug bastards, we were twice as good as they were in the air. We would've thrashed them if it hadn't been for the little maniac with the mustache."

There was a moment of stinging, shocked silence, then Hoff shot to his feet, outraged eyes glaring furiously at the pilot.

Lauter had brought his back stiff against his chair, and when he spoke, his words snapped like brittle ice. "Herr Uher. I am not sure at this moment whether or not we will be associated in this venture. But I must ask you never to refer to the Fuehrer in derogatory terms again. Is that clear?"

Uher shrugged as if it were unimportant to him.

"Is that clear, Herr Uher?" Lauter bore down on the question. There was no ignoring him, his stern gaze pinned Uher, forcing an answer.

"Sorry," he said.

It was quite a concession, but then the pilot had been surprised that this drab, clerkish-looking man could speak with such forcefulness. He'd known that his snide reference to Hitler would get a rise out of them—anyone he met through Planckendorf was usually a Third Reich warrior—but it was now abundantly clear that neither this one nor the fat little mouse—what was his name?—Hoff, could be safely teased.

"It is we who are sorry, Herr Uher," Lauter continued in the same cold formal tone. "Sorry that you do not appreciate the fact that the Fuehrer was a saint who tried to save us all. However, it is not necessary that you feel as we do in order to make a success of this job. It's your flying skill we're interested in, not your warped opinions. We are also counting on your discretion, should you decide not to accept this job after you've heard what it entails."

"You don't have to worry about my discretion," Uher said, on his best behavior now. "If I wasn't discreet I would have been a dead man long ago."

"Very well," Lauter said. He glanced over at Hoff who slowly sat down again, then turned back to Uher and told him about the site, what they planned to do, and how they planned to do it. He didn't tell him everything, however; he didn't tell him what he hoped the second buzz bomb would be carrying.

Uher listened with no trace of expression on his face except a slight raising of his eyebrows. "And it's intact? The site?"

"Completely."

"And the missiles?"

"Almost in mint condition."

"Even so," Uher said, "it will still be a tremendous job."

"Let us worry about that, Herr Uher. The question is, what do you think about my anti-radar idea? As a pilot do you think it's possible?"

Uher stood up, took a few thoughtful steps, turned and put his hands on the back of the chair he'd just vacated. "The timing would have to be perfect."

"But given that," Lauter pressed.

"You'd still run a risk of visual sighting."

"Not if we did it at night."

"Forget it. If I tried it at night I'd be committing suicide."

"Then if we chose the right weather conditions through the day. Rain and cloud over the Channel and Southern England."

"It would still mean low visibility for everybody. It'd be a tricky piece of flying."

Slowing his delivery, Lauter said, "How much would you charge for a tricky piece of flying?"

Uher pressed his perfectly white, perfectly even teeth into his lower lip, and looked as if he were giving it some thought. "We're talking about a double risk here, so the odds are doubly against the English believing whatever I tell them. If they find out I'm lying I'd be through in Europe. Worse, if they connected me with this thing I'd go to jail forever. I'd have to be very amply compensated for taking such a risk."

"How amply?" Lauter asked.

Uher hardly even paused. He knew whom he was dealing with, a fanatic, and he'd dealt with that kind before. He disliked being involved with them because fanatics could be wildly unpredictable. But, on the other hand, there was seldom a question of money because it wasn't important to them. If they didn't have it they simply went out and got it.

"I couldn't touch it for less than two hundred thousand marks."

"Two *hundred*?" It was Hoff who'd spoken. He hadn't meant to but surprised indignation had forced him.

"Very well," Lauter said.

"I'll need a third now."

Again Hoff spluttered, and again Lauter took no notice. "As you wish," he said to Uher. He got up. "I'll give you a check on my bank in France."

"No." The pilot produced a pen and a slip of paper, scribbled something on it, and handed it to Lauter. "Have them transfer the money to this account number at the head office of the Swiss Bank Corporation in Zurich. And in dollars."

Lauter took the piece of paper, held Uher with his eyes. "You no doubt think, Herr Uher, that what we are doing is a madcap scheme."

"Perhaps. But as you pointed out, Herr Lauter, you are not interested in my warped opinions."

"Nevertheless, I want you to know that we are doing this to demonstrate that the Third Reich still has teeth."

When Uher smiled he was careful to make it a small one. "I'm afraid they won't prove very sharp. The flying bomb wasn't much of a weapon, you know. They were never very accurate, and even when they were they weren't very effective."

"I'm aware of that," Lauter said coldly. "The important thing is that we will be carrying on the fight. We have lived with shame for too long, Herr Uher."

Uher forestalled having to comment on that by changing the subject. "How soon before you'll be ready?"

"Impossible to know. There's a lot to be done. But we will contact you."

Lauter moved toward the door and opened it. Uher followed him, nodded curtly to him, ignored Hoff, and left.

Hoff burst out with the thoughts he'd kept bottled up. "I don't understand why you want to use him, Herr Lauter. The way he insulted the Fuehrer, and all that money he's demanding. The greed of the man . . ."

"I agree," Lauter said calmly. "He's despicable, and I loathe the idea of being associated with his type. However, he is probably a first-rate pilot, which is what we're after. And there's something else in his favor."

Hoff waited to hear what that was, watching Lauter, who seemed to be focusing on a point eighteen inches in front of him.

"His plane. A Focke-Wulf. A Luftwaffe fighter for a Luftwaffe flying bomb. How wonderfully appropriate, Herr Hoff, to continue the war with the very weapons that were built for the war. It's exactly right."

"Nevertheless, I'm glad you didn't tell him the truth."

"It wasn't necessary."

Hoff nodded in agreement. "But the other man we need, the engineer, he will have to know."

"Of course," Lauter answered. "That's why we must make sure he's one of us."

When Hoff contacted Planckendorf again, he told him that the pilot he'd sent them was fine, and that they were also interested in contacting another kind of expert. It bothered Hoff to describe to Planckendorf exactly the qualifications they were looking for, but then he knew that if Planckendorf couldn't be trusted he wouldn't still be in business. At any rate it would be hard to guess at the connection between a flier and a V-1 expert, impossible in this case.

Forty-eight hours later Planckendorf came up with two ex-Luftwaffe technicians, but neither proved satisfactory. Without telling them anything of the plan, Lauter questioned them about their political and philosophical sentiments and found them both lacking in zeal. Hoff contacted Planckendorf again and stressed that the man they were interested in talking to had to have been a party member. Planckendorf promised to check his sources and get back to Hoff, but it was some time before he did so. He told Hoff he'd located a man named Bruning who seemed to have all the qualifications Hoff demanded.

As Lauter found out, Bruning's background was perfect for the job he had for him. He'd majored in physics at the University of Berlin, then worked as an aeronautical engineer till the war had intervened. During the war he'd been on the design staff at the Blohm und Voss works, then been drafted into the Luftwaffe as a launching officer at a V-1 site. And a few minutes' talking with him had left no doubt in Lauter's mind that Bruning also qualified in the other area. He understood the meaning of real patriotism, and was enlightened about the true place of the Fuehrer in world history, although for reasons having more to do with his head than his heart.

Lauter and Hoff met him in the miniature grandstand of a soccer field opposite the aerospace factory where Bruning was employed as a systems designer. It was part of the sports complex the firm had built for its employees, and it was deserted at three in the afternoon. They watched him walking toward them across the grass, a tall, slim figure, round shouldered, moving as if he were looking for potholes in the dead-even field. He climbed the steps to where they waited for him, introduced himself, and Lauter got right down to business. He asked Bruning about his personal history, which the man volunteered readily enough, content to wait for Lauter to tell him what he wanted. Hoff said nothing but watched Bruning closely, evaluating his answers.

"Herr Bruning," Lauter said, "we have a job in mind for which we think you'd be eminently suitable. You could name your own price. However, if you're the man we're looking for, the job itself would be payment enough."

"Tell me what it is." Bruning's voice was deep, considered, a twin to his steady open gaze.

"First I'd like to ask you one more question."

Bruning waited for it, his lean face blank, his eyes unreadable behind thin black-framed glasses.

"I would like to know," Lauter continued, "your opinion of Adolf Hitler."

The request had an immediate effect on Bruning and his face took on an instant personality. "He was a genius. Because of him German science jumped twenty years ahead. His influence was incalculable."

"And his aims? What do you think of those?"

"I supported them wholeheartedly. Without them there would have been no reason to push ahead with research, and no way to use the results of that research."

"So you admire him solely because of the influence he had on science."

"I'm a man of science," Bruning said simply. "It's been my whole life. It's natural I'd admire somebody who did so much to advance its cause."

Lauter didn't say anything for a moment, nobody did. The wind drifted across the empty soccer field, swirled through the little grandstand, leaped up at the three men. There was no other movement except for a car way off in the distance speeding toward a neat collection of identical houses gathered around spurs of a suburban street.

"I take it then," Lauter said finally, "that the cessation of hostilities disappointed you not just because Germany gave up but for another reason." It was a shrewd question because Bruning's answer gave Lauter a natural opening.

"I was ashamed at defeat, of course, but also angry and frustrated that some of the things we had on the drawing boards would never be built. Two more years, given the fuel and protection for the factories, and the result of the war would have been vastly different."

"I've read of one thing we were working on," Lauter responded, "that would have put the result beyond a doubt—the atom bomb."

Bruning agreed with a slow movement of his head. "Absolutely. Beyond a doubt."

"It's still possible, Herr Bruning," Lauter said. Then in reply to Bruning's quiet puzzlement spoke uninterrupted for the next few minutes, telling him everything.

The scientist's reaction was neither shock nor excitement nor disbelief, but a long, pensive silence as he thought it through. "Yes," he said after a while, "it would be one of the modified sites. Probably one of the last to be built." He thought some more, his mind already busy with the problems involved. "You say the Fieselers and the propulsion units are in good condition?"

"Excellent condition as far as I could tell."

"In that case, as long as the generator is in a similar state it should be quite possible. All the materials, the fuel and the chemicals, are commercially available. It would take a lot of time, though. Everything would have to be overhauled and tested."

"It has already taken a lot of time," Lauter said. "A little more is of no importance."

Bruning asked him how long he'd spent looking for the site and when Lauter told him, Hoff, speaking for the first time, verified it. "Twenty-three years," he said. He was immensely proud of Lauter, proud to be his associate.

Bruning merely nodded; as a scientist he understood devotion to a project. "There's another point," he said. "The explosives."

"Planckendorf could get them," Hoff suggested. "He can get anything."

"Probably," Bruning agreed.

Then Lauter sprang the question he'd been waiting to ask, the one that really mattered. "How about the bomb? How possible is that?"

Hoff waited on the answer, too, his plump thumbs worrying his fingers anxiously.

Bruning looked out at the empty soccer field and for a while seemed to be checking the accuracy of its white-limed dimensions.

"Theoretically it's entirely possible. But the practical considerations are enormous. Perhaps insurmountable." Bruning paused; the other two could have been holding their breath for all the sound they made. The scientist moved his thin body down a few steps, stopped, and spoke, still facing the field. "There is a man named Jurgen. He's brilliant. If anybody could do it it would be him."

"Do you know him personally? Can you contact him?" Lauter asked quickly.

"Perhaps Planckendorf could, I'm not sure. Jurgen's an outlaw. He was arrested and freed about a year ago in a hostage swap."

Hoff sucked in a fast breath. "*That* man. But he's with those scum, one of those terrorist groups."

"He's only young, not yet thirty," Bruning replied, turning round. "Politically he's a misguided fool, but in his own field he's without question the best."

"Then we must contact him," Lauter said. He addressed himself to Hoff who was looking at him in disbelief. "They're killers, assassins, I know. They're out to destroy Germany, not to make it triumphant. But if it means assuring ourselves a better chance of success then we must have him, regardless of what he stands for."

Hoff, swayed by anything Lauter said, murmured an affirmative.

"It will be a great deal of money," Bruning told them. "They could ask what they like for an order like this. Half a million marks, perhaps more."

"That is not a problem," Lauter said. "We have access to large amounts."

That got a fast look from Hoff, but Lauter didn't respond to it and nothing was said till Bruning walked back up the steps and stood

in front of Lauter. He looked like a different man than the one
they'd first met, or even the one of a few minutes ago. He stood
straighter and moved faster and, whereas before his face had had a
flat, expressionless look, there was now an intense awareness in his
eyes and something like excitement tugging at the corners of his
mouth.

"Herr Lauter, I admire you. You weren't content to sit and brood
like the rest of us. You did something about it. A wonderful thing.
And it's going to work because we'll make it work."

Lauter thanked him stiffly, uncomfortable with praise, then added
a word of caution. "Only four people know about this, counting the
pilot who knows only what he's been told. Nobody else must hear a
word."

Bruning replied that the warning was unnecessary. "I would never
have dreamed in a million years that I'd ever get a chance like this. I
can assure you I'd do nothing to risk losing it."

Lauter accepted that then asked him how he thought the mechanics of the idea might work. Bruning told him he'd have to do a
lot of figuring but outlined something he thought would be close.

They arranged to meet again, then the scientist shook hands with
both of them and left.

Watching him walk back over the soccer field toward his office,
Lauter said, "A good man. We've been lucky."

Hoff agreed, then with Bruning out of earshot asked the question
that had been troubling him. "Herr Lauter, what did you mean
about having access to a large sum of money? How?"

"Money is available to us because of a happy coincidence," Lauter
answered. "Through you, Herr Hoff."

When Hoff didn't respond Lauter said, "Didn't you tell me you
worked in a bank?"

Hoff lost his color, blinked at him, then said with nerves in his
voice, "Of course. Yes, of course."

When Hoff called Planckendorf the next day about getting in
touch with Jurgen, the man told him it would be difficult but that
he'd try. Three days later he succeeded and gave Hoff some instructions. They were understandably complex because the group Jurgen
was part of was hunted night and day, and they'd only agreed to
meet with Hoff because Planckendorf could vouch for him. Even

then there was no question of meeting with Jurgen himself; everything would be done through an intermediary. That was on a Tuesday. On the following Sunday Hoff left for Stuttgart and the rendezvous. It took place on a suburban train.

Hoff limped down the long station, took a seat in the last compartment, and opened his copy of *Stern* magazine to page twelve as he'd been instructed.

At the second stop a youth boarded the train and walked down the aisle toward him. The boy had long, straggly hair and wore crumpled jeans, striped running shoes, and a shabby quilted ski jacket. He sat down next to Hoff and, without looking at him, said, "I hear you have a job for a friend of mine."

"That is correct," Hoff answered, cold and precise. He took out the envelope he'd been carrying in his jacket pocket. Inside was a diagram and some dimensions Bruning had spent a long time over. He handed it to the youth.

"All the information you'll need is contained in this."

The young man shoved it casually into his parka, got up without another word, and left the train at the next station.

It was three days before Hoff was contacted. Planckendorf called to give him a message. The first part thrilled him: the item he was interested in buying could be made available; but he was horrified by the second part—the price would be a million marks, with twenty-five percent in advance. He had to agree to it because he knew Lauter would expect him to, and when he met with him later that day Lauter was concerned only with the practicalities of getting the money.

"Is it going to be any trouble?"

When Hoff replied, the words were awkward in his mouth. "I'll have to make some arrangements. . . . I'll need a few things . . . Planckendorf will get them."

"Then I suggest you do it as soon as possible," Lauter said, fixing him with his stare. "If they say they'll need at least a month, the sooner we pay them the sooner they'll start."

There wasn't much for Hoff to arrange. The gun was no problem, Planckendorf had supplied him with that within twenty-four hours. The letter was the hardest part, the one telling his wife that he wouldn't be home the following evening. Or any other evening.

Hurrying through breakfast the next morning, he checked his

watch for the time and noted the date: December 1—the last day of his old life, the first day of his new one. At the door, as his wife fussed with his overcoat, he muttered something about being late and fled without the usual quick embrace, not trusting himself to hold her, afraid he might not let go. He took the two big suitcases he'd stored in the basement, went out into the cold-weather street, and got a cab to the bank where he worked. It was on Kardinal Faulhaber Strasse, a handsomely decorated nineteenth-century building that had once been the bank's head office. The interior was splendidly baroque, soaring columns, echoing marble floors, florid wrought-iron teller cages.

Schleiemacher, the floor guard, let him in and commented on the suitcases. Hoff told him he was going away for the weekend and would be leaving straight from the office.

"A weekend? Looks more like two weeks," the guard said, joking but still respectful of Hoff's position as head teller.

Hoff crossed the wide expanse of the marble floor, went downstairs to the employees' room, and put the suitcases on top of his locker. Then he went upstairs to his teller's cage to get it ready for business just as he had every other morning for as long as he could remember.

He greeted his associates as they arrived, worried that they might notice something different in his behavior. A minute later Hermann Franck, the guard who watched over the vault in the basement, greeted him as he passed. Hoff couldn't stop himself from watching the man's retreating back, couldn't help but wonder what he'd think if the man had known that he'd just said good morning to his executioner. Hoff did his best to work normally but it was impossible. The tension built inside him till finally he had to rush downstairs to the washroom and throw up.

He got through the rest of the day, and when the bank closed at 3 P.M., he busied himself with the day's accounts till it was time to handle the cash, a job he did every afternoon. Schleiemacher, the floor guard, arrived, pushing a heavy metal trolley. Hoff thanked him and wheeled the trolley down the line of teller cages. collecting from each person a metal cash box that had, taped to the top, the total figure of its contents on a strip of calculator paper. Hoff picked up his own box last of all, took the seven slips, plus his own, and figured the day's cash. He put this figure into an envelope and dropped it into the assistant manager's lock box. Then he wheeled the trolley the length of the floor and took the little elevator down to the vault in the basement. Franck met him at the door, a sliding gate made of iron bars. Fifteen feet behind it, standing open on massive hinges, was the real door, a huge steel monster guarding a large square room sunk into concrete and lined with shiny steel plate.

Hermann Franck was a thin, consumptive-looking man who didn't have the build that usually went with a guard's uniform. He had thick dark hair and very white skin, a serious face with heavy lids over colorless eyes. Hoff had seen his wife once, a buxom, raven-haired Jewess who jiggled when she walked. They had six children, which didn't surprise Hoff; he knew Jews copulated like minks, they were famous for it.

Franck opened the sliding door, took delivery of the trolley, and wished Hoff a pleasant weekend.

The door clanged back into place as Hoff left the vault and took the side stairs up to the sub-basement and the staff room.

At this time of day Hoff knew there'd be only three people in the bank now besides himself: Schleiemacher, at the front door, Freiden, the assistant manager, and Franck in the vault. He opened his locker, took out the gun he'd put there that morning, and tucked it into his pocket. He put on his overcoat, retrieved the two suitcases from on top of his locker, then went back down the steps to the vault.

Through the barred gate he could see Franck putting the trolley into a corner, the cashboxes neatly stacked on a shelf. He tapped on the bars and when Franck appeared said, "Herr Freiden wants these locked away for the night."

Franck, eyeing the suitcases without interest, unlocked the gate and Hoff went through. He put the bags down, reached into his pocket, pulled out the gun, pointed it at the guard, and squeezed the trigger.

There was no explosion, the safety was on, and Hoff had to awkwardly thumb it off and point the gun again.

Franck, frozen in disbelieving horror, only had time to raise his hands in front of his body before the gun went off, a dreadful noise in the steel room, and two bullets smashed through his palms into his chest.

He fell forward, thumping down, his thin body already beginning to pump out bright red blood that pooled underneath him on the metal floor.

Hoff tossed the gun away, picked up the bags, and moved to the rear wall of the vault. He ignored the cashboxes and went instead to a shelf of thick cardboard packages in which bills of large denominations were kept. He filled both suitcases, packing the money in evenly, closed them, walked out of the vault, and took the elevator up to the main floor. Nobody would have heard the shots up there; the vault was buried twenty feet below street level.

Hoff's shoes clicked on the marble floor in an uneven tempo as he limped toward the front door. He'd never realized before just how long a trip it was. He heard himself say good night as he passed the assistant manager's desk. The man, still busy, replied without looking up.

There was only Schleiemacher to get past now.

The guard watched him coming, his eyes on the suitcases.

Hoff suddenly knew he wasn't going to make it; the sweat on his brow would give him away, or his rubbery knees, which were about to go on him. When the suitcase in his left hand bumped into a writing stand, he knew he hadn't latched the case properly, and didn't have to look to know that money was spilling out in bright green bundles.

"Enjoy your weekend, Herr Hoff," the guard said, opening the front door.

When he heard the door close behind him, standing out on the portico of the bank, the two bags intact in his hands, he was amazed. He'd done it! He'd gotten away with it! Schleiemacher wouldn't go and see what was keeping Franck for a good ten or fifteen minutes. He was free and clear.

He got a cab to the railroad station, waited there a few minutes, then, looking like any other traveler, got another cab to a street four blocks from where Lauter lived.

It was only after he'd begun to walk in the cold night air that the enormity of what he'd done washed over him. Franck was a Jew so it wasn't as if he'd killed a person, but the other . . . he'd worked at the bank for thirty-two years, been chief teller for the last seven. . . . The horror, the shame of it forced a quick biliousness into his throat. He'd done an outrageous thing, unthinkable. And even though he'd done it for a glorious and honorable reason, it didn't change the astonishing fact that he, Mathias Hoff, had stolen money from his employers.

Gulping back tears, he moved through the chilly streets toward Lauter's apartment.

CHAPTER TEN

Pelham—London, December 19-21, 1978

"A little bit of the Vaud in the heart of Kensington," Rossi said, coming out of the kitchen. She put down a steaming Pyrex dish, slipped off a pair of oven mitts, and sat down in her chair.

Pelham eyed the food, looked up at the girl. "That's Swiss? I thought Swiss was that hot cheese bowl that everybody dipped their sleeve into."

"Fondue. That's for tourists. When we want to make a cheese dish we make Raclette, or a Croute au Fromage."

Pelham worked a corkscrew into a bottle of wine. "Where's the Vaud?"

"The eastern end of Lake Leman."

"Lake where?"

"Lake Geneva."

"French-speaking?"

"*Oui.*"

Pelham eased out the cork, poured wine into their glasses. "You speak German, too?"

The girl nodded, dishing out food. "The Vaud is right next door to the Valais, and that's German-speaking." She put a plate in front of him. "Now eat."

Pelham tried some potatoes, chewed for a moment, swallowed, said surprised, "Hash brown. The first I've had in London."

The girl looked reproachful. "That's called Rostii."

"Maybe in Switzerland. Back home it's hash-brown potatoes."

"Well that," Rossi said, pointing to the veal cutlets in cream sauce on his plate, "is definitely not hamburger."

Pelham tried it, and wholeheartedly agreed. "Terrific. Hell, I didn't know you could cook."

Rossi smiled, brushed back her long brown hair in an elegant gesture. "You haven't given me time to find out. You know, where I come from a man would have tasted a woman's cooking before he, er . . ."

"Would have tasted anything else," Pelham finished for her.

Rossi laughed, picked up her knife and fork. "You're bad," she said. They ate for a while, drank their wine.

"So," Pelham said, "how's the office without me?"

"All the secretaries are wearing black," she answered, watching him.

Then she said, "You're not really feeling as bright as you sound, are you?"

Pelham was about to deny it but gave in. "I think you're right."

"Because of what happened this afternoon, I would guess," Rossi said. "Although I'm not going to ask what that was."

"Nothing much to tell anyway. I got tossed out of the Ministry of Defense again."

Rossi poured them more wine and waited for him to tell her if he wanted to. It took Pelham a minute to get around to it during which he pressed little circles into the tablecloth with his wineglass, and moodily watched them disappear.

"The thing's got me beat, Rossi. I'm trying to make sense of something that doesn't make sense, although I know there's an answer to it. I've always been rotten at puzzles. Never had the patience to think them through."

"Try me. I've always been good at them."

Pelham sighed. "I'm back to square one. To find out who fired that buzz bomb I have to find out where it came from. And to find out where it came from I have to find out how it got here."

"You're testing my English," Rossi said.

"Okay, I'll simplify it. For that buzz bomb to get here undetected it had to fool the radar somehow. Now that air correspondent I had lunch with told me that some pretty big advances have been made in radar avoidance, but it's all brand-new, top-secret stuff. And it just doesn't follow that somebody who can't do better than a thirty-five-year-old weapon would have access to the newest anti-radar device."

"Then the problem is a scientific one," Rossi said.

Pelham made a hopeless little gesture. "And then some."

"Well then, let us approach it scientifically." Rossi leaned forward, looking serious. "I had a science teacher at school, a very strict man. He said that you should approach a problem by writing down only what you know to be an absolute fact."

"All right, let's try it his way. In my opinion, but nobody else's, it's an absolute fact that a V-1 destroyed those houses."

"Then let us accept that as fact," Rossi replied. "The next question is, how did it reach those houses?"

"The way a V-1 was designed to. It was launched and flew through the air."

Rossi held up a finger. "Supposition, not fact. You're only assuming that it flew. It didn't show up on the radar, and you've just told me that an anti-radar device is probably out of the question. So perhaps it didn't fly at all."

Pelham looked as if he had a pain. "Come on, Rossi, that means that somebody built it on the spot, in one of those houses. And a buzz bomb's not the kind of thing you can build in the backyard without the neighbors knowing. The damn thing had to fly."

"Well . . ." Rossi struggled with it for a moment. "My old science teacher would probably have said that, in that case, the only thing you could say with certainty was that it fell from the sky."

"I think your old science teacher fell from the sky. Anyway, if it fell from the sky it had to be flying, didn't it?"

"Not necessarily. Rain falls from the sky but it doesn't fly."

Pelham rolled his eyes at the ceiling. "So does a man in a parachute. Where does that get us?"

"A man in a parachute is dropped. Maybe . . ." she stopped, the thought dying. "No, that doesn't make sense."

"What doesn't?"

"Nothing. You don't drop something that's designed to fly."

Pelham had his glass halfway to his mouth when he stopped as if he'd seen something swimming in it. He brought it down slowly then said, "What are you, some kind of genius?" He jumped up from the table, took a few fast steps, swung around to the girl, talking fast. "All that stuff I read about the V-1s. Toward the end of the war they stopped firing them from ramps and fired them from aircraft. They'd fit one under a plane, the plane would fly close to the target then release it. And that's what happened this time. That thing didn't fly here, it was carried here. Only something went wrong and it fell on Hayes instead of London."

"But," Rossi said, having a hard time with it, "wouldn't the plane show up on the radar?"

"Of course it would, and it did. Only it was accounted for in some way. Jesus, Rossi," Pelham slapped his hand against his leg, "that's how they did it. They found a way to fool the traffic controllers, the guys who read the radar. God knows how, but that's what happened."

Rossi would have liked to ask a question, several questions, but Pelham was already striding across the room, pulling Jakes's card from his pocket, heading for the telephone.

The man Pelham called the next morning had a heavy schedule and it wasn't till the day after that Pelham could go out to see him. His name was Lane, and his office was near the airport so Pelham took the Underground.

Since they'd completed the extension to Heathrow, the Tube had become, in Pelham's opinion, the best way of getting to the airport —for one thing, he no longer had to give a cabdriver five or six pounds for almost getting him killed twice on the M4. Although the Tube had its drawbacks, too, the main one being what Pelham called The Great English Traveling Public. And he met a charter member of it during the ride.

At South Ealing Station a blind man with a seeing-eye dog got on, and Pelham, being nearest him, got up and took his elbow. "Can I help you to a seat?"

"It's easier if I stand, thanks," the man answered. "I make the trip every day so I'm quite all right. But thanks all the same."

Pelham resumed his seat and, two stops later, watched the blind man confidently get out of the train. Coming into the next station, a middle-aged woman moving toward the door said to Pelham, kindly but firmly, "You shouldn't really have done that, you know."

"Done what?"

"Tried to guide a blind man. It confuses the dogs."

She got off and the doors closed behind her, leaving Pelham massaging the bridge of his nose. He said very distinctly to the row of people opposite him, "The English are slowly driving me bananas."

Nobody took any notice of him. Nor did they take any notice when he spoke out loud again, but this time he spoke for a different reason. As the train pulled into Heathrow Station, and Pelham got up, an advertisement caught his eye. It showed a drawing of a car; the headline read, "Take a Capri for a Trial Run."

He stared at it, a slow change coming over his face. "A trial run," he said.

The sound of the doors opening broke his trance, and he jumped out and bounded up the stairs.

The first cabdriver he asked knew the RAF station at West Drayton, a few miles away, and was pretty sure that the Civil Aviation Authority, which Pelham wanted, was next door to it.

They drove for five minutes through a suburban area, then turned into a long street of small brick houses facing a flat green field. A high security fence ran for one hundred yards to a guarded entrance, uniformed men everywhere, a jet fighter parked a little way inside like a piece of pop art sculpture. The Civil Authority shared the same fence and a similar-looking entrance, the cab dropping Pelham just inside it at the doors of the building. It was a four-story brick and glass structure that could have doubled for any suburban office block if it hadn't been for two things: the center section facing the street had closed louvered blinds covering its long windows and at the rear of the building a spindly radar tower rose up one hundred feet into the sky.

Pelham entered a reception area and told a security man behind a desk who he was and who he was there to see. He had to wait only a few minutes before a tall, very slim man came down the stairs and introduced himself as George Lane.

"Mr. Lane, thanks for seeing me. I know you're busy."

"No problem, I owe Brian Jakes a favor anyway." Lane took the visitor's badge the security man handed him, got Pelham to pin it on, then conducted him upstairs. "It's all offices up here, we can chat in mine if you like. Or I can take you straight to the Ops Room. It's what most people come to see."

Pelham followed his guide down a long series of corridors, and through a door that opened on a sight he wasn't prepared for. "This is where it all goes on," Lane said.

Pelham said, "Wow!" And meant it. They were standing on a high balcony looking down on a room the size of an arena. Three of its sides were taken up by huge radar consoles, two men sitting at each, while a bank of desks ran along the end of the room, and down the center was an array of what looked like catalog shelves. There must have been forty or fifty people either sitting, standing, or walking.

"It looks like an orderly stock market crash," Pelham said.

The tall man beside him chuckled. "Sometimes it looks like the real thing. Come on, we'll go down."

Lane continued his tour as they descended some stairs and came out into the room. "There's not much going on now." He stopped at the first console he came to, an enormous affair with a metal canopy projecting over it, two orange radar drums on each side, illuminated route maps, flight numbers, a secondary radar screen, and a telephone surrounded by a dozen push buttons. Lane nodded at one of the screens that showed a complicated map grid peppered with tiny groups of letters and numerals. As they watched, one of them blinked out, then reappeared an inch to its left. It read, "BF 302," and Pelham asked what it meant.

The operator fielded the question. "Braniff, Flight Three-Oh-Two. It's over the Irish Sea and beginning its approach. We're going to have to stack him." He flipped a switch and said something into a panel mike.

"He's giving him the bad news now," Lane said, moving Pelham along. "We get quite a bit of holding traffic, as you might imagine. There are four airports in your country that handle more flights, O'Hare, Atlanta, Dallas, and Los Angeles, but we're the biggest international airport. We get pilots talking to us in accents you wouldn't believe."

"Some of the ones around Dallas are pretty good, too," Pelham said.

They stopped at the next console, two men manning it, one of them in RAF blue.

"Most of our traffic is civilian, of course," Lane explained. "But there's a lot of military activity, too. Hence, you have an RAF controller sitting next to one of our boys."

Pelham jumped into the opening. "And they trade information . . ."

"That's right."

"So nothing could fly without one of them knowing it."

"Nothing of any importance, anyway."

"Could I ask you how the setup works, say, on a cross-channel flight?"

"That's one of our busiest corridors," Lane answered, moving Pelham toward the other side of the room. "This sector over here would handle it."

"What exactly happens, start to finish?"

"For a start, the pilot files his flight plan at his departure point, in this case, Paris. It's relayed through to his intended destination. It goes on file here." Lane stopped in front of an immense bank of teletype machines that were clicking away in the middle of the room. "Very well, he takes off under Paris control, who pass him on to Calais control, who see him halfway over the Channel before passing him on to Lydd control. Then he would come under Gatwick's jurisdiction and, finally, ours."

"So he's never out of your sight?"

"Not a big commercial jet, no. They carry transponders that flash their code number and is picked up on the radar, like the Braniff flight you saw. With smaller craft it would just be an audial contact."

"Okay," Pelham said. "So he files a flight plan, takes off and flies from A to B."

"Theoretically, yes," Lane answered. "In actual fact, no. He'd request a straight line between A and B, but we can rarely give him that. He'd have to fly a zigzag pattern. Also he might request a certain altitude, fifteen thousand feet, say, but we'd more than likely have to give him a slightly higher or lower one, depending on how crowded the sky is."

Pelham mentally crossed his fingers when he asked the next question. "Do you keep a record of all flights that come under your control?"

"Absolutely. Every completed flight plan goes on file upstairs along with the log of the flight, time and place of departure and arrival, general comments et cetera. Is there a particular flight you're interested in?"

"You guessed it."

"How recent?"

"Four days ago. December seventeenth."

"That should still be on the floor," Lane said. "Shall we see?"

Pelham followed the man down the length of the room, delighted at the treatment he was getting. He realized that Brian Jakes had a lot of clout because he'd clearly been plugged into the Old Boy Network. It seemed to Pelham like the first good break he'd had for ages.

Lane led the way out of the Operations Room and into a long, narrow office somewhere at the back of it. The sign on the door said, "Flight Information Region." There were only two men present, seated at a desk that ran to the far wall. Above it was a display board containing dozens of cards slotted into metal flanges, each card bearing facts and figures written on it in black felt tip. There were no radar screens in the room; it was, as Lane explained, solely voice contact in this section, as was demonstrated when one of the men had a short conversation with the captain of an aircraft coming over the North Sea.

They waited till he was free, then Lane introduced him to Pelham who told him what he was after.

"The seventeenth," the man said, turning and reaching for a big clothbound entry book. "That'd still be in the day log." He began to leaf through it. "You think it originated somewhere in Northern France, and it was in the Croydon vicinity at around three-forty P.M., is that correct?"

"Right. A noncommercial flight."

"That's a heavy traffic area. There are quite a few."

Pelham said, "There could be something special about this one. Something different, maybe."

The controller tapped his finger against an entry. "Here's one that fits. And it's really special. He flew Beauvais-Elstree and would have been over the Croydon area at about the time you mention. He reported rudder trouble and we had to hold up traffic at Gatwick and Heathrow for fifteen minutes till we got him through."

"Beauvais," Pelham repeated, trying to place it.

"Northwest of Paris," Lane told him. "About fifty miles from the coast."

"That's certainly the area," Pelham said. He thought for a moment, looked up at the controller. "Does the log record the type of plane, or the registration number?"

"Both," the man replied. "G478D is his number. The G is our code letter for the plane's nationality."

"It's French?" Pelham asked.

"German."

"*German?*"

Both men looked at Pelham, surprised at his instant reaction.

"And the type of aircraft?" Pelham waited.

The controller consulted the log. "Six-two-eight-four," he read out. "Every kind of aircraft has a code. I'll just check that for you." He reached into a drawer, pulled out a small book, flipped through it till he found the place. "That'd be a Focke-Wulf 190."

"Is that some kind of small jet?" Pelham asked.

Lane answered him. "That's the famous fighter bomber. One nearly shot me down once."

Pelham stared at him. "Are you telling me that plane's a World War II aircraft?"

Lane nodded. "Best kite the Jerries ever came up with."

When Pelham just went on looking at him, Lane said, "It's news to a lot of people that planes like that are still flying. But there are more around than you'd think. Mosquitoes, Messerschmitts, Spitfires, Hurricanes. They cost their owners a fortune to run, but they love them. Like the people who own vintage cars."

Pelham, hearing him out, coughed and said, as evenly as he could, "Mr. Lane, could I use your phone?"

"Brian? Jim Pelham."

"Hello," Jakes said. "Did you get to see George Lane?"

"I'm calling from his office now. Brian, I've got something that's dynamite."

"Oh?"

Pelham's words tumbled out. "I found a flight that was over the Croydon area at the time when those houses went up. It flew from Beauvais in France. German registry. But get this, Brian. It was a Focke-Wulf 190, a World War II aircraft."

"I don't quite see—"

Pelham explained, cutting through Jakes. "When I did some homework on the V-1 I found out that later in the war they were launched from planes. That's what happened at Hayes, Brian. That V-1 was launched from the Focke-Wulf. That's how it got through the radar, because the pilot filed a flight plan in the normal manner, so the plane was expected. Only nobody figured it was going to be carrying a buzz bomb."

"I'm afraid I can't buy it," Jakes said.

"What do you mean you can't buy it?" Pelham was talking loudly.

"Check with Lane if you don't believe me. He's right outside. He'll tell you himself about that plane."

"Jim," Jakes's voice was placating. "I'll admit it's quite a coincidence that a 1944 German aircraft was in the vicinity at the same time that, in your opinion, a 1944 German weapon destroyed those houses. But—"

"Coincidence? Come *on*, now . . ."

With a quiet firmness Jakes said, "Hear me out, please. Lane says it was definitely a Focke-Wulf 190?"

"Better than that, a controller says so."

"Then I'm afraid your theory won't hold up."

"Why the hell not?" Pelham couldn't understand why Jakes was being so obtuse.

"Because a 190 was basically a fighter. True, it could carry a bomb load, and an exceptional one for a plane of that size, but there's just no way you could fit a buzz bomb underneath it. And even if you could, I don't think a 190 would even be able to taxi, let alone take off. It'd be trying to lift twice its own weight."

Pelham was shaking his head as if Jakes was telling him something in a foreign language. "You sure about all this?"

"You're right about the V-1s being carried, Jim, but it took a big, lumbering bomber to do it. Heinkel 111s, I think they used. They could carry a five-thousand-ton bomb load, ten times what a Focke-Wulf fighter could handle."

There was a crushed moment of silence from Pelham, and Jakes sympathized with him. "It was a smart conclusion you made, Jim, because, as I said, it's a huge coincidence a German fighter being around at that time."

"It's more than a coincidence, it's a big fat connection. I've thought of something else, Brian. And it ties right in with something you said."

"What was it I said?"

"All that about a buzz bomb being such an old weapon, and wondering why anybody would use one just to blow up a couple of houses. You said they couldn't even be sure it would get off the ground, remember? Well they weren't sure, so they had a trial run, a test shot to find the range. These people, whoever they are, must be planning to fire a second one."

"It doesn't follow, Jim. Even if they hit Oxford Street at high noon it still wouldn't do that much damage."

"What if they used more explosives? A bigger charge than they used at Hayes?"

"Not possible. The warhead in a V-1 is only so big."

"A new kind of explosive then. Something a lot more powerful."

The same thought at the same time seemed to flash down the wire between them.

"Jim, you're not going to suggest what I think you're going to suggest, are you?"

"A nuclear bomb." Pelham's voice could barely be heard.

Jakes tried to chuckle. "Radford said you had a vivid imagination and I'm inclined to agree with him."

Pelham hadn't heard him; he was still stopped by his conclusion. After a moment he said, "Brian, just tell me this. I read somewhere that they're making nuclear bombs no bigger than beachballs these days. Is that true?"

"Look . . ."

"Is it true?"

The reply was reluctant. "Yes, it's true. Now please don't ask me if you could fit a beachball into a V-1. You're just trying to scare yourself. And you're trying to scare me, too."

"Could you?"

"The whole thing's outlandish, Jim."

"Answer me."

Jakes didn't have to.

Pelham said, "Listen, Brian, could George Lane find out the name and address of the guy who owns that plane? I assume he lives in Germany."

"Yes, he could do it. But as I've already told you, that plane's too small to do what you think it did."

"I'll be in touch," Pelham said, and hung up. Immediately he began to dial again. "Miss Studer, please."

When she came on the phone he spoke fast.

"Rossi, it's me. Go in and tell them you have to take a few days off. Tell them your father's very ill."

"What? I can't do that."

"Yes you can. Then go home and pack a bag. Don't forget your passport."

"Can't it wait for a few days? At least till Christmas?"

"No. This thing's big. So big you wouldn't believe. I really need you."

She hesitated for a moment then said, "I couldn't leave before tomorrow afternoon. There's just no way."

Pelham cursed. "Okay, tomorrow afternoon then."

"Jimmy, at least tell me where we're going."

"Germany for starters," Pelham answered. "And I'll eat my hat if we don't end up in France."

CHAPTER ELEVEN

Lauter—Rouen/the Site, December 9-11, 1978

On the Monday following the robbery, Lauter met with Planckendorf and handed over the down payment for the group in Stuttgart and, at the same time, paid for the large brown envelope that Planckendorf had ready for him. In it was Hoff's new passport. The photograph was new and so was the name.

Tuesday, Lauter phoned his office to tell them he'd been called away on urgent family business. Wednesday, he and Hoff flew to Paris, arriving in Rouen that evening.

As per their agreement, the concierge had looked after Lauter's apartment while he'd been gone. He knew she hadn't been able to touch his workroom, but even so it was the first thing he checked. Asking Hoff to wait outside for a moment, he let himself into the room, closed the door, and turned on the light. Everything was exactly the way he'd left it, and with the window being shut tight and the door fitting closely, the smell of candle wax had built up and now permeated the air with its high, sweet aroma. Lauter reached for the matches, got the candles burning, turned out the light, and breathed a deep sigh of contentment. He'd missed this sight, missed the warm, protected feeling it brought, the sense of grace that flowed through him like a healing drug. He could feel proud this time, too, meet the Fuehrer's gaze unflinchingly because everything was proceeding so well.

He went to the door, opened it. "Herr Hoff. There is something I would like you to see."

He stood aside as Hoff approached the darkened room, entered, and stopped with a tiny gasp. The candlelight reflected in his glasses as he slowly advanced toward the little altar, entranced by the silver frames and marveling at the play of light on the red and black swastika flag that made it appear to be waving in triumph.

"Beautiful," he breathed. "You've done a beautiful job."

Lauter murmured his thanks, turned on the light, snuffed out the candles, and let Hoff explore the rest of the room. Hoff recognized two of the photographs on the corkboard as the ones Lauter had shown him in Munich, the Spitfire flying alongside the V-1, and the shot of the two men with the numerals scrawled across it. He examined the diaries in the shelves and the Michelin maps with their crossed-out sectors and was astonished all over again at what Lauter had accomplished.

He said with a touch of trepidation, "It's really going to happen."

Lauter nodded. "You can be assured of that." He picked up a red pencil and bent over a map of central London. He circled Victoria Station and next to it wrote "150 meters," explaining to Hoff what Bruning had told him about the target area. He enjoyed marking the map; it wouldn't be long now.

In the morning they got Lauter's VW camper out of storage, returned to the apartment for the things they needed, locked the place up again, and drove down to the station to meet Bruning's train from Paris.

Traffic was light once they got outside the city and they made Dieppe in a little over an hour, then followed the N25, the coast road, for thirty miles to the Bresle River. Ten minutes later they'd swung off toward the Channel and rolled through the little village perched near the edge of the cliffs, then bumped down the long, curving dirt road till their headlights picked up an open gate on the right. Lauter turned into it, and the damp smell of pines came to them as they went up the track, finally stopping outside the old farmhouse.

Lauter went inside to see the man he'd hired, paid him, and got rid of him quickly. They settled in and spent a restless night waiting for the morning, but it was eight-thirty before it was light enough to see, and by that time they'd been up and dressed for two hours. They hurried out into a cold, overcast day, got pickaxes and a toolbox from a side shed, and walked through the misty pines.

Lauter didn't have to point out the mounds to Bruning, who spotted them right away and began to trot toward them. He was incredibly excited, as was Hoff, but whereas Hoff's excitement showed in his voice, Bruning's was evident only in the quick movements of his tall body and the way he kept moving his glasses on his nose as if they were the wrong size.

They reached the entrance to the main building and made short work of clearing away the earth and the leaves and the broken netting. This time, with the three of them pushing, prizing the heavy door open was a different matter.

The dank, oily smell rolled out at them as the door screeched back, then they fumbled with flashlights and went in.

Bruning made a beeline for the crates against the wall. He attacked the crate that Lauter had opened, levered the slats up, and reopened the hole Lauter had cut in the tarpaulin. They held their flashlights steady for him while he went to work on the missile's access plate, removing it and peering in. He left that and went to the stack of smaller crates, ripped open the end of the nearest one, slashed the tarpaulin inside, and probed with his flashlight into the mouth of a jet engine.

Then he strode back down the long dark building, again poking his flashlight everywhere, hurrying from one thing to another like a child at a fair. Hoff, in contrast, was looking about him as a tourist would on a tour through a beautiful cave.

"Fantastic," he kept saying. "It's fantastic."

But Lauter wasn't interested in his reaction; it was Bruning's, the expert's, he was holding his breath about. He watched the white circle of Bruning's flashlight bobbing at the far end of the building, heard chunky metal-on-metal noises and the sound of wood being broken. Then the beam moved toward him as the man came back.

Lauter and Hoff followed him out of the building and the three of them stood blinking in the sudden morning light.

Bruning touched his forehead, resettled his glasses, spoke without taking his eyes off the building. "We can do it," he said.

They spent most of the day in Rouen shopping for supplies. Apart from bottles of compressed air, the things they bought were mostly everyday items: car batteries, spark plugs, electrical wire, solvents, oil, and cleaning fluids. They arrived back at the site around 4 P.M. and got straight to work on the generator that served the big assembly building. Once they had power and light inside, they began cleaning all the interior surfaces, brushing, sweeping, clearing away the long years of fine dust and grit that had managed to find its way in.

They attacked the huge workbench, washed it down, soaked all the tools in gasoline, dried them thoroughly, hung them back on their freshly cleaned racks. They oiled the big iron gantry, greased its heavy wheels.

When they finished, in the early hours, iron glowed, tools shone, light bounced off cement, and the stale smell of time had been replaced by the bright, cold, metal smell of machines.

The next day they took on the heaviest job they'd face: the construction of the launching ramp.

It was housed in the larger of the two square buildings, in sixty prefabricated sections. They transported all of it down to the track, a major job in itself, cleared the track of dirt and stones, and uncovered the double row of threaded metal sockets that had been sunk into the concrete underneath. Into these they screwed short, stubby pipes that served as feet for the heavy iron trestles they erected. There were ten trestles shaped like flattened As, each one taller than the last. When Bruning was sure the trestles were rock-solid, they began to lay a tube along the crossbars, the tube being made up of long sections of piping eighteen inches in diameter, and slotted at the top. On each side of the tube, and level with it, they laid the wide, flat rail the missile would actually ride on. It was hard, backbreaking work, and it was late in the day when they stepped back and took a look at what they'd built: an iron ramp, twenty feet wide and one hundred and eighty feet long, rising gradually to point at the sky.

Hoff, perspiring, arms aching, said, "We were lucky to get it finished before dark."

"It isn't finished," Bruning said. "We haven't got to its most important part yet, the steam generator. We'll tackle it first thing in the morning."

But it was 11 A.M. before they started; they hadn't realized how much the building of the ramp had tired them.

They removed the generator from its tarpaulin in the assembly building and hauled it along to the brightly lit maintenance bench. It was a curious-looking thing, about ten feet long, heavy and squat, with scooter-sized wheels sticking out front and back. It resembled a howitzer cannon more than anything else, and Hoff said so. "It serves the same purpose," Bruning told him. "It's the power unit for the catapult."

They stripped, cleaned, and reassembled the machine, broke for a fast lunch, then turned their attention to the little firing hut and spent the rest of the afternoon getting it into operating order. Most of the third day was taken up by another trip to Rouen, this time trying to find a chemical supply house that stocked what they wanted. It took a long time to run down.

Finally, on the fourth day, they were ready to run their first test. They fetched the generator from the maintenance building, as well as some other items, including a three-hundred-pound solid iron object flared at both ends like a dumbbell. It was circular, about six feet long and a foot across, and had an eighteen-inch iron fin mounted on its top. They used a small trolley to transport it to the ramp, and a hand crane to lift it into position. It fitted into the ramp tube like a shell in the breech of a gun, its fin sticking up through the slot that ran the length of the tube.

"That's the piston," Bruning told them. "The fin attaches to a hook underneath the Fieseler. When the generator's opened the piston is forced along the tube and the missile is pulled along with it and catapulted into the air."

They watched Bruning lock the generator to the end of the tube, right behind the piston, then reach for the chemicals they'd bought the day before. He opened a gallon can and began to pour the contents into a deep metal flask attached to the generator's combustion chamber.

He finished with the can, picked up a heavy paper sack, ripped open its sewn top, and tipped dark purple crystals into a second flask on the side of the generator.

"What's that?" Lauter asked.

"The catalyst. Calcium permanganate."

Hoff squinched up his eyes, certain he'd missed something. "How heavy is the Fieseler?"

"Fully loaded, over two tons."

"Forgive me, Herr Bruning, but just those two chemicals? That's all it takes to launch the Fieseler?"

"That's all," Bruning answered. "Plus these." He'd finished with the bag and had picked up a long, slim canister of compressed air.

He screwed it into a pipe on the generator, then added two more in the same way.

"A simple chemical reaction," Bruning explained. "But the gas that results will blast the Fieseler the entire length of the ramp in about a second and a half. I'll show you."

He led them into the assembly building and uncovered the tester. This was a cigar-shaped cylinder that approximated the missile in size and weight. They used the four-wheeled gantry to get it to the doors, then lowered it onto a wooden dolly designed to carry the real missile, and pushed it down to the ramp. They towed the gantry down, too, hooked up the dummy once more, lifted it out of the dolly, and swung it over the launching rail.

They placed a short sliding carriage on the rail, then lowered the dummy onto it, positioning it so that the hook in its belly latched onto the piston's fin.

Lauter towed the gantry away, came back on foot, and asked Bruning an astute question. "How will you know whether or not the catapult's working up to full capacity?"

"By the distance we get. With no wings and no power it will just be momentum, so the dummy should travel about the same length as the ramp, fifty or fifty-five meters."

The scientist dispatched Hoff to measure off the distance into the field, and to mark it in some way. Hoff took a handcart, filled it with old fruit boxes, stepped off the distance, and placed the boxes in line with the ramp.

Bruning picked up one of the electrical leads he'd run through the wall of the firing hut and connected it to the generator's starter valve. He made a last-minute check of everything, waited till Lauter and Hoff had taken shelter behind the hut, then went inside, sat down on a box, and looked through the slit window. He rested a finger lightly on one of the switches he'd rigged up to a car battery, raised his wrist, and followed the sweep hand on his watch. As it advanced toward the twelve he began to count in reverse under his breath.

"Five, four, three, two, *one*." Then he snapped down the switch. There were two noises at the same instant: a tremendously loud prolonged roar, and a bang like two freight cars clashing together. A volcano cloud of hissing, exploding steam shot up obscuring everybody's view so that they saw nothing.

But they heard.

There was a shrill metallic screech that ended a second later, the roaring noise vanished and there was dead silence for a moment. Then, from far out in the field, there came a huge thud that shook the ground, and another noise right on top of it: the triumphant, heart-lifting sound of splintering wood.

CHAPTER TWELVE

Lauter—Paris/the Site, December 12-18, 1978

Besides the main uncertainty of the nuclear bomb there were two other things over which there hovered a question mark: fuel for the two missiles and conventional explosives for the first one. Getting the fuel proved to be easy, once Bruning decided that low-grade gasoline would do just as well as aviation spirit. Lauter and Hoff went into Rouen the following day and found a small service station whose owner was only too happy to call his supplier and get a dozen new fifty-liter cans sent over. They called Planckendorf about the explosives and were told that they'd be ready within twenty-four hours. As for the bomb, he'd heard that things were progressing well, and that delivery should be on time.

They stayed the night at Lauter's apartment and picked up the gasoline the next afternoon. It took two trips to transport it all to the site, and they got back too late to do anything but go to bed. Bruning hadn't been idle while they'd been gone, as they found out in the morning. He'd been working on a propulsion unit that was mounted on a testing frame and ready for an ignition trial. The unit was about eleven feet long and tubular, broadened at the front to encompass a combustion chamber.

Bruning played with throttle and pressure valves, and turned the taps of two air bottles, one attached to the fuel supply, the other connected to a pipe running up into the jet. Then, taking up a long lead from a car battery, he touched its end to a spark plug set into the top of the combustion chamber. There was an instant explosion and flame spurted out the back of the jet. The explosions continued like a slow string of firecrackers, and as Bruning adjusted the fuel supply, the detonations increased, becoming closer and closer together until there was a steady roar and a noise like a jackhammer.

The sides of the jet began to change color, and Lauter could feel the heat being given off.

The jet's exhaust flame flared into a blue-white blaze, and the testing frame shook violently.

Bruning ran it for another minute, listening, watching, tinkering with the fuel control, then cut the gasoline supply. The jet wound down, coughed twice, and cut out, and the silence rolled back in.

"Good enough," Bruning said. "We can start on the big job now."

The bright lights beating down from the assembly building's ceiling lit up the missile's interior machinery with a garish intensity. All its access plates were off and it lay in three separate compartments, its lethal torpedo shape no longer evident. "You'll be able to help me a lot more if you understand what you're working on and the role it plays in the overall design," Bruning told them. "Starting here and working backwards . . ."

He spun the little six-inch propeller that struck out on a spike on the missile's nose. "This is the range control. An airlog. It drives a counter in the rear compartment. When we've calculated the distance we want the missile to fly, we set the counter at that figure, and when the propeller has turned a corresponding number of revolutions the counter trips a relay that fires two detonators." Bruning pointed to the elevators in the tail planes. "That deflects those two flaps that tip the craft into a dive."

He directed their attention back to the propeller. "Right behind the airlog is an impact switch that's connected to the main fuses. Now, the nose cone itself. This is where the compass is located. It polices the master gyro and uses an air pickup device to correct any deviation from the course we'll give it."

He rapped his fingers against the last section of the first compartment; it made a hollow sound. "The warhead," Bruning said, looking pointedly at Lauter. "Empty as yet."

Lauter said that they'd be calling Planckendorf about it that afternoon. He watched Bruning move on to the second of the dismembered compartments, this one divided into only two sections, but big ones.

"The fuel tank. That hole through the center is for the wing spars. This second section here houses the compressed air supply."

Through the open maintenance hatch Lauter and Hoff could see two large cylinders, pipes running in and out of them. Both were bound tightly with wire and held in place by wide metal belts. "Very well," Bruning said, "the last compartment. This first section takes the fuel control mechanism and the auto pilot, the brain of the missile. It monitors height and range settings as well as the servo units in the last section here that operate the rudder and the elevators."

He crouched and stuck his finger into the maintenance hole. "That's the master gyro. It governs roll, pitch, and yaw. The two secondary gyros control the rate of climb and the initial turn."

"This is the big problem, isn't it?" Lauter said. "This section here."

Bruning told him he was right, enlarged on the problems inherent with the automatic controls and ended by talking himself out of the idea of handling that section first. He decided to leave it till last and to start at the front of the missile and get the easier jobs out of the way.

The little windmill and its cable needed only greasing. The compass they removed; it would be replaced later with a new one Bruning had bought in Rouen.

That brought them very quickly to the empty warhead and Hoff was sent into the village to do something about it. He called Planckendorf who had some instructions for him.

Hoff hurried back to the site, and an hour later he and Lauter packed a bag, drove into Dieppe, took the late afternoon train to Paris, and spent the night there.

They had to wait till the next evening, but Lauter used the time well, calling Uher and speaking with the pilot at some length. They also used the time to buy a light UHF radio transmitter they'd be needing. At seven Hoff tried the number he'd been given, but the voice on the other end told him delivery would be a day late.

There was no problem the next evening, however. The voice gave them an address, told them what they'd find there, and hung up. It turned out to be a café in a working-class section near the Port de la Chapelle. There was an old Citroën van parked outside with the words "H. Lannoy et Cie." in faded white on the corrugated body, no hint of the type of business, although with the battered rack on the roof it could have been a plumber's or an electrician's van.

Hoff found the keys where he'd been told to look for them, taped to the rear axle, and opened the loading doors. The street lighting lit up two big cardboard packing boxes, each with a full-scale drawing of a washing machine on the side with the name "Brandt" printed across it. There were some smaller boxes at the rear but nothing else. Lauter put the radio transmitter in, locked the doors, let them both into the front seat, and started the engine.

It was when they were moving through traffic in Saint-Denis that the trouble happened: Lauter drove through a red light he didn't see in time.

They didn't get more than a block before the speed cop pulled them over.

He got off his motorcycle, big and lumpy in his leather jacket, and slowly walked back toward them, pulling off his gloves like an executioner.

There was nothing Lauter or Hoff could do; it was just a terrible piece of luck. They watched him moving on them, a cold, empty churning in their insides.

"You think they're Christmas decoration? The lights?" He was a typical Paris cop: insolent, tough, dispeptic.

Lauter told him that a truck had obscured his view.

"License," the cop said. He didn't want an excuse.

He checked it over when Lauter handed it to him. "You live in Rouen?"

"Yes."

He glanced at Lauter again then stooped to get a look at Hoff, noticed their white collars and ties under their topcoats. They didn't fit the van they were driving.

"Whose van is this?"

"My partner's."

"That him?" the cop asked with a rude lift of his chin.

"No. He's a friend. He doesn't speak French."

The policeman's grunt said that anybody who didn't speak French was an imbecile. He eyed the van again. "What kind of business you in?"

Lauter felt the damp of perspiration on his ribs and was sure it was showing on his brow. Beside him he heard Hoff swallow and he could sense the rigid tension in him.

"Pardon?" Lauter asked.

"Business. What kind of business?"

Lauter thought of what they were carrying and the way it was packaged. "We own a laundry," he said.

The cop started to walk toward the rear. "Open up the back."

"My God," Hoff said under his breath. "Herr Lauter . . ."

Lauter shushed him with a quick movement. The motorbike was parked twenty feet ahead; if he ran it down, moved quickly into the traffic—hopeless. The van was old and heavy, the policeman had a gun.

"Come on. I don't have all night."

With his legs a long way beneath him Lauter got out and unlocked the rear doors.

"What's the radio for?" the cop asked.

"Short wave. A present for my wife," Lauter told him, surprised at how easily the answer had come.

"And the two big boxes? They presents, too?"

"They're for the laundry."

The cop had assumed that; he could see they were washing machines but he hadn't finished bullying this driver yet.

"Let's take a look," he said.

Lauter's breath stayed in his throat, caught on something. He got up into the van, the policeman climbing in, too.

"This one," the cop said, giving the nearest box a soft kick.

Lauter fiddled with the band of plastic tape that held it closed, deliberately making a long job of it, hoping the policeman would reach over to yank it himself, and give him a chance at the gun. Lauter flicked his eyes to it. It was in a large black holster, the flap held down by a leather strip.

"Pull it, for God's sake, it's only tape."

He'd have to be quick, have to surprise him, jerk the pistol out before the cop knew what was happening.

"I'm pulling it."

He got ready.

"Here . . ." the policeman lumbered sideways, reaching for the flaps of the box, pulled them open.

Lauter had to look in spite of his plan and saw, as he'd expected, flat gray metal. But it wasn't a bomb casing, it was a big tin trunk.

The policeman snapped it open. "Hey," he said.

Inside, completely filling the trunk, were a dozen fat clear plastic bags, all of them full of a white crystalline powder. The cop stepped back quickly, his hand suddenly near his pistol, and Lauter saw that he'd missed his chance. The cop's face had paled. He looked from Lauter to the sacks and back again, his left hand grasping for something under his jacket, a clasp knife. He levered up a blade and with an almost timid movement slashed open one of the bags.

"What's that?" he asked, his voice higher, stretched out.

"Bleach," Lauter answered.

The cop, certain he'd found a major drug haul, dipped his fingers into the powder, scooped up a handful, brought it close to his nose and sniffed.

His reaction was a quick gasp and a barking sneeze. Then another. He coughed violently, cleared his throat and spat out of the van's doors. With his eyes watering, his breath wheezing, he said, "Why the fuck didn't you tell me?" He threw the ammonium nitrate back into the sack, coughed and spat again.

Lauter said nothing; he knew he was still dangling on the precipice because there was still the other box and the cop was just mad enough to make him open it.

Which was exactly what the cop made him do.

Inside was an identical tin trunk containing the same number of clear plastic bags, but the powder was a pale yellow color. The cop perversely cut open one of them and stabbed the knife blade into ten pounds of TNT.

"Solvent," Lauter volunteered. "For dry cleaning."

The policeman knew he'd wasted his time and wasn't going to waste any more of it by writing out a ticket. "Okay, get out of here," he said. "And next time you see a red light stop and take a look at it." He jumped out of the van, walked to his motorcycle, started it, and tore off. But it was a good five minutes before Lauter and Hoff followed him. Lauter was trembling; an unseen red light, a little thing like that, and it had come close to ruining his life's work.

He resealed the boxes then drove back to the farm with both eyes on the road.

Even with the three of them working as a team the overhauling of the missile was a lengthy, painstaking job. Everything had to be stripped, cleaned, checked, replaced, checked again. It took them two whole days and most of two nights before they finished, and the best part of a third day before Bruning was satisfied with the tests they ran.

Then they started making up the explosives they'd come so close to losing.

They began by emptying out ten one-hundred-pound sacks of fertilizer they'd found in one of the sheds. The sacks were bright yellow and made of a heavy quality polyethylene. They also found an old milk vat, left from the days when the farm supported cows. They washed, scoured, and dried it thoroughly, then carried it, with the yellow bags piled inside, into the assembly building.

Bruning prepared a length of fuse tape, stuffed it into the exploder tube in the center of the warhead, then combined the ammonium nitrate and the TNT in the vat. He poured in water, added gum arabic to act as a gelatinizing agent, and an equal amount of borax for a binder.

They ladled the mudlike mixture into one of the sacks, packed it in full and tight until the double sack bulged evenly, closed off the interior wrapping, and fastened the outside with a box stapler.

It took the three of them to heft the sack that they placed in the bottom of the warhead as far forward as it would go. Bruning made up two more batches of the mixture, and by the time they'd finished, the warhead was solid with yellow bags jammed in a double row around the exploder tube. They replaced the warhead's cover, went outside, and started toward the farmhouse, the evening coming on fast.

"How soon before we launch?" Lauter asked.

Bruning asked him a question back. "What about the pilot?"

"He's waiting for my call in Beauvais."

Bruning looked at the rain spattering down. "If the weather holds we could launch tomorrow."

Inside the farmhouse Bruning sat down over the atlas and took them through some figures.

"I make it one hundred and ninety kilometers to central London. Allowing for the climb, that will give the Fieseler a flying time of around twenty-five minutes at four-sixty kilometers an hour."

Lauter, scanning the map, asked Bruning how accurate he thought the missile might be.

"Impossible to predict. With any Fieseler, even this one, all you can do is do your best and hope." He then explained his course calculation, stood up and suggested they get some sleep.

It was wishful thinking as far as Lauter was concerned. He lay in the dark for hours, listening to the rain on the roof and worrying about the pilot he'd be calling in the morning. Uher was an unknown quantity and Lauter had a nagging fear that his behavior might turn out to be just as unpredictable as the missile's.

The weather the next day was a repeat of the kind they'd been experiencing for almost a week: low, slate-colored skies that drizzled on and off, and sharp gusts of wind carrying the smell and the chill of the winter sea.

They attended to the compass first, treating it like royalty. They set its course inside the little square building that had been built iron-free solely for that purpose, then suspended it on rubber springs inside a wooden sphere, carried the sphere back to the assembly building, and cushioned it in the nose cone.

Bruning connected it to the battery and auto pilot leads, attached the little propeller to the counter lead, then announced that he was arming the warhead.

It was a sobering moment; as he finished with the nose fuse, they found themselves standing in front of a thousand pounds of primed, high-density explosive.

They bolted the nose cone onto the warhead, filled the fuel tank and compressed air cylinders, bolted on all the access plates, and hauled the missile to the ramp on the tractor.

From the large square building they carried out a set of stubby wings and secured them to the missile's body.

Lauter towed the big gantry down to the ramp and fifteen minutes later they had the buzz bomb reclining on the launch rail, its belly hook gripping the fin of the dumbbell piston snug in the ramp tube. When he'd checked the positioning, Bruning loosened the rear access plate and began to adjust the controls. He set the kilometer counter for the figure he'd computed then moved to the altimeter gauge.

"What height?" Lauter asked, watching him set it.

"The same as we used to fly them at, nine hundred meters."

At 2 p.m. Uher called to test their radio. Beauvais was only fifty miles away, so they could hear him clearly: everything was on schedule; he estimated takeoff at three-fifteen. The weather report was excellent: light rain and low ceiling over the Channel and Southern England, negligible head winds. They told him they'd be ready and got back to work.

Bruning left the missile and set up the generator unit as he'd done before, pouring in the chemicals and attaching the compressed air bottles. He connected the leads running from the firing hut, one to the generator's air valve, the other to an exterior fuel valve in the body of the missile, and made the final adjustment to the throttle.

Lauter towed away the gantry and Hoff cleared the rest of the equipment, then they came back and waited with Bruning at the ramp. They were all looking at something few people had ever seen before, and something Bruning had never thought he'd see again: a V-1 ready to be fired from its launching rail. He ran his eyes over the machine. "I congratulate you, Herr Lauter. This must be a proud day for you."

"It's a proud day for Germany," Lauter answered.

"A historical day," Hoff said. "December 17, 1978, the reopening of hostilities."

It was a strange time for them; ten days of intense work, of snatched meals and interrupted sleep, all culminating in an hour in which there was absolutely nothing to do.

Lauter waited it out by walking the length of the ramp, raindrops sprinkling down from the tunnel of trees, plastering his thinning hair to his forehead. The fields were deserted as always; nobody would see the missile taking off, the village was too far away, and the low clouds would hide it from any shipping in the Channel.

At two-forty-five the radio leaped into life. Uher reported no change in plans, so they went straight into the prelaunch procedure.

Bruning opened the main air supply valve and made a long, slow check of the rear compartment. He started the propulsion unit, which caught the first time, exploding cleanly, the flame building up, spurting in pulsating flashes from the stovepipe orifice. He bolted on the remaining hatch covers and the missile was ready.

They watched the jet's chamber start to glow, the noise building into a steady, roaring drumbeat.

Bruning waved Hoff and Lauter behind the firing hut, entered it, and put the radio at the door, its volume all the way up. He sat down on the wooden crate in front of the bench, checked the missile through the slit in the concrete wall, laid his watch down on the bench, and waited.

The radio cracked. Uher was in the air.

Bruning estimated a fourteen-minute flight.

He was happy to have the time; it would mean that the jet would be good and hot and receptive to constant self-ignition.

Fourteen minutes became ten.

Then five.

Then one.

Uher's voice was partly masked by the noise of the pulse jet but the message, a single code word, was crystal clear.

Bruning reached out to the firing box and snapped down both switches together.

As before, when they'd tested the generator, there was a tremendous sustained explosion, but this time, a fraction of a beat behind it, came the thunder of the jet leaping to full power as it responded to the opening of the fuel supply. Metal shrieked and the ground trembled for a second. Bruning rushed out of the hut, Lauter and Hoff right there with him, and through the roiling swirl of steam they could just make out the missile soaring up into the sky and banking into a turn before the trees hid it from their sight.

It was six hours before they found out the result of the launch; Lauter drove to a hotel in a nearby town where Uher called him from England. They got a more detailed report from the pilot when he arrived at the site the following day.

He drove over from Beauvais in a rental car, following the directions Lauter had given him, and sauntered into the farmhouse as if expecting to be decorated. Bruning, who hadn't met him before, disliked him instantly, and Lauter, despite Uher's demonstrated talent as a flier, was still uneasy about him and didn't mind letting it show. Hoff would have been more hostile than either of them if he'd been present, but he'd gone to Dieppe to buy an English newspaper, and to call Planckendorf.

The pilot took in the room as if he were amused by it, let his eyes travel over the unswept floor, the rumpled beds, the dishes in the sink. He picked up a cane chair, bouncing it lightly on the floor to jar the dust away, hitched at the knees of his tailored leather pants, and sat down.

Lauter said, "I take it you had no trouble?"

Uher waved the thought away. "A piece of cake, as our English friends say. I told them I had a jammed rudder, requested special clearance, and the idiots gave it to me, just like that."

"I was worried they might send a jet to check on you if they got suspicious," Lauter said.

"They were lucky they didn't."

"What do you mean?"

Uher made a gun of his hand and pulled an imaginary trigger.

Lauter didn't understand, but Bruning did. He said, startled, "Your plane is armed?"

"Of course it is." Uher's mouth lifted in a tiny smile. "I never fly into enemy territory without guns."

Lauter saw that he was mocking them, but that he was also telling the truth.

Bruning saw it, too. "How can you get away with a thing like that?"

"Easy. They're inboard. I had the barrels shortened and the gun ports plugged." In the silence that followed Uher said, "Why are you so surprised? You know my line of work. The guns were a present from a grateful government."

Anger made Lauter's words come out in a whisper. "You could have jeopardized everything. If they'd sent a jet to check on you, and you'd opened fire, it would have shot you down and—"

Uher didn't let him finish. "Shot *me* down? A jet?" He made a sound of humor in his teeth. "That'll be the day. I flew against jets in Biafra. The Nigerians were flying MiG-15s, twice as fast as my 190. They took one look at me, a 1945 piston-engined aircraft, and thought I'd be easy meat. The next thing they knew I'd turned inside them and they found themselves flying a burning wreck."

Bruning spoke up. "The MiG-15 is a twenty-five-year-old aircraft. The English are flying today's jets, with the latest air-to-air missiles."

Uher dismissed that with a shake of his head. "No matter how fast or how well armed a plane is, it still has to be flown by a pilot. And there are no fighter pilots anymore. They're button pushers— computer operators."

"Herr Uher." Lauter's voice had ice on the edges. "Getting the missile to London safely should be your only thought. If this time luck is against you and you're intercepted, remember, your role is a defensive one, nothing else."

"I agree," Uher answered. "And you know what they say the best defense is." He rushed on, not giving Lauter a chance to respond. "You don't have to worry. I snuck it in yesterday and I can sneak one in again. I'll probably be asked for a written 'Please Explain', which they won't accept, but that's what I'm being paid for, or so I've been led to believe."

It was a crass way of asking for his money, but Lauter didn't comment. He went into the other room and returned a moment later with a plastic supermarket bag, which he handed to the pilot.

"When do you think you'll be ready?" Uher asked. He didn't look at the money in the bag; these people were too stupid to think of cheating him.

"Soon," Lauter said. "I will call you in Munich when I know."

Uher moved to the door but couldn't resist a parting shot. "I suppose you'll be sorry when it's all over," he said, looking round the grubby room. "You'll miss the healthy farm life."

He left on that note, but his visit stayed with them for some time. An hour later Hoff returned with a copy of the London *Times* opened at a report of the explosion. Lauter translated it. "A gas main explosion," Bruning said. "I was wondering if they might think it was something like that. I knew there'd be nothing left of the Fieseler, not with a five-hundred-kilo warhead."

Hoff also had big news: they'd have the bomb in six days' time. Delivery would have to be direct, so he'd given Planckendorf directions to the farm.

"Six days . . ." Lauter checked a calendar on the wall. "That's excellent. Perfect." He asked Bruning when they'd be ready to launch.

The scientist figured it for a moment. "Two days for the propulsion unit, four for the missile. We should be able to launch on the day of delivery. The twenty-fourth."

CHAPTER THIRTEEN

Pelham—Munich, December 23, 1978

The morning flight to Munich boarded quickly and took off on schedule, but it still wasn't fast enough for Pelham. He was having a hard time sitting still in his seat, and Rossi wasn't finding it easy, either. Pelham's theory had been nagging at her ever since he'd explained it, and she admitted her problem.

"I'm still not sure, Jimmy. The idea of a trial run sounds plausible, but I just can't believe the other part."

"Why not? What stops you?"

"I just can't see how they could steal a nuclear bomb. I mean, they must be the most closely guarded things in the world."

"Maybe they didn't steal it. Maybe they bought it."

"That sounds even more impossible."

"It's been done before," Pelham said. "Israel got the bomb that way. Bought the plutonium under the counter. You can get anything if you've got enough bread."

"Then you're supposing they've got money."

Pelham's answer was a touch irritated. "I'm supposing a lot of things. As far as Brian Jakes is concerned I'm supposing everything. But what if I'm right, Rossi? The hell of it is, I'm not sure there's going to be much we can do about it anyway. We need help and nobody's going to believe us. And they're not going to want to because tomorrow's Christmas Eve and they'll be starting the holiday."

Pelham recrossed his legs, shifted impatiently. "For the first time in my life I'm dying to be wrong. The English won't be able to stop that thing once it's in the air. They didn't know about the first one, so they won't know about the second one until it hits. It has to be stopped on the ground. But where's it coming from? And when are they going to launch it? For all we know they could be planning on

Christmas Day. A nice little gift-wrapped bomb for London. And meantime all we have is the name and address of one man in Munich, and two seats on the world's slowest jet."

"You're doing your best, Jimmy," Rossi said, trying to soothe him.

"And we'll be landing in less than an hour."

But it didn't make Pelham feel any better. Nor did the customs man who insisted on going through his suitcase.

Rossi had to trot to keep up with him as he went through the terminal and out to the cab rank. He thrust Uher's address at the driver of the first taxi he came to.

"Let's go," he said, jumping into the back seat. "We're in a hurry. Is it far?"

The driver gave him a cold look.

"Tell him to step on it," Pelham said to Rossi.

The girl spoke to the driver in soft German. The man nodded and took the cab away.

"I forgot they don't speak English," Pelham said.

The driver shifted gears angrily. "I speak English. I just don't like being ordered around."

"Sensitive, huh?" Pelham replied, then set back and dropped the conversation.

The cab moved swiftly through the outskirts of the city, then into the downtown section. Rossi, who'd never been to Munich before, saw that it suffered from the same visual malaise as most of the other big cities of Europe: the beautiful old buildings smothered by modern office blocks. But she didn't give it much thought; she was worrying about the man they were on their way to see.

"Jimmy, what are you going to say to Uher? If he is tied into this then whatever we say could be dangerous."

"I know that. I also know we don't have time to play games with him." Pelham turned to her looking serious. "Incidentally, if he speaks English, you don't get to meet him."

Rossi started to protest but the cab pulled into the curb, and Pelham jumped out. They paid the driver and took a look at where they were. It was a smart area: antique shops, small boutiques, a glistening jewelry store. Uher's apartment house was a handsome nineteenth-century building with pale yellow arched windows picked out in white. The front entrance was guarded by double doors made of heavy plate glass with a shiny brass lock firmly in place. Through them they could see the foyer: two Bergère sofas set each side of a richly worked coffee table, a large wall tapestry, a Spanish tile floor in a pink and green floral pattern.

There was a row of call buttons set into the wall on one side of the doors, a speak box above it. Uher's name was opposite apartment number 3A. Pelham pressed the button and they waited. He pressed the button again, hard and long this time, but there was still no response.

Rossi couldn't disguise her relief. "He's not in."

"Then we'll just have to visit without him," Pelham said. He eyed the bank of buttons. "Try this one, 4B. Tell whoever answers that you're Elspeth Hauser in 1A and you've forgotten your key. Ask them to let you in."

Rossi wasn't crazy about it but she did as Pelham asked. The call was answered almost immediately and Rossi said something in German into the voice mike. There was no query, just a buzz from somewhere. The door clicked, they pushed it open, crossed the lobby, and rode the elevator to the third floor. There were only two apartments to each floor, one on the front of the building, one on the back. Uher's apartment was on the front. Pelham pressed the bell and knocked hard but there was no sound from inside. He bent down, examined the lock, and said, "I'd sell my soul for five minutes in there but we won't be opening that with a hairpin. I'll have to bust it open."

"How?"

"Simple. Find a hardware store, and buy a chisel and a hammer."

"Noisy, Jimmy. People would hear us."

"Too bad. We've got to get inside that apartment."

Rossi thought for a moment then said, "I was locked out of an apartment once when I lost my keys. But I got in without breaking the door down."

"That's no trick. It was your apartment."

"Why couldn't this be my apartment?" Rossi explained what she had in mind, but Pelham thought it would take too long.

"Not as long as it would take us if we're in jail because somebody heard us breaking in."

Pelham couldn't argue with that and reluctantly agreed to do what she suggested. But he made sure it was done at top speed.

They hurried downstairs to the lobby where Pelham jammed a pen under the front door to keep it from locking behind them. Then they took a cab to the nearest store, shopped in the stationery and the toy departments, and got a postage stamp from a machine. When they found a quiet corner Pelham took an envelope they'd bought, wrote Rossi's name on it, put Uher's address underneath, and stuck on the postage stamp. Then he dug into the store bag again, brought out a red ink pad and a child's rubber stamp, inked it, and very lightly, touched it to the envelope.

The result wasn't bad: it came out looking like a poorly franked letter.

Rossi made a fast phone call, then they got back to Uher's apartment house.

Pelham went to the bank of mailboxes mounted on the lobby wall. There were no names on them, just the apartment numbers. He dropped the fake letter into Uher's box.

"Don't forget his card outside," Rossi said.

Pelham pointed a finger at her, went out and removed the card from the bank of call buttons. He didn't come back in again.

Fifteen minutes later a man rapped on the doors.

Rossi opened them.

"Locksmith," the man said.

"Thank heavens you're here." Rossi's switch into German was effortless. "I've got a real problem."

The locksmith went by her looking a bit grumpy at being pulled out of his nice warm shop.

"I left a spare with somebody in 4B," Rossi said, "but they won't be home till late tonight."

The man was unimpressed, and more than a touch suspicious. "How did you get in here if you've lost your keys?"

"The door was open," Rossi said truthfully.

"What's your name?"

"Rossi Studer."

"I'll need identification."

"Of course." Rossi dipped into her tote bag, handed him her passport. "Lucky thing I was carrying it."

The man checked the name and the photograph inside, flicked his eyes to Rossi's face, handed the passport back. "I need proof that you live here."

Rossi began to rake around in her bag, frowning down at it. "I've only been here a week. I've been living in London. I don't think I have anything with my new address on it."

The locksmith shifted the satchel he was carrying to his other hand. He said dourly, "I'll have to have something. Or somebody in the building to vouch for you."

"There's only the woman in 4B but as I told you, she's not home." Rossi bit her lip, said uncertainly, "You could call the rental agent."

The man's expression made it plain that making phone calls wasn't part of the service.

"Or," the girl continued, brightening, "there's my mail. If I showed you—" She stopped in mid-sentence, her face falling. "The box key was on my key chain." She looked at him hopefully. "If you'd open the box for me . . ." She trailed off because the man was shaking his head.

"I can't open a mailbox without proof of residence." He transferred the satchel again, getting ready to go.

"Wait, let me try something." Rossi raked through her tote bag, pulled out a nail file. "This might do it. I hope you can't get arrested for stealing your own mail," she said. The man watched her slide the file into the slot of the mailbox. Rossi, probing carefully, felt the envelope, and slowly drew it up till she could grab it with her fingers. She gave a little cry of triumph, and handed the letter to the locksmith who checked the name and address on the front. "You were lucky," he said. He sounded disappointed.

They rode up to the third floor together where the man went to work on Uher's lock. It took him the best part of ten minutes to pick it, and she didn't even know he'd finished till he straightened up and began to put his tools away. Rossi thanked him, paid what he asked, added a large tip, and watched him head for the elevator. Then she took a big breath, fought down the nerves in her tummy, and eased the door back.

She knew right away that nobody was there; the apartment had a dead, empty sound. But she didn't go in; she waited till Pelham joined her.

"Good girl," he said. He stopped to examine the lock, took out a tissue, and wiped away a blob of oil. "He'll never know it was picked."

They walked into a little hallway, closed the door behind them, then took a tour. The hallway angled into a large living room with a dining area at one end and a kitchen off. Through an opposite door was a bedroom with big walk-in closets, a dressing room, and a bathroom. The bed had been made, the quilted spread folded neatly over a chair. In the bathroom two fluffy towels lay on a rack, almost dry. More towels in various strong colors were stacked up in the bathroom cabinet on top of which stood several bottles of after-shave lotion and body cologne. All of them had a strong lemony lime smell, nothing like the sweet perfume Pelham had noticed in the bedroom. When Rossi wandered in he said to her, "I'd say he had company last night."

"I'd say he has company every night," she answered. "Have you noticed the photographs?"

Pelham saw what she meant. On the dressing table were four framed shots, each showing Uher with his arm around a different girl. In the background was the same white sports car. Pelham took a closer look at it. "A Ferrari. Uher does okay for himself. You should see his closet, it looks like a men's store."

They moved into the living room. Like the bedroom the furniture in here was all modern Italian, very stylish as was the whole decor. But there was something too pat about it, as if it had been carefully arranged for a magazine photograph. The walls were papered in a dark brown and silver pattern that was matched exactly by the fabric covering the cushions on the leather sofa. The deep cream-colored broadloom had American Indian throw rugs scattered over it. There were no fussy touches, no lamp shades or stacked side tables; the whole effect was hard edged and very masculine.

"What do you think of him so far?" Pelham asked.

Rossi was examining the smoked glass bookshelves. "A rich bachelor, likes the good things of life. Clothes, cars. There's a cupboard in the kitchen full of vintage wines, and I don't think this stereo could have cost less than four thousand marks."

"Rossi, you're doing okay," Pelham said, crossing to the bookshelf. But it wasn't the set which interested him, it was the photographs underneath it. These were much older than the ones in the bedroom, black-and-white shots showing Uher as a young man with crinkly fair hair. In one of them he was looking straight at the camera, standing in front of a fighter plane and wearing a cloth jacket with a knitted collar and embroidered shoulder patches.

There was an Iron Cross hanging over the knot of his tie. In the photograph next to it he wore a more formal uniform, a single-breasted blouse, breeches, and high knee boots. Again he was posing in front of the same aircraft.

"He certainly loves that plane," Rossi said.

"He sure does. He even left himself out of this one." Pelham had picked up another photo showing the fighter from a three-quarter angle. It seemed to be mostly engine with a big three-blade propeller in front mounted on a fat propeller hub. The cockpit was short and functional, the body tapering down to a rounded tail fin. The wheels on the wide-spaced undercarriage were half covered, giving the craft a thirtyish racing-plane look, but the overall impression was one of strength and power.

There was a drawing of it in another frame, beautifully done in colored inks. The fighter was in profile, big yellow numerals on each side of the black-and-white cross behind the cockpit. The swastika on the tail was very much in evidence and a fierce-looking black hawk, outlined in white, had been painted on the forward fuselage.

Pelham read out the legend underneath the illustration. "Focke-Wulf FW 190 A 4."

Rossi pointed to another group of photographs displayed on a higher shelf. These were much newer, and the first showed the fighter again, or one very much like it; it was silver, not dark colored, and there were no markings except a registration number. The engine looked different, too, longer and slimmer. Uher stood behind the wing with another man, a black man wearing a flight suit and carrying a helmet.

"Does the number check?" Rossi asked.

"You better believe it. That's the plane that flew over Hayes six days ago. And it's the same kind our boy flew for the Fuehrer." Pelham studied the photos some more, peering at them up close. "Do you notice anything special about this plane in these recent shots?" Rossi waited for him to tell her. "See here in the wings? They're machine guns. And Uher looks only, what, seven or eight years younger than he does in the shots in the bedroom, the ones with the Ferrari, which is a fairly new model. So you have to ask yourself what a guy was doing with machine guns in his plane around 1970 or so. I don't know but I'd say our boy is for hire."

He couldn't tell whether or not Rossi accepted his theory so he strengthened his case a little. "Look at the other pilot, a black man. Okay, there are lots of black pilots. But look at the background, hot and dry. Could be Africa. And the guy he's with in this one, wearing the shorts. Looks like an English type, but with all that sunshine it wasn't taken in England. South Africa or Rhodesia, maybe. And this shot here, the one with the girl in that sarong thing. She could be Filipino or Indonesian. And in all three shots the guns are showing. I think he flies for whoever's paying."

Rossi didn't give him an argument, but she didn't agree, either. "You don't buy it?" he asked.

She made a neutral gesture. "I just don't see who'd hire him with such an old plane."

"It may be an oldie but it's a goodie. Hell, there are all kinds of border disputes and mini-wars going on in the Third World, and most rebel groups can't afford ten-million-dollar jets. A man with a fighter could name his own price. And," Pelham concluded, sweeping his arm at the lush apartment, "I'd say that Uher isn't shy about naming it."

"Then he's a *mercenaire*. I think you call it a 'mercenary.' "

"That's exactly what we call it. He worked for whoever launched that flying bomb. And we've got to find out who that is."

Pelham crossed the room to a desk against the wall. It was an old-fashioned rolltop, out of place with the rest of the decor but still a handsome piece, and it wasn't locked. Pelham pulled out the chair in front of it and invited Rossi to sit down.

"What do you want me to look for?"

"Bank statements, check stubs, personal correspondence, anything that'll tell us where his money comes from. And anything connected with France."

If the outside of the desk was different from the rest of the apartment, the interior was a perfect match. Everything was neat and tidy and in its proper place, papers and forms filed evenly in three rows of pigeonholes. Rossi started on the upper row, pulling out papers, scanning them, putting them back exactly as they'd been.

"Insurance policies," she said. "Car registration, a copy of his lease." She read something quickly. "A letter from a lawyer about a ski cabin in Austria. Obergurgl."

"Austria's no good, we want France. Try the next row."

Rossi dug into another slot. "Here's a contract of some kind. Looks like he owns a bar."

"Where?"

"Here in Munich. In Schwabing. It's the nightclub area."

"Keep going."

Straightaway Rossi said, "This is better, his bank statement. A local bank. On the thirtieth of last month his balance was just over eight thousand marks."

Pelham considered it. "No, this guy's got to have more than that, unless he's living on credit. What else is there?"

"Cancelled checks." Rossi flicked through them. "One for utilities, one for rent—"

"Skip it. Try the next hole."

Rossi had more luck with this one. "This is better, Jimmy, a letter from a bank in Zurich."

"He's got a Swiss bank account?"

"Looks like it. The Swiss Bank Corporation. It's addressed to Karl Uher and or Freida Uher. So I was wrong, he must be married. Probably separated."

"What's it say?"

"Nothing startling. Something about adjusting his account."

Rossi picked up a stack of forms and frowned at them. "I'm not sure exactly what these are." She struggled to translate one, confused by all the figures and the different entries. "*Abschlussdatum* that's trade date, eighteenth of the second, Seventy-eight. *Stückzahl*, amount, twenty thousand U.S. dollars."

"Twenty thousand," Pelham echoed. "We're getting somewhere."

"*Kurs*, that's price, ninety-nine, twenty-five. Then it says eight-and-three-quarter percent *Montaunion Hohe Behoerde der*—"

"Bonds! That's a buy confirmation for bonds. Uher bought twenty thousand bucks' worth on February eighteenth."

Rossi pulled out the rest of the forms, checked through them quickly, knowing what to look for now. "He bought fifteen thousand dollars' worth in May, ten thousand dollars' worth in July."

She got to the last one and Pelham read the figure over her shoulder. "Thirty-three thousand dollars on November twenty-fifth. A month ago. That's the one, Rossi. We have to find out where that money came from."

She was already pulling forms from another section of the desk, pink ones, and from the same bank, but with a different layout and not as many figures.

She translated again. "*Gutshrift*, credit notice, or credit advice."

"They're the ones, keep going."

"February eighth. *Wir bestätigen den Erhalt*. . . . We acknowledge receipt of, then the figure, twenty thousand dollars. *Rimesse der Barney MacNeil*, Commonwealth Bank of Australia, Darwin, N.T."

"Australia. He gets around. But look at that date, Rossi, and that amount." Pelham leafed through the purchase confirmations and picked out the first one. "The dates are close and the amounts match. This guy MacNeil in Darwin remits twenty grand to Uher's account in Zurich. The bank credits his account and sends him the notice, and he writes back and has them buy Eurodollar bonds with the money. There are probably debit notices there somewhere, but that doesn't matter. . . ." Pelham was scattering through the pink forms, snatching them up, putting them down. "What we need is the credit notice for that thirty-three thousand dollars."

They looked but it wasn't there.

Pelham tore through the notes again, but there was no thirty-three-thousand-dollar figure.

"Goddammit! The one thing we're after!" He hurled them down onto the desk.

Rossi, ignoring his impatience, made another search and found something she hadn't noticed before. "Jimmy, take a look at this. I think it's his accounts book. See here? He's written the figure twenty thousand, then the initial M."

"MacNeil," Pelham said. "M for MacNeil. The name and the amount check. Keep going."

The girl's fingers flicked through the book and stabbed at a page. "Here it is! Thirty-three-thousand. Then the letter L."

Pelham grabbed it from her. "We've got to have more than that. What's this say here?"

Rossi tried to make out the writing, then she said, excited, "It's a name. It looks like . . . Hoff."

"Hoff."

"I can't read the other part, but I'm sure that name is Hoff."

"That's all? No address?"

"Nothing," Rossi answered. She checked all the way through the book, but it was the calendar on the last page that stopped her. Pelham saw it at the same time: two dates circled in December, the seventeenth and the twenty-fourth. He didn't have to remind Rossi that the seventeenth was the day of the explosion in Hayes.

When he spoke, his voice sounded different, flattened. "The twenty-fourth. That's tomorrow. They're firing that thing tomorrow."

Neither of them said anything for a moment, then Pelham snapped out of it. "We've got to have more to go on than one name and one initial. There must be thousands of Hoffs in Germany. How are we supposed to find the right one in twenty-four hours?"

"What do we do, Jimmy?"

"Concentrate on Uher. Try to find him."

"Go to Beauvais?"

Pelham said no. "He may use a different airport this time. Let's check the apartment again. Check the pockets of his clothes, everything."

It was ten minutes before they found something; Rossi came out of the bedroom holding a crumpled piece of paper she'd picked out of a wastepaper basket.

"It's a phone message. No date. Looks like a woman's handwriting." She read out a man's name and a number.

"Call him," Pelham said. "Tell him you're a friend of Uher's. See if this guy knows where he is."

Rossi went to the phone, dialed, and waited.

Pelham heard the answering voice on the other end.

Rossi, puzzled, asked a question, and got a reply. She looked up, her face open in surprise. "It's the police," she said.

The precinct house was an ugly stone structure built to look like a fort. A desk sergeant led them through it to an office at the end of a corridor, and the man inside stood up to greet them. He did so with some effort. He was a large man with a soft, jowly face, close-cropped iron-gray hair, and a braided uniform that stretched over his stomach.

"Jim Pelham, Captain. This is Miss Studer. I hope you speak English."

"I do," the man answered, "but I'm afraid I make many mistakes."

"It doesn't sound like it," Pelham said.

The policeman pointed to chairs, sat down himself, and got straight down to business.

"You told me on the phone, Miss Studer, that you are interested in talking to Karl Uher."

"Yes, that's right."

"I'm trying to contact him myself."

"I don't understand," Pelham said.

The policeman smiled an apology. "Karl Uher went to jail for a year on a smuggling charge. I was with the narcotics division at the time. As his arresting officer he's supposed to report to me every month till his parole is over, but he missed his visit this month so I tried to jog his memory with a phone call. When he still didn't come in we went looking for him, but he'd gone."

"Have you tried France, Captain? Beauvais?"

The policeman sat a little straighter. "You have reason to believe he's there?"

"We know for sure he was there last week."

"Mr. Pelham, perhaps you'd be good enough to explain your interest in this man."

"Miss Studer and I work for an insurance company in London. About a week ago three houses covered by our firm were destroyed in an explosion, and we think Uher was involved. We also think it's going to happen again. Tomorrow. But on a much larger scale. Perhaps a colossal one."

The policeman's eyebrows rose. "Uher must be expanding. What else have you found out?"

Pelham told him about the accounts book and the initial and the name they'd found in it. The captain reacted sharply.

"Hoff!"

"You know him?"

"Three weeks ago a man by that name robbed the bank where he'd worked for twenty years. Killed a guard and stole more than a million marks, then disappeared."

Rossi was the first to speak. She said softly, "They bought it . . ."

The captain's eyes swiveled to her. "Bought what?"

"If I told you, Captain, you wouldn't believe me."

Pelham's chair went back. "We've got to find Uher. Can you check with Beauvais airport?"

"I'll call immediately. If he is there I'll have the French police hold on to him." The captain got up, too. "I want to thank you both. If Hoff is with Uher the arrest would be quite a feather in my cap."

Pelham gave him a hard look. "I wouldn't worry about that side of it. What Uher's doing is a hell of a lot bigger than robbing banks."

"Of course," the policeman said, but he didn't sound too concerned.

"How long will it take you to get an answer?"

"Say, two hours. We may have to check all the other airfields in the vicinity."

Pelham hated the idea of just waiting around, and he wondered if they could use the time to find out more about Hoff and the bank robbery. The police captain suggested the microfilm newspaper files at the public library, showed them out, and told them to call him in two hours.

When they'd gone he went straight to the phone, snatched it up, and barked an order into it. "Send Max in. Immediately."

Out in the lobby the desk sergeant called to a big man sitting on a bench. "Hey, Max! Planckendorf wants you. On the double."

CHAPTER FOURTEEN

Pelham—Munich, December 23, 1978

As they emerged into the cold of the street, Rossi found she'd left her gloves in the waiting room of the precinct house.

She looked thoughtful when she came out again.

"A funny thing, Jimmy. When I went back inside, a man stopped as if he'd recognized me, then turned away and pretended to read a bulletin board."

Pelham looked over her shoulder. "A big guy? Head like a bullet, brown duffel coat?"

"Yes."

"He's just come out of the door."

They started walking, and almost immediately spotted an empty cab. As they climbed into it, Pelham saw a gray car, an Opel, pull in front of the precinct house and pick up the man in the duffel coat. Rossi asked the cabdriver to take them to the library.

"We're going to have company," Pelham told her. "I think Captain whatshisname . . ."

"Planckendorf . . ."

"Yeah. I think he sees us as a springboard for a promotion. He doesn't want to lose us."

"What if he can't find Uher, Jimmy?"

"He'd better. If he doesn't we've had it." Pelham made a fist and thumped his knee. "Lousy, bloody thing; one little piece of paper from that bank and we'd know who this guy 'L' is. And where he lives. He paid Uher thirty-three grand on November twenty-fifth, and that was *before* Hoff stole a million marks. So what do you figure, did they need the money to buy the buzz bombs? Or did they need it for something they're going to put on board? I know what I think."

In a nervous gesture Rossi flicked a strand of hair away from her face. "So do I," she said.

Five minutes later the cab stopped outside of a big, impressive-looking building with the facade of a Greek temple. Going through the doors, Pelham saw the Opel pull up, and the man in the duffel coat get out and start up the stairs.

"Slick, isn't he," he said.

They crossed the vestibule into an immense room with a domed ceiling. In the center of the marble floor was a circular desk built around a book elevator, people sitting near it waiting for books to come up from the basement.

A librarian directed Rossi into a wing of the building, and they followed a high, echoing corridor, then went through double doors. The room was long and narrow, three rooms actually, one leading into the next. A gallery ran all the way around the walls that seemed to be built of books. They climbed the stairs to it and found the microfilm machine, and the catalog files. It was quiet in the room, only a few people on the floor below, no sound save for the soft thump of somebody stacking books in a shelf.

If it hadn't been so quiet Pelham wouldn't have heard the door squeak open, wouldn't have looked down and seen the cop in the duffel coat slip into the room.

He was about to go and tell him to get lost when something about the man's attitude stopped him. It was the slow, cautious way he was moving his hand toward his coat pocket, as if there were something in that pocket he planned to surprise.

Drawn by Pelham's stillness, Rossi had spotted the man, too, and when his hand came out holding a gun she thought the same as Pelham: that he was there to arrest them, at gunpoint, which didn't make sense.

But what he did next did make sense; a horrible, heart-stopping sense. He reached into his other pocket and brought out something that looked like a short, slim telescope, and fitted it onto the barrel of the gun.

Rossi didn't know what it was, but by the way the man slid the gun back into his pocket, and kept his hand on it, she knew that he was there to kill them.

Pelham understood the moment he saw the silencer; understood quite at bit. He pressed Rossi back against the bookstacks, moved her down the gallery, creeping along. But he knew they were only buying time: the gallery ended sixty feet ahead; once the cop had seen that they weren't on the lower floor he'd know there was only one place they could be. He'd come up the stairs and it would be all over.

Pelham forced his numbed brain to figure it. He could hide between the stacks, jump out at the man—and then what? Tangle with a big guy like that, a killer with a gun? Insane. He needed a weapon of some kind, but everywhere he looked there was nothing but books. That books would make a splendid weapon didn't occur to him until he saw the trolley.

It had been left at the end of the gallery, a heavy metal trolley, its three shelves jammed with thick volumes. He whispered into Rossi's ear. She nodded and kept going. She made the end of the gallery and started around the turn of the rail.

Pelham, with no idea of where the man below was, watched the girl work her way around behind the stairway.

Very cautiously Rossi raised her head.

She saw the cop; he was almost to the stairs, the gun out of his pocket now. He knew they were hiding up there. He was coming up. Rossi surprised herself; she was trembling, the fear inside her like needles of ice, yet she found herself thinking that when the man started up the stairs he'd be directly below her, and have his back to her.

She glanced around; they were in a reference section, the books all big, heavy tomes. To her left, on a stand of its own, was a huge one-volume encyclopedia.

Below her she caught the sound of a soft footstep.

She shifted her position, hefted the encyclopedia, inched forward, and looked down.

The cop was creeping up the stairs.

Rossi sprang up, intending to hurl the book at him, but she underestimated its bulk and was way too slow.

With phenomenal reflexes the cop spun, the pistol jerking up with his head, and there was a sharp, quick sound like a cork popping from a bottle.

The bullet would have killed the girl if it hadn't had to travel through twelve inches of pages. It slapped into the encyclopedia in front of Rossi's chest, staggering her, but she still managed to fling the book over the stair rail.

The cop dodged it easily, and charged up the stairs.

Rossi cried out, "*Jimmy!*" but Pelham was already moving.

He kicked away from the wall, grabbed the handle of the trolley, rammed it ahead of him and, as hard as he could, shoved it down the stairs.

The trolley, too heavy to fly, nose dived halfway down, and landed with a tremendous impact, books exploding out of it. They slammed into the cop, peppered him; one of them, the size of a dictionary, caught him flush in the face and stopped him cold. The trolley spun end over end, crash banged down toward him, side-swiped him, and sent him tumbling back to the bottom of the stairs.

But he wasn't out of it; half buried by books, he was trying to struggle to his feet. And he hadn't let go of the gun.

Pelham grabbed for Rossi.

They raced back down the gallery, back the way they'd come, ran all the way to the end, down the stairs, and onto the floor.

Pelham risked a look behind and saw what he was afraid he'd see: the cop was up, wobbly, but coming fast.

They charged through the door, ran down the long corridor, and out into the vestibule.

They didn't get any further—the driver of the Opel, another hard-faced cop, was coming through the front doors, and he'd spotted them.

Pelham wheeled, dragged Rossi with him, and ran into the main room.

He realized his mistake immediately: the room was circular, there were no exits, no way out of it.

Not for people, anyway.

Rossi didn't understand when Pelham jerked her toward the center of the room, but she got the message when they rushed through the iron gate of the librarian's desk. A young woman unloading the book elevator stared in amazement as Pelham ducked under the hatch, pulled Rossi with him, then reached around and hit the Down button. The shaft swallowed them up, and they had to huddle together to escape the walls as the elevator clanked its way down. Above them a ring of astonished faces watched their descent, then the cop's face appeared, and vanished, and Pelham knew he'd be heading for the stairs near the front door. Light burst in on them as the elevator bumped down onto the basement loading dock. They scrambled out, fled past a gaping man, sprinted down a long wall of books toward an exit sign.

They charged into what had to be a staff lunchroom, spotted a door, and almost collided with a man coming through it carrying a milk crate.

Then they were outside, running down steps to a narrow service road at the back of the building. But there was nowhere to hide, and the only vehicle in sight was the milkman's van, a little electric van that looked like a toy.

But it was there and it had wheels.

They jumped into it. There were no doors, no seats, either; the van was supposed to be driven standing up.

Pelham stamped on the only pedal he could see, and they shot forward with a jangle of milk crates, the electric motor whining. But the speed was laughable; the little van, designed for door-to-door delivery, wasn't going much faster than a man could run. Pelham knew the cop couldn't be far behind, but he was still surprised when he glanced back and saw him burst out of the door.

"Get down!" he yelled, and pulled Rossi with him, steering blind but still keeping his foot on the pedal.

The bang of the gunshots and the crash of shattering glass sounded together. In a single sustained burst the cop emptied his pistol, and the bullets, spraying into the van, demolished half the bottles in the back before they took out the windshield inches above Pelham's head.

Pelham checked Rossi, jumped up, straightened the wheel, kept them rolling. They went through an open gate, and swung out into the avenue traffic.

Cars slowed, their drivers staring at the incredible sight.

Milk poured from the van, a white river of it gushing over the sides, splashing down onto the street, chunks of broken glass everywhere. The windshield looked like a rock had gone through it. None of it would have mattered if the van had had any speed, but at that insanely slow pace Pelham figured they had perhaps three minutes before the cops overtook them. They had to dump the van, get inside somewhere, but the buildings they were passing looked like embassies, or government offices, most of them forbiddingly shuttered. All he could think of to do was to keep going, cross his fingers, and hope, but a hundred yards farther on Pelham knew that wasn't going to be good enough: from back up the avenue came the sound of honking horns, the kind of din indignant drivers might make at a car cutting in front of them.

Pelham tried to grind the pedal through the floor, but it made no difference; there was just no way the van could go any faster, and they really needed speed now, because ahead of them was a traffic light, which meant a cross street, which meant maybe a place to hide. A minute later it didn't seem to matter; the gray Opel was suddenly just three cars back.

It was a bus that sprang them loose. It slanted in behind the van, heading toward a stop, and the Opel, trying to go around it, was hemmed in by traffic.

It gave Pelham and Rossi the fifty yards they needed to make the turn and reach the store that came up on their right.

Then they were out of the van and running for the doors, pushed along by the sound of tires screeching into the curb.

At any other time of the year the two cops would have grabbed them easily, but the store was jammed with Christmas shoppers, and two men as big as they just couldn't slip through the crowds as fast as Pelham and Rossi.

Pelham didn't know where he was heading; all he was doing was keeping a wall of people between them and the two men, so it was a suprise when he saw the elevator waiting. He couldn't have said why it stopped him; maybe because an elevator had got them out of trouble earlier on. Whatever the reason, he pulled Rossi into it.

But it wasn't going anywhere. It was jammed with people, and the operator was waiting for something. They could see the two cops coming fast, bulling their way through the crowd, the one in the duffel coat leading.

Pelham cried out, "Let's go! Let's go!" The operator ignored him, and said something Pelham didn't understand.

But Rossi did and was frozen by it.

"One more, please. Just one."

The cop, ten feet away, called out, "Wait!"

"Hurry on, please." The operator held the doors.

The woman came out of nowhere. Fat and dumpy, loaded with shopping bags, she bustled into the elevator.

The operator stretched out a protective arm. "Next car, please," and the glass doors hissed closed.

The cop almost ran into them.

For the briefest moment the elevator hung there, and Pelham and the cop stared at one another, the big man's face cut and bruised, a murderous expression pulling at his mouth.

The elevator dropped away, then slowed almost immediately as it arrived at the basement floor. But Pelham, looking at the store directory, held Rossi back. Beneath the basement was a parking garage—an exit—and they needed an exit badly because the cop would already be on his way down.

They rode one more floor and ran out into the garage. Pelham knew what the odds were against finding a car with the keys in it, so he made straight for the exit ramp and, clutching Rossi's hand, started up it on foot.

The ramp curved around in a shallow spiral, and they kept to its inner edge, their shoes clanging on the steel surface. They made the first turn, then another, then had to leap out of the way of a car that came swishing around at them, the surprised driver blasting his horn.

They got going again but it was awful. The ramp was featureless, claustrophobic, and they felt as if they were circling the same part of it over and over.

They were panting now, their lungs starting to burn, and when Rossi had to stop to catch her breath, they heard a metallic drumming coming from below.

Somebody was running up the ramp.

Pelham bolted, pulling Rossi with him. He didn't have to tell her who it was, or what had obviously happened: one of the cops had covered the basement floor, the other had taken the garage, spotted the exit ramp, and known without a doubt where they'd gone. The ramp curved around, unending, the incline slowing them to a trot. Rossi was gasping again; Pelham, a stitch stabbing into his side, wasn't much better off.

They slowed, unable even to trot anymore, forced back to an exhausted walk.

And they might have stayed at that deadly pace if they hadn't noticed something: the yellow glare that had been hammering down from the ceiling was dimming slightly, diminished by what had to be daylight. It got them going again, got them trotting up the incline and around a curve that expanded suddenly into an entrance, a ticket machine, sidewalks, and people.

They ran by a barrier, plunged into the crowd, took the first turn, and came out onto another street.

At the curb a woman was closing her handbag, the cab she'd just got out of beginning to move away.

Pelham lunged, thumped his hand on the rear fender.

The cab stopped and they piled into it.

Rossi wasn't able to speak so Pelham said one of the few words he knew of German. "Barnhoff. The Barnhoff."

"Late for a train?" the cabbie asked.

Pelham didn't understand him, but it didn't matter, because the man took the cab away fast.

Pelham swiveled, checked the rear window, but there was no cop plunging out into the street, stopping a car, coming after them; there was nothing but the Christmas crowds.

They sank back into the seat, gulping for air, and stayed that way for some time. Then Rossi moved, slumped against him.

"Jimmy . . ." The tremor running through her body shook her words. ". . . I was so frightened."

"So was I," Pelham said.

"I could feel the bullet, feel it hit against my chest."

He pulled her close, gentled her. "It's okay. He can't touch you now. You'll never see that guy again."

He held her to him till the cab reached the railroad station. They got out because it was as good a place as any, and it was jammed with people, which had to be safer for them.

They went downstairs to the main concourse and into the first cafeteria they saw. Their order was a strange one: two big tumblers of water each, and two cognacs. They drank the water on the way to a table, then sat down and began on the brandy. Pelham recovered enough to start berating himself.

"Boy, what a dummy I turned out to be. Why did I think that a captain of police would be above suspicion?"

"Don't blame yourself, Jimmy. He was very convincing."

"Sure he was, very smooth, the bastard. But I shouldn't have rushed into it like that."

"Do you think what he told us about Hoff is true?"

Pelham, finishing his cognac, nodded. "We could have been testing him for all he knew. And as he was figuring to get rid of us anyway, the truth could hardly hurt."

"Then that's four people we know about," Rossi said. "Uher, Hoff, somebody whose name begins with L, and now Planckendorf."

"It still doesn't get us any closer. All Planckendorf has done is prove we're right. Jesus, this thing's really going to happen. Tomorrow afternoon around three-fifteen."

"How can you pinpoint it so closely?"

"Because the first buzz bomb hit Hayes around ten of four. It must have come from somewhere in Northern France, just the way they did in the war, and the average flight time then was around thirty minutes."

"They'll fire it at the same time as the other?"

"If they're smart. It'll be twilight then, the hardest time to spot anything in the air."

Rossi said quickly, "We'll have to go to Beauvais. Try to intercept Uher."

Pelham shook his head. "He won't be there. Planckendorf will get a message to him. The only thing we can do is go back to Uher's apartment and look for that credit notice."

"But that's one place Planckendorf might look for us."

"You're right." Pelham slumped in his chair, leaned his head back. "Hell, we're beat."

It was a long moment before Rossi said, "No we're not. We can check on that credit notice by calling the bank."

Pelham didn't even raise his head. "They're not going to tell you about somebody else's account. No bank would. especially a Swiss one."

"But it's a joint account, remember? I'll say I'm Freida Uher."

Pelham sat bolt upright.

"I'll tell them I've mislaid the credit notice for the thirty-three thousand dollars that went into the account in November, and ask them for the name of the remitter. It won't work if they know her voice, but they may not."

"But you'd have to talk to whoever looks after his account, Rossi. The guy who signed that letter. You'd have to know his name, the name of the bank, everything."

"It was the Swiss Bank Corporation in Zurich. And the letter was signed by two people. One of the names was . . ." Rossi squinched her eyes shut, fought her memory for a moment, then shoved her chair back . . . "*Holtzen.*"

Pelham beat her out of the door. They spotted a telephone sign and ran for it.

There was a desk, a switchboard, several glass booths. Rossi spoke to the switch girl, and had to wait a nervous few minutes while she checked the number and placed the call. Then she nodded at Rossi and pointed to a booth.

Pelham, hovering close to the glass, saw Rossi talk into the phone, hold for a minute, talk again, and hold once more. She gave him a look that could have meant anything, then swung back to the phone, reached into her tote bag, and wrote something down. Pelham had the door open, and the note in his hand, even before she'd cut the connection.

"Wilhelm Lauter. Credit Lyonnais, Rouen." His head snapped up.

"Rouen. Smack dab in the middle of Northern France."

Rossi had the phone off the hook again and was speaking rapidly to the switch girl. Pelham caught the word "Lufthansa."

She slapped her hand over the mouthpiece, turned to him. "We'll get the next plane to Paris, fly on from there, check with his bank first thing in the morning. We can find him, Jimmy."

"Sure we can," Pelham said. "Question is, can we do it before three o'clock?"

PART THREE

THE LAUNCH

CHAPTER FIFTEEN

Lauter—The Site, December 24, 1978

The second missile had been a lot easier than the first one because for one thing Lauter and Hoff were doing something they'd done before, and Bruning, knowing exactly what he required, was better prepared.

As he'd predicted, the propulsion unit and the fuel system were ready and tested in two days and the missile itself in four. The only major things they had to replenish were the fuel and the compressed air. Hoff went to Rouen to get them, but he brought back something else besides the supplies: some disturbing news. "I called Planckendorf," he said, walking into the farmhouse. "We can expect delivery around one."

"And Uher? You spoke to him?" Lauter asked.

"Yes. He's standing by in Compiègne. A few kilometers from Beauvais."

"Why the change?"

"Just a precaution," Hoff said. He looked embarrassed. Lauter could see he was hiding something, and demanded to know what it was. Hoff didn't quite know how to put it. "It seems we've been found out."

There was a moment of stinging silence in the room. Bruning, who'd been busy with some figures, slowly looked up. And Lauter, the color shocked from his face, gazed at Hoff as if he'd never seen him before.

"It can't affect us," Hoff babbled. "It won't change a thing."

"Exactly what did Planckendorf tell you?"

"An insurance man from London. An American. He traced Uher and got into his apartment, found a message from Planckendorf, and went to see him. Planckendorf says he could tell that the man . . .

well, he seems to know about the Fieseler, and that we plan to launch it today."

As if he were collapsing in slow motion, Lauter sank down onto a chair. "Who is he? What is his name?"

"Pelham."

Lauter repeated it, exhaling the name in a long breath.

"But it's only one man," Hoff rushed on. "And a woman with him. Planckendorf is certain that it's a private investigation. Nothing to do with the English authorities."

Bruning spoke, sounding puzzled, far away. "I can't understand it. The Fieseler should have been pulverized."

Hoff said, "What?"

"This insurance man must have found a piece of it in the wreckage of those houses."

Lauter said leadenly, "Where is Pelham now?"

"Planckendorf's not sure. He said he assumed we'd want him out of the way, even though he's no real threat. But he eluded Planckendorf's men."

Lauter put his hands up to his face, slumped his shoulders. Hoff and Bruning traded looks; they'd never seen Lauter like this.

"He can't affect us," Hoff said again. "He can't find us here."

Lauter didn't appear to have heard him. He stood, walked to the door, turned. "We'll contact Uher again. We'll move up the time of the launch."

Bruning answered him sharply. "No! It's imperative that we keep to the same program as the first one. If we try to rush we'll be guaranteeing failure."

Lauter remained silent, his eyes on the floor, and the scientist softened his tone. "I can understand your concern, Herr Lauter. You've worked half your life for today, and you are quite naturally horrified that anything might jeopardize it. But you searched for this place for twenty-three years before you found it. Surely you don't expect this man, this Pelham, to accomplish the same thing in"—he checked his watch—"less than five hours."

Almost painfully, Lauter nodded in agreement. "Yes. You're right, of course. He could never find it in time." But his head stayed bowed, the look of doubt remaining.

They got back to work, then, doing the things they'd left till last. The weather was the same as it had been when they'd fired the first buzz bomb—gray and rainy, with little wind to move the cloud mass, so Bruning set the missile to fly at the same height and speed, but increased the range setting by ten kilometers, the distance between Hayes and London.

Nobody mentioned the disturbing news again, least of all Lauter, but the change in him was striking. His previous air of confidence had been replaced by a watchful uneasiness, a nervous uncertainty that showed in the way he kept checking the time, and in the fact that he asked Hoff twice what Planckendorf had said about the delivery of the bomb.

This had been the only question mark of the last few days, not so much the delivery but whether or not the bomb would work.

Curiously enough, it was Bruning who'd first sowed the seeds of doubt. When Hoff had begun talking about the devastation they would wreak on London, Bruning had reminded him that there were no certainties they could count on.

"You must remember," he'd said, "that this will be an original design. Jurgen has a brilliant mind, and I have every confidence in him, but there is, of course, no way to test a device like this."

That had troubled Lauter, who'd never questioned that side of the project. "But you'll have some inkling, won't you? When you see his design?"

"It's not what it looks like that's important," Bruning had answered, a bit enigmatically, "it's how he arrived at it."

Bruning got his chance to find out shortly after 1 P.M.

They heard the sound of a heavy truck laboring up the rocky road and Lauter hurried into the farmhouse and got the shotgun he'd readied that morning. It belonged to the farm and Lauter had been glad to find it because he'd been worried about the delivery. He was aware that the people they'd be dealing with belonged to an organization that desperately needed money, and because they knew there was money at the farm there was always the chance they'd simply try to steal it.

Lauter cocked the gun and stayed in the house behind a half-opened window; Hoff and Bruning went outside and watched the truck lumbering toward them in low gear, a big beer truck loaded with aluminum barrels.

The driver was the straggly haired young man Hoff had spoken to on the train in Stuttgart, the passenger was an older man, and the way he quickly got out and stood with the door open in front of him like a shield, it was apparent that he held some kind of weapon.

Lauter spoke up, making no bones about the situation—a fortune was about to change hands between two groups, both of which were outside the law, so the climate had to be one of mutual distrust. He called to the shaggy haired youth who was now standing beside the truck. "Do you have the diagram? The description we asked for?"

"Yes."

"Give it to the gentleman on your right."

The youth looked at Bruning, then looked back at what he could see of Lauter and the shotgun that was pointing directly at him.

"You got the money?" he asked.

"You'll have it once we're satisfied."

The youth didn't move, neither did his partner whom Bruning was sure had a machine gun.

"It's in the cab," the youth said. "I'll get it."

"No!" Lauter's sharp command stopped the boy. The youth could see they'd chosen the right man to hold the shotgun; the other two—the roly-poly guy he'd met on the train and the tall, thin one who looked like an undertaker—were obviously noncombatants.

"Have the other man toss it out," Lauter called.

The gunman did so and a long brown envelope landed with a smack in front of Bruning who picked it up, ripped it open, and unfolded three sheets of paper. He read each one carefully while they waited in a tense silence, checked them over again, then looked back at Lauter and nodded.

"Unload it, please," Lauter told the young man.

"How about we see some money first."

"After we see the bomb." The shotgun came up fractionally.

"Unload it, please."

The young man made a show of being nonchalant, but he was clearly not about to fool with Lauter; he recognized an amateur behind that shotgun and amateurs were dangerously unpredictable.

The truck had its own pneumatic crane that lay like a thick protecting arm over the barrels. It was operated from a little seat mounted directly behind the cab and the young man hopped up into it, pulling at levers. There was a loud hiss of air as the heavy crane arm came alive. He maneuvered it over one of the barrels that looked like all the rest, a fat silvery container large enough to take fifteen gallons of beer. He was very good with the crane and easily got its steel claws into the barrel's handgrips, but when the crane took its weight the big truck shuddered and looked as if it were going to rear back.

Hoff wheeled up one of the large wooden dollies they'd gotten ready, and the barrel was swung slowly out and lowered onto it lengthwise. The jaws of the crane were detached, and the crane arm raised and folded back down onto the barrels.

The young man dropped to the ground, reached into the cab, brought out a cloth sports bag, which he zipped open. He produced a big T-shaped key, inserted it into the top of the barrel, and removed a plate that had been cut into the metal.

Bruning peered inside for a long moment then motioned to the young man who replaced the panel, locked it, and put the key back in the bag.

Bruning turned to Hoff. "Pay them," he said.

Hoff hurried inside and was out a minute later carrying a suitcase. The young man clicked it open and examined the bundles of bank notes, not bothering to count them but flicking through each bundle making sure that all of it was money. When he was satisfied, he snapped the suitcase closed, threw it in the truck, got in, and started the engine. The truck backed and filled and clanked down the track on its way to the front gate and the road.

When Lauter walked out of the house to join the other two, Hoff saw that he'd left the shotgun inside.

"We should be careful," he warned. "They could creep back and surprise us."

Lauter said no. "If they'd wanted to take the money and keep the bomb, they would have."

Bruning agreed. "They want us to use it. And when we do they'll let it be known where it came from. That way they'll get the publicity they thrive on but escape the blame."

"They're fools," Lauter said. "They don't have leaders, they have nonentities, brainless idiots. They're trying to bring down the existing German government and replace it with a new order. They don't realize it's the old order that's needed."

He made a sour noise in his throat, dismissing them, and bent down to examine the barrel. He said to Bruning, "You're quite satisfied?"

"It's extraordinary. Better than I ever hoped for. Jurgen's done a remarkable job."

Hoff tried not to look so dubious, but he couldn't help it; he'd expected something long and lethal, a deadly, evil-looking thing, not this fat, bland beer barrel. "I thought an atom bomb would be . . . bigger," he said.

"It's not an atom bomb," Bruning answered. "It's a hydrogen bomb."

Lauter swiveled. "He's given us *that*? It doesn't sound possible."

"It's all here." Bruning read the letter again and began to smile. "It's a landmark in physics, a homemade fusion bomb." He shook his head in admiration.

When both men looked at him blankly, Bruning explained. "To build an H-bomb, you first have to build an A-bomb, because that's the only thing you can use as a detonator. But you have to explode the A-bomb first and for that you need about two kilos of plutonium in two separate containers. When they're plunged together the blast has to explode in two directions, one before the other, or there's no big bang, and for that to happen the geometry of the main canister has to be absolutely perfect."

Bruning ran his hand over the aluminum casing in a manner that was almost affectionate. "Do you know how Jurgen solved it?"

It was a rhetorical question and they waited to hear.

"He stole it from a computer."

Hoff, who thought of computers as things that only figured bank statements, had trouble with the idea.

"He stole the math," Bruning said. "There's an enormous amount of it involved, and it all takes a great deal of time, far more than we had, so Jurgen took a shortcut and broke into a computer."

Bruning dipped into the sports bag the youth had left, brought out the metal key, and removed the plate from the top of the barrel.

Lauter and Hoff craned forward and saw part of a smooth, dull-colored canister jammed tightly into the barrel. There was a circular well sunk into it about six inches deep at the bottom of which was a long copper wire.

"I'm beginning to appreciate what he's done," Lauter said. "It must be extraordinarily difficult to gain access to a military computer. The security must be very strict."

Bruning smiled again, proud of Jurgen, his own personal recommendation. "He didn't even try. He found a government computer doing research into nuclear reactors. They handle the same kind of problems the military ones do, but the security isn't anywhere near as tight, so Jurgen was able to tap it."

Hoff still found it hard to believe that the beer barrel had anything to do with the colossal mushroom clouds he'd seen on film. He said to Bruning, "I take it that the barrel is only for a disguise." Bruning nodded. "It was a smart way of getting it across the border."

"Then what exactly is inside it?"

"More things that I could explain, but basically there's an A-bomb surrounded by a shell of hydrogen fluoride. The heat from the A-bomb explosion will fuse the hydrogen into helium, and the release of energy will be enormoous."

Bruning dug into the bag again, produced what looked like a can of beans with a clock face on top. "The altimeter," he announced.

Hoff examined it. "It's American," he said, spotting the brand name and the place of manufacture.

Bruning told him that American aviation instruments were the best you could get. He pointed to a hole drilled into the bottom of the dial just to the right of the figure 5. "It's set for fifteen hundred meters. Five hundred feet on this."

Bruning reached into the bomb, got hold of an exposed copper wire, connected it to a similar one at the base of the altimeter, and placed the altimeter into the well. With no particular emphasis in his voice he said, "We'll arm the bomb now," and brought out from the bag, not something with switches and wires, but an ordinary matchbox. Inside it, lying on cotton wool, was a rubber-covered metal pin no thicker than a pencil. Deftly, Bruning screwed it into the hole in the altimeter's dial, leaving only a half inch protruding.

"Jurgen's modified the instrument; there's only the one hand as you can see, the hundred-feet pointer. The altimeter will only function during the descent, and then only when the Fieseler reaches eleven hundred feet. It will be in its dive at that point, of course. The hand will spin down the dial and when it contacts the pin the bomb will be triggered."

When Bruning slipped the rubber cover off the pin they knew that all that stood between them and a thermonuclear explosion were the three inches of space between the pin at the 5 and the pointer at the 1. The altimeter stuck up from the barrel like a tiny chimney, but Jurgen had taken that into account and made a cover for it. It was a piece of heavy-raised steel with a small square of thick-armored glass in the center.

Bruning was delighted with the thinking behind it. "I didn't tell Jurgen what the bomb was for, of course, but he knew it would be airborne because of the altimeter, so he's made it tamper-proof."

"He assumed we were going to put it on a plane," Lauter said.

"Why the glass?" Hoff asked.

"So we could monitor it visually if we wanted to. He thought of everything. He's even supplied rivets and a punch gun."

They watched Bruning drop a fat rivet into a presunk hole in the cover, take the gun, which looked like a giant stapler, and press it down onto the rivet head. There was a sharp bang as a small explosive charge drove the rivet into one of the holes drilled for it in the barrel.

When he'd fastened all four corners, the cover was airtight, bonded on flush, the altimeter visible just below the armored glass.

"All set," Bruning said.

CHAPTER SIXTEEN

Pelham—Rouen, December 24, 1978

The travel schedule was disastrous; it seemed to Pelham that half of Germany was trying to get to France for Christmas. Rossi spent an age on the phone calling airlines, but the flights were jammed. Finally, they went to the American Express office to see if they could help, but there was nothing they could do. It was too much for Pelham.

"Look," he said to the man behind the desk, "we're not going to Paris for Christmas dinner. This is a goddamn screaming emergency. You must have some pull; call up Lufthansa and get them to bump somebody off a flight."

The man politely said he couldn't do that.

Pelham turned away, took a few fast steps, turned back again.

"A train, then. What time would the train get us there?"

"It's completely booked, sir. I'm afraid you've chosen the worst time of the year to travel."

"What if we drive? Rent a car and drive?"

The man had bad news again: a blizzard in Eastern France, the roads already swelled by Christmas traffic, nothing was moving. "You don't understand," Pelham said loudly. "We've got to get to Rouen."

"Jimmy." Rossi tried to shush him. "He's doing all he can."

"Well, it's not enough."

Rossi turned from him, spoke quietly to the travel agent. The man got on the telephone, made a series of calls, then spelled it out for them. "I can get you on a charter to Frankfurt at six A.M. tomorrow. Then the morning Paris flight, which gets in around ten, and a rental car from there. That's the best I can offer."

"We'll take it," Rossi said.

*   *   *

They went to a hotel, but there was no question of sleep.

Rossi dozed on the bed, and Pelham restlessly prowled round the room, constantly checking his watch. They left for the airport at four, were in Frankfurt at seven, Paris by ten, and were driving north thirty minutes later.

When they joined the autoroute, Pelham swung straight into the passing lane and stayed there, pushing the car along far above the speed limit. As the miles melted away, he began talking.

"I asked myself a lot of questions in that hotel room last night, or this morning, or whenever it was. Trying to get a handle on this thing. You want to hear some answers?"

Rossi waited.

"Firstly, who are these people? Not terrorists because there's no blackmail. So I wondered who else would be in a position to get their hands on a couple of buzz bombs. The obvious answer is somebody who helped fire them in the war. Maybe Hoff and Planckendorf and Lauter are old air force buddies who thought they were robbed in 1945 when Germany lost the decision. And now it's time for a little revenge."

"But why now? What have they been waiting for?"

"Technology. They wanted to do a job on London like we did on Hiroshima, but you couldn't have put a nuclear bomb in a V-1 in those days; the early models were huge. However, their own scientists had said that, eventually, an A-bomb would be no bigger than a pineapple, so they decided to wait and do the job properly."

Pelham honked the horn at a car in front, and when it refused to move, roared by it on the wrong side.

"Jimmy, take it easy."

"I'll tell you something else," Pelham said, ignoring Rossi's fright. "I think Lauter's running things. He paid Uher, and the man who pays the bills is usually the boss. Also, if Lauter has a bank account in Rouen it's ten-to-one he lives there, because Rouen's buzz bomb territory. He probably lives there just so he can keep an eye on the ones he's got stashed. So it all sounds like it's his show. What's the time?"

"Almost eleven."

"Four hours," Pelham said.

They made Rouen around noon where a quick phone call to Lauter's bank got them his address. They drove as far as they could into the Old Town, and ran the rest of the way to Lauter's apartment house.

It was on a narrow crescent bordered by tall ancient houses with tent-shaped roofs and wooden shutters closing off high windows. The entrance to number 49 had a grimy doorway, no call buttons, no mailboxes. Rossi spoke French to the concierge, a large, tired-looking woman, then turned to Pelham.

"She says he's not in. She hasn't seen him for some time."

Rossi spoke again to the concierge, saying something that made the woman look doubtful, but kept at her until finally the woman reached for a bunch of keys.

They followed her to a small wrought-iron elevator, crowded in, and let her take them up to the top floor. Walking down a gloomy corridor, Pelham asked Rossi what she'd said. "I told her we're friends of his from Munich, and that he was supposed to be here today to show us his apartment."

"Why would he want to do that?"

"We're subletting it from him."

The concierge stopped outside an apartment, jingled through her keys, and opened the door.

The room was dark, a straggly piece of daylight slanting in through the louvered blinds across the front window; no paintings, no ornaments, no decorations of any kind, just crinkly cream wallpaper dulled by age.

Pelham took a quick tour, checking the kitchen with its few cheap pots and pans, and the tiny bathroom devoid of toiletries. The place told Pelham quite a bit about Lauter, but it was what he couldn't see that intrigued him—the room behind the locked door.

"Ask her if she has the key," he said to Rossi. She did so, then translated the answer.

"Lauter has the key. It's his study. She cleans the apartment twice a week but she's never allowed in there."

"Tell her we're going to have to break it down."

Rossi said, "I don't think she'd go for it. I think she'd call the police."

The woman was glaring sullenly at Pelham, not understanding his words but recognizing his tone.

Pelham reconsidered. "Okay. See if you can get her into the kitchen for a moment."

Rossi moved out of the room, saying something to the woman, who waddled after her. A minute later Pelham joined them. "All through," he said.

Rossi thanked the concierge for showing them the apartment, they went down to the street floor with her, and left.

But they were back almost immediately.

They sneaked up the stairs to the second floor, rang for the elevator, and rode it the rest of the way.

The top floor was just as quiet as it had been before, no music playing, no sound coming from the other apartments. Pelham stopped outside Lauter's door, swung his hip against it, and popped it open. He dug out the wad of tissue he'd stuffed into the lock slot, went straight to Lauter's workroom, and inspected the door. Then he crossed the room to the only table in the place, a poorly carved oaken piece, and hefted it. It weighed a ton. He hurried into the kitchen and returned with a pot of water and a piece of soap, splashed the water on the dark parquetry in front of the door, and ran the soap over the water, getting the floor good and mushy.

"Rossi," he said. "Give me a hand with this table." With some effort they turned it on its side and laid its edge in the middle of the soapy track, as far away from the door as they could get it. They took a breather, got a good grip on the table again, and at Pelham's cue started it moving over the soapy floor, pushing it as hard as they could.

It didn't travel more than ten feet, but it was enough. The table slammed into the door with a terrific impact, smashing it open as the lock was ripped away from the frame.

Pelham squeezed past the table, found a light switch, and got his first look at Lauter's secret room.

He said nothing for a full thirty seconds, neither did Rossi; they just gazed around them at the pinned-up photographs, the maps on the drafting table, the open atlas, the long row of diaries in the shelves. The silver-framed face of Adolf Hitler challenged them again and again, and the thick, gutted candles on each side of the little altar filled the stale air with their sour-sweet smell.

In two strides Pelham was bending over the maps, the one of central London with the red circle around Victoria Station and the two big Michelins with their pencil-shaded squares. A quick scanning of the Michelins told him that no city, town, or village was picked out in any way, and there was nothing on the atlas, either.

He looked above him at the row of diaries, grabbed one, and opened it at random. "What do you make of this? It's in German, isn't it?"

Rossi checked a page. "Abbreviated German." She flipped to the next page, then another. "It's a diary. Weekly entries."

"Can you read any of it?"

"March second, third. Then the letter B, then the words 'de Lorain.' Bois de Lorain, perhaps." Rossi read the shortened German to herself, then translated. "*Versprechen* . . . promising at first, but too *hügel*, hilly. Too hilly."

"What's the next entry?"

"March ninth, tenth. Saint Claircourt." Rossi paused, struggling with it. Pelham squinted at the writing and saw what looked to him like *Kl. Wa. neben Dorf.*

"Something near village," Rossi said. "Picnic area only." Then she said in a fast burst, "*Klein Wald.* Small forest near village. Picnic area only."

"It's a record of a search," Pelham said. "I was wrong, he didn't know where the site was. He had to look for it. What are the dates?"

"This one's January to December, 1972." Rossi looked at some others.

"Each one's for a year, and there must be a couple of dozen. Can you believe it?"

The same thought occurred to them at the same time, but Rossi beat him to the last diary on the shelf. "October 3, 1978, that's the last entry. He searched the Bois d'Arques and found nothing."

"And the next entry he didn't bother writing up," Pelham said, "because he found the site."

Rossi was studying one of the maps. "I've been through Arques, it's just outside Dieppe. Somewhere . . . here!"

"What's the entry before that?"

Rossi checked the diary. "Fécamp. That's down the coast from Dieppe."

"Got it," Pelham said, reading the map. "About fifty miles away. He was obviously working his way north, but look at all that green territory. Where did he go after Arques, Rossi?"

Pelham searched the map for the answer, but there was nothing. He went back to the map of central London again and saw something he hadn't noticed before, something written on the white border: L B D C L, 103, 87, 190.

"What the hell does that mean?"

"Coordinates perhaps. Or a telephone number."

Pelham left the map and went to the corkboard. "Maybe there's something here." He skimmed the photographs of the buzz bomb but came back to the one that showed it wing tip to wing tip with the Spitfire. Directly underneath it was the old photograph of the two men with the numerals written across it.

Pelham peered at their faces, asked Rossi if she recognized them, but got a negative reply. He pointed at the sheet of writing paper pinned up next to it.

Rossi read the words, and thought for a moment. "I think it's a German saying, or a quote. 'Vengeance is sweeter when it comes at the right time.' 'Appropriate time' would be closer."

Pelham pulled out a card, pushed it at Rossi. "Get Brian Jakes, quick."

Lauter had had little use for a telephone, but as the previous occupant had put one in, Lauter had left it there. It took Rossi only a few minutes to get through.

"Brian? Jim Pelham. Hold on to your hat, we're in big trouble."

He told him everything, where they were, how they came to be there, and what they'd found.

With a long space between each word Jakes said, "My God!"

"And listen, I think I know how they fooled the radar." Pelham looked at the photograph on the wall. "Uher's Focke-Wulf would be about the same size as a Spitfire, wouldn't it?"

"About the same, yes."

"He must have been directly over the site when they fired the buzz bomb. He picked it up and flew right on top of it all the way so that there was only one radar echo. He'd filed a flight plan, remember, so he was expected."

"Could be," Jakes said. "It's possible. You sure there's nothing that could tell you where the site is?"

"Nothing I can see on the Michelins. There's an atlas, but it's no help, either. But there's a map of London with some figures on it that could be something." He described them, as well as the other markings. "There are some more things, too. A German proverb tacked up on the wall, and an old shot of two men I can't identify."

"What do they look like?"

"In their forties, both slightly built, they could be doctors or college professors. There are numerals scrawled across the bottom in red. Looks like 8,938."

"What about the proverb?"

Pelham told him how it read.

"All right," Jakes said crisply. "Give me the exact address. We'll get somebody there as soon as we can."

"Brian, you don't understand. We found the pilot's diary. They're going to launch that buzz bomb in a few hours. And I still think it's going to have a nuclear bomb on board."

"I doubt it, Jim. Something that big, we would at least have had an inkling, heard a rumor."

"Christ, Brian, will you listen to me? Rossi and I almost got killed today. We told the wrong guy what I'm telling you and they tried to kill us. Face it, you've got a class A emergency on your hands."

"I can assure you we'll treat it as one. I'll get the experts on to these numbers right away. Stay in touch, Jim."

Pelham slammed down the phone, swore at it, ran back into the workroom, scooped up the atlas and the Michelin maps, and bolted for the door, Rossi right behind him.

He didn't tell her what Jakes had said till they'd reached their car, fought their way through the city traffic, and hit the road that ran dead straight toward the coast.

"The guy still doesn't believe me. He doesn't think I'm lying about Lauter's room, but he's shut his mind to any bomb threat."

Rossi held on as the car zipped by a truck. "Where are we going?"

"Dieppe. The launching site has to be either east or north of there. If Jakes's boys come up with anything at least we'll be close. What's the time?"

"Five to two."

"Jesus God, we're not going to make it." Pelham slapped down a switch, and the windshield wipers went to work against the rain that had begun to spatter down.

Rossi had the atlas in one hand, open at the page showing France and England, and the London map in the other. She read out the letters written on it. "L, B, D, C, L."

For a moment Pelham thought he had it. "They're Roman numerals."

"No. They don't have a B." Rossi tried to make something out of the numbers next to the letters, 103, 87, 190. She checked the atlas and said, "They don't work as coordinates. Eighty-seven degrees would be up in the North Pole."

She worried the problem while the car ate up the road, tearing through little villages shuttered against the rain.

Ten minutes later Rossi caught a glimpse of a sign—Dieppe, with a numeral next to it—and instantly saw the answer: 103 and 87 totaled 190. "Distances! Jimmy, they're distances. Whatever L, B, D, C, L is it's 103 kilometers from something else. Altogether, it's 190 kilometers from London, which has to be one of the Ls."

Pelham swerved off onto the shoulder of the road and braked hard. They fumbled at the maps and the atlas, but there was just no room to open them properly; the Michelins alone were twenty inches deep.

Pelham shot the car away again, sped to the next village, and skidded into the curb outside the first bar he saw.

They snatched up everything, barged into the place, and spread it all out on a table.

Pelham needed a ruler but made do with a long envelope. He laid it along the distance key of the England-France page of the atlas, and marked off 190 kilometers. He placed one corner on London and, using it like a compass, swiveled the envelope over the map of Northern France, putting dots wherever the 190 mark fell. Then he drew an arc connecting the dots, and redrew it on the Michelin maps Rossi had butted up together.

He slumped when he saw the size of it. "Hopeless. There must be two thousand villages along that line."

Rossi was still playing with the letters, L B D C L. She was getting nowhere till she remembered Lauter's diaries.

"Jimmy! The last L stands for London. Lauter was only interested in forests or woods. L B D stands for Le Bois de something. Something beginning with C."

It suddenly wasn't a puzzle anymore. Pelham realized something he should have thought of, too: that if Uher had flown directly over the site, the site would have to be reasonably close to a line between London and Beauvais.

He used the edge of the envelope to draw a line between the two cities, then carefully transferred it to the bottom Michelin map. It was either a remarkably accurate transfer or he was just lucky, because at exactly the point where the line crossed the arc was a small village on the Channel named le Bois-de-Cise.

They didn't move at all till Pelham had verified the distance from the village to the English coast. It was 103 kilometers. And the distance from the coast to London was exactly 87.

Then they did move.

They jumped for the phone at the rear of the bar where Rossi called Jakes again.

"Brian? Hello?" It was a bad connection, and Pelham had to shout. "We've found it. The site."

When Jakes answered he sounded different. His voice buzzed with an unfamiliar tenseness, and his words came much faster.

"Le Bois-de-Cise, correct?"

"How did you—"

"Same way you did, probably. Jim, you were right. It looks very much like we're in big trouble. That photograph of the two men with the figure written on it . . . 8,938 didn't mean a thing to anybody so we tried it as a date, put another comma in and it came out as eight, nine, thirty-eight, September 8, 1938. And that did mean something. We think those two men are Hahn and Strassmann, the German physicists. That was the date they split the atom."

"You can bet your bottom dollar it's them," Pelham shouted.

Jakes raced on. "That figure you said was written on the map of London, the one next to Victoria Station, are you sure it was 150 meters?"

"Positive. I'm looking right at it."

"Then that makes it worse than ever. We thought it meant a target 150 meters from the station. But it must mean 150 meters *above* the station."

"Brian, the French police . . ."

"On their way, I hope. And they'd better hurry, because there's something else you could be right about. That German proverb, 'Revenge is sweetest when it's most appropriate,' we checked the records for a date they might see as being suitable. We found that the prototype V-1 was launched at Peenemünde on December 24, 1942. And one year later, on the same date, the Eighth Air Force crippled the launching sites in France. So Christmas Eve sounds extremely appropriate. And that's today."

"It's more than today, Brian, it's now. That thing's going up in fifty minutes."

"Where are you? Where are you speaking from?"

But Jakes was talking to thin air. Pelham had gone.

CHAPTER SEVENTEEN

Lauter—The Site, December 24, 1978

When Bruning turned away from the bomb and began walking toward the farmhouse Lauter started to protest.

"Herr Bruning, if the bomb is armed, why not load it now? Surely you're not going to just leave it here? Out in the open?"

The scientist stopped, came back to where Lauter was standing. His answer was delivered quietly but with a firmness that made it clear who was in control.

"We agreed to stick to a timetable. We are doing so. We have ninety minutes till launch, which is plenty of time to do what we have to do. If we get ahead of ourselves we could make a vital mistake."

Hoff, who knew the problem was only Lauter's nervousness, tried to be reassuring. "It's airtight, Herr Lauter. The rain can't hurt it." Although Hoff knew very well that it wasn't the rain Lauter was worried about.

He and Bruning started for the farmhouse again, and Lauter, after sweeping his eyes around the trees, reluctantly followed.

Inside, Hoff made coffee, Bruning stood over the map, and Lauter stayed near the door, leaving it open and staring out.

Because of Lauter Hoff had been trying to act normally, to appear calm, but he was tremendously excited, and couldn't stop from asking Bruning how powerful he thought the bomb would be.

"Our first shot delivered five hundred kilos of TNT," Bruning replied. "This one will deliver the equivalent of a million tons."

"A million *tons*?" Hoff forgot about the coffee, and crossed the room to look at the map.

Bruning picked up a big compass, spanned it to a measurement on a ruler, put the point on Victoria Station, and described a circle.

"About fifty square kilometers," he said. "That will be more or less the area of devastation."

Hoff sucked in a breath; the circumference of the circle touched Euston Road in the north, Paddington and Kensington in the west, crossed the river to Battersea and Clapham in the south, went through Stockwell, Camberwell, the Elephant and Castle in the east, crossed the river again at Blackfriars, curved through Fleet Street and Holborn, and passed Bloomsbury on its way back to Euston.

Bruning tapped the map. "Anything within five kilometers of the impact point will be a blackened ruin."

"That's everything. All the famous places," Hoff said. He looked like a child in front of a birthday cake.

The nature of the conversation had drawn Lauter away from the door. He came and stood over the map, and recited the names he knew so well. "Mayfair, Hyde Park, Piccadilly. The Houses of Parliament, Whitehall, Westminster Abbey, Buckingham Palace, Leicester Square, Berkeley Square, Trafalgar Square. All their precious museums, their famous art galleries, their Park Lane hotels, their West End theaters, their libraries, their banks, and their businesses."

Bruning concurred. "All the central part certainly." He ran his finger around the circle. "Even outside this ring you'll get the residue of the blast effect, and instant fires from the colossal heat. If the wind springs up the fires will burn their way right through to the outer suburbs. And even if there's only a gentle breeze, from the east, say, it will still spread the fallout all across the country."

Bruning could hardly hear Lauter when he said, "What do you estimate total deaths at?"

The scientist considered the question dispassionately. "I'd say a million in the first few minutes. Another half million twenty-four hours later. Within a month or two, again depending on the winds, perhaps ten million dead or dying."

"Ten million English." Lauter looked up at Hoff. "They danced in the streets in 1945 celebrating what they thought was the end of the war."

Hoff nodded slowly, his breathing shallow. "They won't be celebrating the real ending."

Bruning said that they should get started on the missile. They'd fitted the wings and set the compass the day before, so it was merely a matter of towing the missile down and putting the bomb on board.

Bruning first removed the central exploder tube from the warhead so that the section was nothing but empty space, then they lifted the bomb with the gantry and lowered it in with great care. It fitted with only six inches to spare at either end, which allowed them to chock it in tight by wedging in pieces of wood. They bolted on the warhead cover, slipped the gantry's hook through the lifting lug, and raised the missile onto the launching rail. Bruning ducked under the ramp to verify the positioning on the piston, and as he finished, the hiss of static coming from the radio was interrupted by Uher's voice repeating a code word twice. Everybody checked the time.

"Forty-five minutes," Lauter said. He was watching the road, listening.

The rain had thinned to a fine mist. There was a faint smell of the sea in the air, and no sound except the soft dripping of the trees and the hiss of the radio. Hoff looked at the missile poised on its catapult, then followed the direction in which it pointed, as if he were seeing the metropolis waiting 190 kilometers away. He asked Bruning: "How long will it be before they can rebuild?"

"Impossible to say. The radiation will still be measurable for perhaps a hundred years. Unless they flood what's left and start again they may never be able to rebuild."

"It's strange," Hoff said. "The Fuehrer wanted to destroy Stalingrad and replace it with a lake. He never dreamed that one day he'd be doing the same to London."

"It should have been possible in '45," Bruning said with bitterness. "We would have had a fission bomb long before the Americans. It was our work they used, Hahn and Strassmann's brilliant achievement."

Lauter spoke, but without turning round. "September 8, 1938."

"We were ahead of everybody," Bruning went on. "And with a bit more luck Germany would have had a nuclear bomb."

Lauter moved his head then, and gazed at the V-1. He said, just above a whisper, "Germany has one now."

The rain stopped a little while later, or perhaps the wind, which was wafting it inland, died down; it didn't matter. The three of them stood by the radio, waiting for it to break its scratchy silence.

It seemed to take forever before it did.

"Thirty minutes," Lauter said. He had his arms tucked around himself, and was moving from one foot to the other, but not because of the cold.

Bruning, beginning the prelaunch procedure, checked over the auto pilot and the other controls in the rear compartment, left that and opened the flow valve to the compressed air. When he was sure the gyros had reached operating speed, he bolted on the two remaining hatch covers and turned his attention to the propulsion unit.

It fired and held and threw a fierce blue flame behind it, then settled down to a steady rhythmic roar.

As he seated himself inside the firing hut the radio crackled again: Uher, ninety kilometers away in Compiègne, was beginning his run-up.

Hoff thought about him with a strange feeling of regret. What a shame that the man was the way he was. If only he'd thought like a true German, what a wonderfully privileged position he'd be in: to actually shepherd the missile, take care of it, look after it, be there as it dropped away to the city spread below. Surely it would be possible, if only for the briefest part of a second, to see the incandescent brilliance boiling up, to ride the billowing mushroom cloud higher than any plane had ever flown before, and die in the sky a true flier's death. Instead he would never know. The minutes ticked by.

Lauter and Hoff took their places behind the wall of the firing hut.

Lauter, following the sweep hand of his watch, looked up above him, trying to pierce the tent of trees arching overhead, trying to hear the sound of Uher's plane over the roaring thunder a few yards away. Hoff glanced at him and held up a trembling hand, the fingers spread wide, cried out something that was torn away by the sound of the jet, glowing now, ready.

"Five minutes," was what Hoff had said. "Five minutes to victory."

CHAPTER EIGHTEEN

Pelham—The Site, December 24, 1978

He whipped the car down the narrow highway, leaning on the horn, overtaking, darting back onto his side of the road a few feet in front of oncoming cars. He sped through little villages scarcely slowing, floored the gas pedal again on the other side, and charged ahead.

The signs began to flash by, ads for hotels in Dieppe, the traffic already beginning to thicken.

They made it through two red lights, Pelham hammering the horn, braking, swerving around cars, but the center of the town stopped them. It was a nightmare of Christmas crowds, jammed streets, solid lines of automobiles. The bridge over the river reduced them to a crawl, and Pelham thumped the dashboard, yelled at the windshield. "Come *on!*"

It was twenty minutes before they were out of the city and on the highway heading north. The road followed the coast for several miles, elbowed slightly, then went straight again for a similar distance. Pelham hunched over the wheel, flashing the hi-beam, rocketing the car along.

Rossi, the road map on her knees, watched for a village sign, spotted it, yelled at Pelham. "Go right!"

He swung the car into the fork and they got a few more miles of flat-out speed before they had to brake for a town. It was a smaller version of Dieppe, with the same infuriatingly crowded streets, and a bridge that slowed traffic to a series of stops and starts. They were forced to cross through the center looking for their turnoff.

"Next right!" Rossi cried.

They took it, picked up speed through the outskirts of the town, sped past a small airfield to a crossroads.

"Left! Go left!"

Pelham braked, changed down, threw the car into the turn, saw a sign saying "le Bois-de-Cise 1.5."

The little D road ran straight for half a mile, curved, then brought the village rushing toward them: a small church, a few old stone houses, plane trees bent by the sea winds, a strip of channel in the distance.

They tore into a small square set around a war monument, a few shops, a café bar at the end.

"Stop there!" Rossi said, and was out and running into the bar as the car slammed to a halt.

Three old men were watching two others at a billiard table.

Heads came up as Rossi burst in, the man behind the bar lowering his newspaper. Rossi asked him a fast question then repeated it when the man just looked at her.

"German?" he said. He folded his newspaper, took the cigarette out of his mouth, ashed it thoughtfully. "Not in this village."

Rossi couldn't speak. It couldn't be the wrong village, Jakes had said it was this one, too. The wrong village . . . it was unthinkable.

"Are you sure? His name's Lauter."

The barman called to one of the billiard players. "Dadou, you know somebody named Lauter? A German? Lives near here?"

The man waved his cue in silent denial.

"Who else might know? In the village?" Rossi asked.

The barman shrugged as if to say if he didn't know, nobody would. Rossi swung around, started for the door.

"German?"

The word stopped her. One of the old men sitting at a table was scratching the stubble on his chin. "The one who comes in for the telephone. Isn't he German?"

The barman shook his head heavily. "Belgian."

"No, he's German," the old man insisted. "Out at Chennard's place. The man he hired told me."

"What kind of place?" Rossi said. "Is it a wood, a forest?"

"It's mostly all woods in that part."

Rossi gunned words at him. "Which part? How do I get there?"

"It's about two kilometers along the old coast road."

"Chennard's?" the barman said. "No, no. It's faster to go back to the highway and take the road to Mers."

Then everybody had an opinion, but Rossi put her trust in the old man at the table. "Take the road to the end of the village," he said, "then follow the track till it becomes a road again. You'll see a gate and a farm sign."

Rossi threw her thanks at him, ran for the door, called the instructions to Pelham as she jumped into the car.

He burned rubber taking it away, zipped the short length of the village street, and made the turn. The road petered out and they bounced and skittered over a rocky track, dirt and stones spraying up behind them. Ahead, the road began again, and they could see it snake dancing toward a green clump of trees, a small wood standing by itself, open fields around it.

"Where the hell are the cops?" Pelham cried.

The road smoothed out; the tires dug in, and they clicked off another kilometer.

"There it is!"

Pelham spotted the open gate, stood on the brakes, skidded the car through it, stomped the gas pedal.

The farmhouse appeared and he went for it, rushed toward it, slammed to a locked-wheel stop outside of it. He'd given no thought to what he'd find or what he'd do, he was simply swept along by his own momentum. As he leaped out of the car, the roaring sound hit him immediately, a noise like a blast furnace coming from somewhere in the trees. He didn't stop; he plunged into the farmhouse, saw that it was empty, spotted the shotgun propped against a chair, and snatched it up. He checked the load going back out through the door, raced down the pathway leading into the trees, the noise sounding louder and louder.

Pelham knew what it was, what it had to be, so he wasn't surprised when he ran into the clearing and saw the ramp and the missile with its jet spurting flame.

Then he saw the two men standing behind the hut, and even though they couldn't have heard him, one of them seemed to sense an intrusion and turned.

Pelham was never able to explain it, but he knew instantly that it was Lauter he was looking at.

And there wasn't the slightest doubt in Lauter's mind that the man rushing toward him was the one he'd been expecting.

"Pelham." He said it almost with relief; perhaps because the awful tension of waiting was over—the threat that had haunted him for the last five hours had at last shown itself.

But the shock still froze his body, and it was a moment before he started to run for the other side of the hut.

"LAUTER!" Pelham's shout was whipped away by the jet noise. He pulled up, jerked the shotgun to his shoulder, and fired at the running man's legs.

As if he'd stepped onto slippery ice Lauter's feet flew from under him, and he went down hard on his back.

Pelham bolted by him, got a fast glimpse of leads snaking from the missile and the contraption behind it, then lunged through the open door of the hut.

He saw a tall man at a bench, a radio crackling beside him, a voice coming from it, saw the man's hands poised above twin switches. He didn't seem to see Pelham, ignored his shouted command.

"Hold it!"

The shotgun went off in his hands as something or somebody smashed into his back. But even in the confines of that little room the roar of the gun was masked by a shattering explosion from outside.

Pelham was on the floor, the world full of noise, a hissing cauldron of steam, the stench of gunpowder and gasoline, a kick as somebody went over him.

He pulled himself up, staggered groggily out into a hellish white cloud, thunder somewhere in the sky. He could see the iron ramp vibrating and, beyond it, soaring up toward the overcast, the missile rising like a bird, a silver fighter plane right behind it. He gazed around, floating in a sea of horror, dimly aware of the hee-haw sound of a police siren.

A chubby little man, his glasses broken and dangling crookedly, had his face turned to the sky, and next to him, the man who'd been at the bench, his left side peppered with little red blobs, was watching the same thing.

Lauter had crawled around the hut and was lying on his side looking up at the blue flame vanishing in the distance. Blood was pooling around his leg, but there was a look of peace on his face, of perfect contentment.

Pelham gaped at them, standing there, lying there as if he didn't exist. The words crept out of his mouth, stunned, totally bewildered. "What have you done?" he whispered. "What have you done?"

Lauter answered him in accented English. "Our duty," he said.

CHAPTER NINETEEN

Southern England, December 24, 1978

The windows of the Air Force Operations Room, high up in the Ministry of Defense building, were fake. The room was sealed tight and air-conditioned, and lit only in the areas that needed light. It was a smaller replica of the Ops Room at Strike Command, fifteen miles away at High Wycombe, which had been named the James Bond Chamber because of the maze of computers and screens and flashing numerals all buried fifty feet below the ground.

At 2 P.M. the atmosphere in both rooms had been one of relaxed watchfulness. High Wycombe had been keeping an eye on a Tupolev Blinder flying a patrol north of the Shetlands, but apart from that not much had been going on.

Everything changed a few minutes later when the call came through from Whitehall.

Jakes had informed his own Ops people first, and the reaction there had been exactly the same: a humming tenseness quivered in the room as if it had been fired in from a bow. Jakes was in the room himself, along with several members of the duty staff. The RAF Undersecretary of State was present, too, talking intently into a phone. He was a young man for his job, not yet forty, short and broad shouldered like a boxer. He'd been a name in the business world until he'd entered politics, and right then he would have given anything never to have changed jobs. He came off the phone, nibbling at his lip, fighting down the panic that wanted to bubble up and swamp him. The senior officer, an Air Vice Marshal, immaculate in his heavily braided uniform, finished speaking into another phone.

"No action yet, sir."

The Undersecretary, whose name was Hurley, looked disgusted.

"Damn Frogs. They have five police departments, each one more bloody-minded than the other. What about Beauvais?"

"They said they'll see what they can do."

"How nice of them. They'll see what they can do. Are the French sweet to everybody, or just us?" Hurley brooded about it, wondered again if he could handle the incredible responsibility that had landed on him just like that. But he was the boss unless the Deputy Minister or the RAF Secretary of State got there, and they'd both left hours ago for Christmas at their country homes. "I'll talk to Strike now," he said firmly.

Another officer said something to a technician at a console, then nodded at the Undersecretary who spoke up for the unseen microphone.

"Hugh? Can you hear all right?"

The voice of the senior officer at High Wycombe came in clearly. "Go ahead, sir."

"No joy yet from the French police. They may find them before they launch that thing, or they may not. We may be wrong, it may not be today, it may not be at all, but we'll proceed on the presumption that there is a threat, that it is nuclear, and that they do intend to fire it very soon. You agree?"

"Absolutely."

"I've been on to Evaluation. If a nuclear device has been stolen somewhere in the world they reckon they'd know about it so they're certain it's homemade. If that's so then according to what we know it was probably made in Germany, which is bad news. The experts say there are one or two people there who could produce a bomb of considerable size that's not going to fizzle. You with me?"

The reply was affirmative. Though they were fifteen miles apart, both rooms could hear the silence in the other.

Hurley went on. "So if the device gets into the air and starts coming our way there are only two alternatives. One is to shoot it down, tip it into the drink. But if we're right and it's primed to go off at five hundred feet, that'll give us a nuclear explosion thirty miles off the coast, midway between England and France. Depending on the winds, and assuming severe fallout, millions could be affected in either country, and probably both. I think this solution is unacceptable."

When the Undersecretary paused, the silence, once again, stretched between the two rooms in an almost physical connection.

"As I see it, the best plan is the one that's already been put into operation. It's Jakes's idea, he's been on top of this business for some time, so with your permission I think he should run it. I suggest we let him call the shots from here, contingent, of course, that you agree with his decisions."

The answering voice offered no argument, the summation was correct—Jakes's plan was the only alternative. The problem was that Jakes's plan had never been tried before.

Hurley turned to the senior officer beside him and got his okay as well, then said to Jakes, "Right. It's all yours. What's the position?"

For an answer Jakes signaled a Flight Lieutenant waiting in front of a console. The man punched buttons lighting up a big yellow screen, a map like a blueprint outlined on it. Hurley recognized the coastline of East Sussex by the names of the towns: Eastbourne, Bexhill, Hastings. Colored dots danced over them, and Jakes explained.

"The white blip's a Hercules on its way from Farnborough with the bomb man on board. They're getting another Hercules ready at Lyneham. The yellow blip's a helicopter, a Sea King, standing by in case it's needed. The pink blip is an Early Warning Nimrod. The green is an interceptor from Strike, a Phantom. As you can see the Phantom and the Nimrod are over the Channel on the edge of U.K. airspace."

"How much can we see of the other side?" Hurley asked.

Jakes directed his attention to a screen on another console.

"That's a TV picture from the Nimrod. The dark patch is the twin towns of le Tréport and Mers-les-Bains. Le Bois-de-Cise, which you can't see, is about a mile to the north. If he comes he'll fly a beeline to London and cross the coast halfway between Hastings and Fairlight."

"So we're all ready?"

"Just on," Jakes said. "The Hercules won't be in position for about another ten minutes."

"What happens if they launch that thing before that?"

"In that case we've had it," Jakes answered. "However, we have only an hour to get through. It's two-thirty now. The French were told at two. Even they can't take more than an hour and a half to cut the red tape."

They were comforting words but they didn't apply because after fifty-five minutes of inaction, of watching the screens in an almost unbroken silence, the room was suddenly full of buzzing phones, radio talk, voices calling over each other.

"West Drayton has a flight plan for a Focke-Wulf 190."

"Beauvais, sir. He's in the air. Took off from Compiègne. The tower couldn't hold him."

Hurley swore, a quick moisture breaking out on his forehead. He watched the screen, moved from one foot to the other, listened to Jakes ask for the name of the man flying the Phantom, heard High Wycombe respond.

"Patch me into him," Jakes said to somebody. Then, a few moments later, "Control to Sister Yoke."

The reply came back through a mushy static.

Jakes spoke quickly. "Phillips, he's on the way. Now listen to me. You can't shoot him down because he's too close to the buzz bomb and we can't risk tipping it. You'll have to get him away from it somehow. But watch your efflux. If you get too close it'll upset the gyros and the thing will dive, and that's the last thing we want. Do you read me?"

"I read you, Control."

They looked at the Phantom's position on the screen, the green blip hardly moving as the jet circled, waiting. The white blip, the Hercules transport, had turned and was moving very, very slowly back toward the English coast. As they watched, a new blip popped onto the screen, enemy red, just off the coast of France. On the TV picture it registered as a faint blur.

Hurley, his eyes glued to it, spoke to the senior officer. "This man Phillips. Do you know him?"

"No sir. He's a duty pilot. There was no time to choose anyone in particular."

"I hope he's good."

Jakes would have seconded that; it was something he was wondering about, too. He tapped a technician on the shoulder. "Let me talk with the Herc," he said.

The timing was perfect again. Uher only had to gun the plane a little to overhaul the missile, position himself underneath it, and follow it up into the cloud layer.

This was the tricky part, the clouds were so thick that they obscured the missile's blue flame. But it was the part that Uher enjoyed because he knew that an ordinary pilot might have climbed too quickly and run right into the Fieseler. Only a seat-of-the-pants flier like himself would intrinsically know where the missile was. He wondered, as he had the first time, how many other pilots could have done this job—not many. He was a natural, had been from the start. He'd soloed after only four and a half hours and, on top of that, brought the plane down in a perfect dead-stick landing. Maybe there were younger fliers, but there weren't any better ones and never had been. The record, like all records, didn't tell the whole truth. Joachim Marseille, seventeen planes in one day. Eight was Uher's best, but then Marseille had had the targets; four sorties had come over with inadequate fighter cover, so he'd heard. A milk run, ducks on a pond. Not like where he'd been stationed at Vannes, where you lined up on a bomber and bang, you had two Spitfires on your tail. Still, they had fliers then: Barkhorn, over three hundred victories. Schnaufer, the top night-fighter pilot, over one hundred twenty. And Hans Baetcher, six hundred fifty-eight operational sorties, six hundred fifty-eight! The effete RAF didn't know what flying was, and they never had. In the Luftwaffe you went up again and again until you didn't come down. There was no rest, practically no leave—you were a flier so you flew.

The clouds thinned and broke and he came into a pale blue sky, the sun low on his left. It sparkled dully off the V-1 one hundred feet above him, still climbing, still gaining speed. Uher eased the throttle forward, moved the stick back a fraction, and the plane effortlessly crept a little closer.

He flicked his eyes over the instruments, once for a pilot's check, a second time for the pure pleasure of it. He remembered a man who'd tried to sell him a Lamborghini once. "Have you ever *seen* such a dashboard," he'd said. The fool didn't know that a 190 had the prettiest, the most exciting arrangement of dials and switches ever designed. There never had been a fighter with a cockpit or a canopy like it, everything perfectly visible and within easy reach, comfortable, plenty of room to move, and excellent vision all around. Uher had often said that he wouldn't have gotten into a Messerschmitt on a bet. A deathtrap that 109, with its cramped little cockpit sunk so low you couldn't see anything, its undersized fuel tanks that might not get you home, and those lousy aileron slats that often snapped open in a high-speed turn. They'd never got the Messerschmitt right, while the Focke-Wulf had just gotten better and better, reaching its final peak in the model he was flying. Uher had met the designer, had shaken his hand: Kurt Tank, a genius. He'd given the Luftwaffe a plane so good they'd renamed it after him, the Ta 152. It was recognized as the ultimate World War II fighter, period. Today, tomorrow, or yesterday.

Uher checked the altimeter, something he'd never really had his eye off; another three hundred meters and the Fieseler should level off and settle down to its flying speed of four hundred and sixty kilometers an hour. That wouldn't even make his big Jumo engine breathe hard. Its top speed was seven hundred eighty-seven; four hundred seventy-two miles per hour, a speed, he loved to remember, that wasn't bettered by a single-engined piston aircraft for twenty-four years, and then only by a measly eleven miles per hour.

He hit another patch of cloud but thin enough so he could still see the missile's flame. He checked the clock, checked his airspeed, calculated that he should be about halfway across the Channel. He'd give it a few more minutes then call up and tell them he was having control problems. They'd have to clear a path for him again, but he wouldn't be around to get into trouble because he didn't intend to land at Elstree, didn't intend to land in England at all. Why take the risk? This time the fools might catch on to what had happened and tie him in. Uher reached out to turn down the heat a fraction; he liked to fly cool and was dressed lightly. In fact he looked more like a skier than a pilot in a white machine-knit sweater and a body-hugging leather jump suit. He wore a ski cloche over his yellow hair, gold-framed oval-shaped glasses tinted blue, string-backed racing driver's gloves, ankle-length boots he'd had made for him in Rome, slim in spite of their fleecy lining.

The plane drifted through the clouds into blue sky again, the missile chugging steadily along, their positions unchanged. He saw the elevators flatten as the craft reached its flying height, and with an expert movement Uher took his plane up and around and on top of the V-1, leveling out fifty feet above it, ten feet behind it. The cloud layer would protect him from a visual sighting from below, and he'd have to be very unlucky for another plane to spot him in the next fifteen minutes.

It was while he was thinking this that he saw the jet.

He felt no stab of fright, no sudden tightening in his stomach; on the contrary, a pleasant tingling feeling settled over him: this job wasn't going to be so boring after all. He just hoped he could get close enough to see the look on the pilot's face—they'd probably have the boys in white waiting for him when he landed: a Focke-Wulf 190 ferrying a V-1 . . . oh, sure. And how many gremlins did you see today?

He watched the plane coming toward him to check him out, getting very close now. Uher marveled at its ugliness, the fat, ungainly body with the air scoops on each side like giant vacuum cleaners, the swept-up gull wings, the fin like a sailing boat's jib, the tail planes drooping down at an absurd forty-five-degree angle. When it banked around him it looked even more awkward, as if it had crashed and been hurriedly put back together with another plane's nose stuck onto it.

It drew level with him, crept nearer, looked even worse close up in its filthy green camouflage and its garish Day-Glo insignia. Two domed heads peered over at him like robots from another world. Two men it took to fly the thing, although that was the wrong word; you didn't fly a jet, you operated it, like a computer. They weren't pilots, they were button pushers, console jockeys who couldn't even blow their noses without electronic help.

The Phantom was flying in tandem with him now, the pilot making motions, pointing his finger at the ground. Uher replied in kind, only his finger was pointing the other way in the international gesture of insult.

The Phantom rose and fell behind probably to radio London for instructions, Uher thought. Let them, he knew the English: they'd have a cup of tea before they'd actually do anything, and by that time he would have delivered the Fieseler and be back in the cloud layer on his way to France. He'd refuel in Limoges and Tangier, then hop down to Mauritania where there was a nice little war that could use a pilot like him. After that, he'd see.

In his rear-vision mirror he saw the jet moving over him, leading him by about fifty feet, and he wondered what he was playing at. He found out in the next minute. The Phantom dropped right in front of him and went into reheat in a tremendous burst of power.

It happened before Uher could do anything about it: a wild maelstrom of air shot back from the Phantom's twin turbojets, forty thousand pounds of thrust corkscrewing straight into the Focke-Wulf. Instantly the fighter was tossed up and away, then pitched forward into a spinning dive, tumbling down through the clouds.

By the time Uher had the plane under control and flying straight again he'd dropped a thousand feet and was heading east instead of north. He'd been lucky to pull out at all.

His initial surprise was quickly replaced by a surging anger. The *bastard!* The stinking Tommy *bastard!* He brought the nose up, and in three swift movements cut the automatic airscrew control, fined off the pitch of the propellers, then shoved the throttle arm all the way forward in a slam acceleration. The big engine shook with power, bored the fighter up through the sky.

But it was a sky empty of everything but clouds. The Phantom had disappeared. And the V-1, too.

As soon as Jakes had known what they'd be up against he'd rushed his idea into the works. It hadn't taken him long to figure out; it had been self-evident: the V-1 was like a deadly insect buzzing through the air, and if you couldn't kill an insect on the wing, all you could do was try to catch it.

His first call had been to Farnborough in Surrey, seventy miles northwest of Hastings where the missile would cross the coast. It was the nearest base that had a Hercules standing by.

The plane was one of the biggest things flying, more like a freight car than an aircraft, with a gigantic hold that was nothing but enclosed space. Five minutes after Jakes had spoken with the base commanding officer, men had swarmed all over the Hercules, inside and out, worked on it solidly for an hour, then got it into the air. It had reached its point over the Channel ten miles off Hastings less than fifteen minutes before Uher's plane had been picked up on the radar, then had turned and flown back toward the coast on a dead-straight course in line with London. When the Phantom had relayed Uher's height and speed, and confirmed his course, the Hercules had matched them exactly, and was now approaching the coast level with the missile and the Focke-Wulf, which were somewhere in the clouds a few miles behind. But the Hercules didn't look the way it normally did. The loading ramp, which ordinarily hinged closed thirty feet beneath the high-raised tail, had been removed, leaving a gaping hole in the rear of the plane, while inside the hold two big winches had been rigged up on either side of the craft. The winches had been no problem, and the dismantling of the ramp, although cumbersome, was hardly a job that had never been done before. But what had taken the time, and was still a source of concern, was the net they'd rushed to make.

The construction was simple enough: three big cargo slings cleated together then joined widthways to three more cargo slings cleated together. Thick cable had been run around the edges, one end being secured in the hold, the far end secured to the winches' own cables. When they'd tried it with the plane on the ground the net had hung out of the open hold like a long tongue. But the real test was going to be its behavior in the air, because to be of any use the net would have to "fly" behind the aircraft, and not flap and ball up hopelessly in the wind. The loadmaster had an idea of how to accomplish this, and it seemed better than anybody else's. He'd taken two drogue chutes, the starters for the big cargo parachutes, and attached them to the other end of the net, one at each corner. He felt it would work, and so did Jakes when it had been described to him, but the problem was they wouldn't have time to run a test until shortly before they had to use it.

The sound was deafening inside the plane at three thousand feet, the four massive turboprops churned through the air, vibrating the craft in a steady quiver. The wind whipped into the hold, darted its length and swept out again chilling the men even with their thick immersion suits zipped up tight.

Besides the loadmaster there were two winchmen, a man who sat with a large tool belt on his lap, and another who was nervously running his hand over the stock of a rifle. A Flight Officer was in overall charge of the team, six men in all. They waited for the loadmaster to finish adjusting the chutes. When he'd had a last word with the winchmen, he and the officer buckled themselves into safety harnesses attached to a long overhead brace and got down to the hard part. They crouched over the net, rolled up at the lip of the open hold, swapped a signal, then shoved the net out of the plane. The winchmen kicked off their cable brakes and the net hissed out into the sky, dropping away. The two drogue chutes blossomed and snapped open like twin white rockets as they filled with air, and when the cables were tightened the net rose up behind the plane looking a bit like a rickety jungle suspension bridge. But it worked— the net was stretched out in a deep basket shape and flying nicely.

When the news flashed back to the Ops Room in Whitehall the Undersecretary tried not to let his relief show too much.

"Well," he said, hiding behind an attempt at levity, "we seem to have the net. Now let's see if we can catch anything."

It didn't help his temper when Uher realized his mistake. The few times he'd ever lost an aircraft he'd been dogging he'd had to try to guess the course the pilot might have switched to, and decide whether he'd dived or climbed, slowed up or poured on the speed. But the Fieseler didn't have a pilot, it was flown by a mechanical brain, and automatons just went on doing what they were doing until they were ordered to do something else.

He found it easily with a simple course and time calculation and a fast burst of his supercharging engine. The Phantom was shadowing it as he knew it would be, but this time he was ready for it.

He could see that it wasn't ready for him.

The fool just sat there almost innocently, as if tumbling a man out of the sky wasn't throwing down the gauntlet. He caught the filthy kerosene reek flowing back from the jet, those whining, stinking jet engines. Jets had killed aviation by destroying the very symbol of flying, the propeller with its beautiful curving symmetry, one of the prettiest parts of a real aircraft.

Uher didn't even have to look when he moved his hand. At the top left of the raised instrument panel were five vertical gauges making up the armament switch and the ammunition counter control. The button he jabbed flashed a red light, telling him that the cannon in his wing had been electrically armed and was ready to fire.

Just that simple movement thrilled him, coursed the blood through his body, made him feel more alive than he had in ages. He knew why: he'd been a fighter pilot without a fight for too long.

The Phantom reacted at last, moving up and away to the left.

Uher could see the pilot's plan: he was going to try the same sneaky maneuver with his jetwash again.

Uher continued his climb, slackened his speed, but as the Phantom began to bank, he slapped the throttle forward, nudged the stick over, turned easily inside the jet, and flew at it at a three-quarter angle.

The gunsight unit picked up the plane and projected its image onto the windshield target plate. The jet slid slowly across the circular markings, swam toward the crosshairs.

With feather lightness Uher rested his thumb on the flap button on top of the control stick and could have blasted the jet right in the middle of its fat, ugly body, but that would have been letting the Tommies off too easily. He wanted them to know how it felt when control was suddenly wrenched away at low altitude and the sea rushed up at you. He waited till the fin came into his sights, that insane fin that must have been three meters high and almost twice as long.

His thumb danced on the firing button.

The Focke-Wulf bucked slightly as, in the left side wing stem, a plastic plug was blown out ahead of a dozen thirty-millimeter high-explosive shells.

Like any professional killer one gun was all Uher needed to carry to feel comfortable. When he had his choice—flying for somebody who could get him any armament he wanted—he opted for two MG 131 machine guns mounted above the engine cowling, and four five-chambered Mauser revolver cannons in the wings. But when he had to keep his armament a secret, one gun was easier to hide than several. He'd chosen Rheinmetall's old 108 cannon, which was stubby enough to be hidden in the wing. It was slow firing with poor velocity severely limiting its range, but range didn't matter to a pilot like Uher who was expert enough to get in close. What mattered was what the shells did after they'd hit, and with the explosive 108s it was like putting a bomb on board your opponent's aircraft.

The three quick bursts straddled the Phantom in a slow, looping trajectory, four shells ripping into the tail fin and blowing it away as if it had been dynamited.

The jet shuddered like an animal shaking itself, then dropped its nose and spiraled down in a dive.

Uher saw the twin canopies explode off, then the two men shoot out in their ejection seats, the seats falling away as parachutes blossomed. It was too bad, he thought, that the cloud layer was so heavy, otherwise the English holiday makers who'd come to spend Christmas at the seaside hotels down below would have been treated to a pyrotechnic display. In fact, if the layer hadn't been so low they could have witnessed some more aerobatics, because if those Tommies thought they were just going to float gently down into the Channel and be picked up five minutes later to be wrapped in blankets and mollycoddled, they'd better think again. Nobody embarrassed Karl Uher in the air without being severely reprimanded.

He took the plane down in a steep dive, leveling off half a mile away from one of the dangling airmen, who was swaying from the strings of his parachute. His flying helmet had come off, and his look of shocked horror was plainly visible as the Focke-Wulf swept toward him. At point-blank range his body wasn't enough to impact the shells, which tore through his chest leaving him spinning like a manikin.

Uher banked the aircraft violently, a wing tip missing the bell of the parachute by a few feet. As he turned to begin his run on the other man, he expected to be amused at the sight of him trying to claw his way up the strings, or hunch himself into a ball, but he wasn't doing either of those things. Instead he was looking around him, fumbling at his harness release. Then he was free and falling like a stone.

Uher fumed with anger. The bastard was trying to get away, risking a four-hundred meter drop to the water rather than face the same treatment his partner had been given. Oh, no, that wasn't playing the game. If you played, and lost, you had to take your medicine. Uher dropped the nose and roared down after him at three hundred miles per hour.

The falling man had had the presence of mind to try to control his plunge with his arms and legs. He was plummeting down, his body spread-eagled facing the water. The wind screamed past his helmet so he never heard the fighter tearing down at him. He felt something like a heavy rock strike his back and then, for a brief second, the freezing air, which was rushing by him, seemed to be rushing through him, too.

In a single smooth movement Uher brought the plane out of its dive five hundred feet above the water, turned in his seat to watch the body fall out of the clouds and splash into the slate-colored sea.

He barreled up into the sky again, thinking about his new situation: London would be wondering what had happened to their jet and they'd send another to find out. It would take care of the Fieseler first then come looking for him. Uher checked the ammunition gauge: forty rounds. He'd never yet returned from an action flight with any ammo left, and he didn't see why he should start now. He flipped open a map, adjusted his course and turned on the speed.

He'd decided to make himself easy to find.

When Uher's cannon burst had smashed into the Phantom, the navigator had yelled into his mike before ejecting, but the message never reached London because the plane's R/T had been blown away. But when the green blip simply disappeared from the radar in the Ops Room and the red one remained, and they couldn't get any response from the jet, they knew what must have happened.

"Dear God! . . ." The Undersecretary looked stunned.

In a dead voice Jakes said, "I should have realized that plane might be armed. I didn't think."

They heard High Wycombe ordering another jet into the air, this time with different instructions, and most explicit ones.

Nibbling at his lip again, Hurley listened, then swung around to the senior officer. "Where's that jet coming from?"

"Wattisham, in Suffolk."

"How long will it take?"

"About five or six minutes."

"And the German? How far is he away from the Hercules?"

Everyone was watching the red blip on the screen slowly converging on the white one, which represented the transport. Jakes was first to answer. "About four minutes," he said. Then he shook his head knowing what the Undersecretary was going to say next. "If he shoots it down the bomb will be on top of us in about twelve minutes."

"But the second Hercules . . ."

Jakes's lips hardly moved. "It won't make it in time."

As a young man the captain of the Hercules had flown a Douglas-Boston in France in the closing stages of the war, so he knew only too well what it was like to pilot a lumbering, underarmed bomber while a four-hundred-mile-an-hour Focke-Wulf took pieces out of you. When the message came through from High Wycombe he couldn't believe he might be in for the same experience once more.

He broke the news to the cabin crew—co-pilot, navigator, engineer—and let the Flight Officer know, pretty sure that the man would keep it to himself; they had a hell of a job to do back there and it wasn't going to be made any easier if they were watching the skies for a marauder. Meanwhile he did the only thing he could do, kept going and prayed for the sight of the jet, which was on its way.

The captain had been right about the officer in the hold keeping the news to himself, and for exactly the reason he'd thought. His team had seen nothing of Uher or the Phantom, and nothing of the missile, the only thing they were watching for. And when the clouds broke as they crossed the coast they spotted it, burbling along less than a mile behind them.

The captain, taking directions from the hold, cut his airspeed a few knots, then the Flight Officer's voice sounded in his earphones again.

"Up fifty. . . . more . . . more . . . okay! It's dead astern. About a thousand yards."

The captain, eyes on the altimeter, snapped out a word. "Navigator."

"Twelve minutes," the man called.

That was another thing the captain found hard to believe—that they could grab that thing in such a ridiculously short time. There were some flying chores that were damn difficult, but something like this where he wouldn't be able to see what he was trying to catch, couldn't even see the net . . . how the hell was he supposed to do it?

Behind the plate the wind slammed through the center vents in the two drogue chutes, bobbing them wildly like balloons, but they were doing their job: the net flowed through the sky about thirty feet below the mouth of the hold, the winch cables slack on each side, ready.

The chutes were too low to obscure the view of the man with the rifle, who was now lying on his stomach on the floor of the hold. He was a young man, a corporal, chosen for this job because of his prowess as a sharpshooter, and he was scared and jittery. He hadn't been told what was on board the thing he was supposed to shoot down but he could see from the grim look on the Flight Officer's face that the job was pretty important.

The officer had to crouch down and shout right in his ear for him to hear anything above the noise racketing around the hold.

"I want a bullet straight down the throat of that jet unit. If you miss, miss high. For Chrissakes, don't hit the body, we want to bring it back alive. Understood?"

The corporal moved his head up and down.

"Set it at five hundred yards. Remember, hell of a crosswind."

The officer straightened, looking at the rifle as the man cocked it. It was too light for the job, a standard issue FN. They needed a sporting rifle, a big Remington with a heavy grain bullet, something that could power its way through the wind. He checked the missile; it was much closer now, flying steady, its fiery trail dazzling in the afternoon light. It crept toward them, gaining.

The officer tapped the rifleman on the head.

The crack of the weapon was smothered by the rush of noise, but it could have been a dud he'd fired for all the difference it made in the buzz bomb.

"Aim off!" the officer yelled.

He saw the rifle recoil, but with the same negative effect.

"Four hundred yards!" he cried. Christ, the thing was coming fast.

The corporal adjusted the rear sight, cocked the gun again, and got off two more rounds, but the bullets missed—by an inch or a yard, there was no way of telling.

The Flight Officer had known it would be a tough trick to pull off, and the way the buzz bomb was beginning to behave wasn't going to make it any easier. It was starting to pitch and yaw, rolling from side to side like a boat in a sea. It was partly because of the wash from the turbojets, but the real villains were the vortices produced by the giant plane's airframe as it pushed the air ahead of it. The whirlwind lashed back at the missile, tossing it around, threatening to flip it over.

"Automatic!" the officer yelled. "Spray it!"

The airman flicked down a lever, hunched over the rifle, squeezed off three two-second bursts.

The V-1 kept coming, the beat of its jet plainly audible now, driving the machine toward them.

The gun stopped. The rifleman whipped out the spent magazine, shoved in another, cocked the weapon, and started firing again. He had to wave it like a garden hose, trying to follow the propulsion unit in its crazy dance.

The missile edged closer, burrowing further into the slipstream, which bucked it back, making it wave its wings in an exaggerated salute. The Flight Officer could see that it would go any second, and it would have if a bullet hadn't found its mark.

The jet coughed, the flame hesitated, stopped, then streamed out again but with only half the force of a moment ago. It had been a lucky shot, but like a lot of lucky shots it had been a perfect one, taking out one of the fuel nozzles.

Everybody yelled at once, a cheer, but the officer was doing his yelling into his throat mike.

"Skipper, we hit it! But it's still under power. Throttle back fifty."

Because it was losing speed, the buzz bomb was also losing height, and as the captain cut his revs, the transport dropped, too, staying roughly level with the missile. The slower speed had reduced the wash and the missile was steadier now, still buffeted though, and still in danger of tipping.

The Flight Officer held up a fist, pointed to both winchmen in a "get ready" signal. He crouched down again with the corporal, who'd fitted a new magazine. He could see that there wasn't another; somebody had thought that sixty rounds should be plenty, but they were down to their last twenty now.

"Okay. A hundred yards. Let's get it this time." He talked again to the captain, bringing their speed down a hair, dead level with the missile once more.

Again the rifleman fired in quick bursts and holes starred the air intake. The gun chattered a second time and everybody could have sworn that the bullets went straight into the mouth of the jet, but the flame stayed bright, and the missile kept coming.

Fifty yards, they needed a point-blank range of fifty yards.

The captain gave it to them, throttling back again.

"Hold it." The officer steadied the rifleman. "Wait for my signal."

The man took a deep breath, let it out, slapped the rear sight flat, tucked the rifle into his shoulder.

The V-1 was close enough now to see the bolts in the steel sheeting, and the anvil hammering of the pulse jet reverberated in the hold like an echo in a hall.

It swam toward them like a great blind shark, nosing forward as if it had caught their scent.

The loadmaster cried out. "Get it! Get it!" He snapped his eyes to the Flight Officer, but the man was just standing there watching the monster, just letting it come for them. Why wasn't he shouting into his throat mike, yelling for more speed? The officer moved then, but very slowly. He raised his hand, pointed at both winchmen again, called into his mike. "Skipper! Right rudder . . . okay! Get ready, she's coming on board."

He meant it. The missile was just fifty feet behind, overhauling them fast.

"On your feet!"

The rifleman didn't need to be told twice; the thing looked like it was going to crush him. It filled the sky, came in past the drogue chutes and over the net, rolling around twenty feet beneath the raised tail.

The officer dropped his arm.

Winches sang, cables snapped taut as the net began to rise.

"*Now!*"

The corporal banged off two bursts, two more, another. They couldn't hear the gunfire, didn't see the spray of ejected cartridges bouncing across the floor, their gaze was fixed on the tiny whirling windmill on the missile's spike, and the dark maw of the engine intake coming in to get them.

And the missile *was* coming in. Its huge head had actually entered the hold, thrashing around as if it had been cruelly hooked.

It was its left wing that stopped it, catching the edge of the gaping door frame, belting into the transport. It shuddered and slewed round, half of it in the hold, half of it in the air, corrected itself and banged into the door frame again.

Even in his shocked state the rifleman was too close to miss. A burst of bullets shattered flap valves and fuel leads; the flame popped, coughed, and vanished.

The Flight Officer shouted into his mike. The net hummed up tight behind the missile, which thumped its nose onto the floor of the hold and slid away as the captain poured on the power. It plunged into the net headfirst, one wing bursting through the canvas webbing, and by rights should have fallen through like a gallon can of paint dropping through a paper bag, but the metal cleats stopped the run—the missile was snagged, nose down and lying on its side, dead.

The wrench was terrific as two tons suddenly dragged behind the plane, pulling the Hercules down in spite of the screaming engines. The captain had to fight to halt the transport's slide, and gently to hold on to the buzz bomb, which was swaying precariously. It took nine hundred feet of sky to do it, and as he gradually flattened it out, the co-pilot spotted a second support helicopter waiting for them up ahead.

The captain blinked at the quivering instruments, said with a break in his voice, "Right now we could use some support," and began to ease his plane upward. He wanted another thousand feet before turning away to the North Sea to let the bomb man get to work, but he got only a little of the height before he felt the heavy thumps.

The transport shook, then shook again, a dragging feeling this time that told him that the missile had shifted—it had moved when the plane had been jounced by something, and a second later he knew what had happened when he saw two things almost at the same moment: smoke curling from the inner starboard engine, and the silver blur of the Focke-Wulf streaking up in front of him.

The first thing he did was yell into his mike. "Get him down! Get that man into the net!"

It had taken Uher longer to find the missile this time because of the patchy cloud layers. With radar he could have found it right away, but he wouldn't have had a unit on board for love nor money; the day he couldn't tell the difference between an aircraft and a flock of birds, as radar often couldn't, was the day he'd quit flying.

He flew along the course two hundred feet above where he estimated the Fieseler should be, and when the cloud break came, there it was below him.

And a fat, lumbering transport plane as well.

When he saw the net trailing behind it, and realized its purpose, he knew that the jet he'd shot down hadn't run into him by chance; it had been waiting for him. Which meant that somebody had found out about those Heil Hitler nuts who were paying him for this crazy job.

Uher wondered why they were trying to catch the missile instead of just shooting it down. Maybe it was because the English always had been great collectors. He smiled at his little joke; whatever the reason it didn't matter much. He watched them trying to grab it, the Fieseler looking like a fluttering butterfly very much aware of the net spread for it and refusing to be lured in. He was quite surprised when they caught it, and impressed, too. It was a funny thing about the English: stiff and formal in spite of their vaunted sense of humor, and yet they were capable of flashes of great ingenuity, like this circus trick they'd just pulled off, plucking the missile right out of the air. Naturally they couldn't be allowed to keep it; it was private property, and stealing private property was against the law in any country.

Uher watched the missile drag the transport down, saw the big plane shudder, then slowly start to climb again. He checked the sky in front of him, all around him, looking for the interceptor that had to be on its way, but the only other aircraft was a helicopter rising up with the transport, a jet-powered one, too, Uher noticed. Ugly bloody thing, it looked more like a van than a plane. It belonged on the highway, not in the sky.

He banked and began his dive, keeping his eyes peeled for the jet. He knew there'd be only one—if it had been an American plane he'd shot down the Yanks would have sent an entire squadron, but not the conservative, parsimonious English. In their thinking one modern jet would be enough to handle a thirty-three-year-old propeller-driven fighter, even one they knew had teeth.

He leveled out five hundred feet below the transport and came up at it in a thundering climb, exactly as he'd done against the Lancasters and the B-17s, except this time there was no annoying belly gunner to worry about.

He hit the plane right where he wanted to, and as he finished up past the wing there was the helicopter, a couple of hundred feet above the transport, practically sitting in his sights.

He squeezed off a burst, but he was by it too quickly to get a really good shot at it. Still, it was something he'd never tried before, two planes on the one pass. He flattened out, looked down, saw the transport's engine on fire, a cheerful blaze in the late afternoon. The helicopter didn't seem to have been affected, although he was sure he'd nipped it.

Uher positioned himself for another run and swooped down, but his gun was quiet this time—away to the northeast he'd caught a flash of reflected sunlight, the one he'd been expecting. He leveled off, came up, and parked right underneath the transport, not far from his ex-charge dangling in the net. The jet would never spot him there, and the transport's crew wouldn't be able to see where he'd gone, and maybe the helicopter would have lost him, too.

He checked his round counter, hoping for more of a workout this time, although he'd heard that the RAF didn't even bother to train their pilots in aerial combat anymore. If that was so he'd be happy to give this pilot his first and last lesson.

The jet was the newest thing in the skies, a Panavia Tornado, one of the first of the air defense versions. Smaller and lighter than the Phantom it had been designed to replace, it was a flying laboratory of electronics and could carry enough firepower to sink a battleship in a single pass.

Five minutes before Uher spotted it, the Tornado had swept into the air eighty-five miles away, folded its wings so that they formed an almost solid V with the tail planes, leaped forward, and reached a speed which was faster than the velocity of a bullet fired from a .357 Magnum.

Uher wouldn't have been impressed by that fact, nor surprised by it—speed was why jets had been invented. But there were two things he would have been surprised to learn: firstly, that part of the craft, a three-nation production, was made by his old distrusted friend the Messerschmitt Company. And secondly, that the Tornado had seen him long before he had seen it.

On takeoff the navigator had inserted a plastic vector card into the plane's computer, which had guided the craft according to track, heading, and altitude information received from High Wycombe. And while Uher had still been watching the transport trying to net the buzz bomb, the Focke-Wulf's presence had been picked up by the Tornado's radar and its position projected in horizontal and vertical coordinates onto the visor of the pilot's flight helmet.

As Uher watched the jet slow, he snickered at the way its wings swung forward, and gave a parody of a cheer when the four big missiles mounted on the wing pylons swiveled to retain their straight-ahead direction. Smaller missiles clung underneath the body like sucker fish. Insane—it could never fly clean. All he had to do was raise his undercarriage after takeoff and his plane was a perfect aerodynamic shape, but these things . . . a junk pile below, a skyscraper above—that tail fin had to be five or six meters high.

It circled around looking for him, the two crewmen in their twin cockpits ignoring the transport with its smoking engine, and the helicopter standing helplessly by. Halfway through its turn, Uher went for it, dropping down then zooming up at it at an oblique angle.

The jet seemed to rear up like a horse surprised by a snake, then rolled over and fled. Uher charged after it, yelling at it.

"Run, you yellow Tommy bastard!"

He was mad at being robbed of his perfect shot, but not so angry that he didn't realize what the Englishman was doing: drawing him away from the transport so he could turn and get off a missile. Well he'd had plenty of practice out-maneuvering missiles . . . the heat seekers, designed to fly up a jet's tailpipe, would swish harmlessly by, the heat given off by his piston engine too quickly dissipated to attract one. And an expert pilot could simply dodge any other kind.

He stayed on the jet's tail; he had it in his sights; sooner or later it would turn and then he'd fake that limey out of his flying boots and, bing, bang, it would be all over.

Uher would have been amazed to know that he was in the Tornado's sights, too, and had been ever since he'd shot out from underneath the transport. One glimpse was all that had been needed; at the jab of a button the Tornado's laser-operated target seeker had locked onto the Focke-Wulf and flashed a simulated picture of it to the head-up display in the twin cockpits. And now that they'd tempted it far enough away from the transport and its nuclear cargo, the jet's pilot flicked a switch that armed one of the missiles under the wing, then punched a button to launch it.

Uher saw the burst of flame and the rocketing black exhaust and laughed out loud: the fools were so scared they were firing missiles ahead of them. But the look on his face changed to a frown a second later—the missile was behaving strangely. It was no longer shooting ahead, it was climbing up into the sky. A dud, a wild one. Even the English missiles didn't want to fight. But he was as wrong about the missile as he'd been about a number of things. The missile was a new generation Sky Flash, twelve feet long and only eight inches across, yet it carried its own computer and its own radar that, at that moment, was locked onto the image of the Focke-Wulf it had been given by the Tornado.

Uher couldn't believe it when he saw the thing looping around and coming down after him, but it didn't stop him from doing what he did best. With a marvelous piece of flying he pulled the plane's nose up sharply in a near stall, flipped it into a Dutch roll, and snatched his plane away. The missile tore through the piece of sky the Focke-Wulf had been in a second before, and streaked on by.

Like a good pro boxer Uher came out of his defensive move thinking about attack. The jet was banking now, just five of those missiles left, and if he could—he didn't get any further with his planning because something had flashed into his rear-vision mirror.

It was such a stupifying sight he was caught between horror and genuine surprise. The missile he'd just slipped was back on his tail.

It had turned around and come after him again.

He tumbled his plane over in a breathtaking lateral movement, but his astonishment had shaved a second off his reflexes and the maneuver came too late.

Striking the plane where the missile did, on the left-side wing stem close to the body, eight ounces of high explosive would have been enough to knock the Focke-Wulf down. But the Sky Flash carried sixty pounds in its torpedo head, and the furious boiling explosion literally tore the plane to shreds, ripped it into tiny parts and violently hurled them three hundred feet in every direction. A moment later, where there had been a slim, elegant two-ton fighter plane, a murky smudge hung in the air like a piece of dark cloud.

Curiously, one single part of the plane had been left intact, shocked loose by the blast and blown away in one piece: the propeller hub and its three perfectly curved blades.

It dropped through the clouds, the blades still spinning, falling toward a green paddock far below.

CHAPTER TWENTY

London, December 24, 1978

If the call had come through half an hour later the bomb disposal man reckoned that some other poor sod would be sitting in the Herc. He'd been running a sweep at Frensham Ponds when the chopper had come for him—as senior man he was "it." He'd bitched to the helicopter's crew all the way back about how he'd been just about to call it a day and go and get the turkey the missus was waiting on, but when they'd put him down at Farnborough, and he'd heard about the job he was in for, Christmas dinner had been the last thing on his mind.

He'd sat in the freezing hold and sweated along with everybody else as they'd tried to land the buzz bomb, which he'd hardly believed in till he'd seen it with his own eyes. Then when they'd grabbed it he'd been ready to settle back for the ride out over the North Sea before going to work, but that plan had changed when the plane had seemed to run into something. He'd thought it was bye-bye buzz bomb then, they all had; the net had parted and it would have gone but for a few strands of straining canvas. Then he'd suddenly found himself being buckled into a safety harness and invited to try his luck down there with the flying bomb. A flying *nuclear* bomb—he was still trying to get his mind around that one. He'd talked on the blower with the experts in London while he'd been at Farnborough, but in the end they hadn't told him anything he couldn't have figured out for himself. All bombs had to be triggered in some way, and if they knew that this one was set for five hundred feet, then that meant some kind of aneroid device. They'd also told him that they hadn't thought it would be booby-trapped— brilliant thinking. Anybody who sends a bomb in a V-1 isn't going to be worried about somebody playing with it on the way. Or shouldn't have been.

He'd done his regulation jumps, which had been a bit dicey, but nowhere near as scary as standing in an open ramp doorway with just a thin wire between you and a whip-round for the missus. He sat down on the lip of the door, turned around and felt with his boots for the net, and began to climb down it, very much aware that the addition of his weight might be all it would take to send the missile through.

The transport was creeping along at about one hundred twenty miles an hour, but it felt more like six times that—he had to thrust both hands through the webbing to keep from being snatched by the screeching wind. It tore into his body, trying to shake him loose, snapped his safety wire wildly around, jerked at his harness. He clambered down a bit more, clutching himself to the net, clinging with his arms and his legs and his feet. It was impossible to do it lightly, it was all he could do to keep from being plucked away by the hurricane grabbing at him from behind. When he looked up, the force of the wind flattened his face, obscuring his vision, but he could see enough to know that the situation was even worse than he'd thought: one of the engines was pouring smoke, throwing up flames, and there wasn't going to be anything the captain could do about it if the wing extinguishers couldn't help, because he certainly couldn't put it out by diving the plane. He couldn't move the plane a single inch, up, down, or sideways without risking the missile, and they couldn't get a cable onto it because two winches were all they were carrying. It was a fine jar of pickles they were in, just like mother used to make, because all they could do was what they were doing: stay dead on course and hope that muggins could defuse the bomb before the missile fell through, or the wing blew up, or both.

He froze when he felt his boot kick against hard metal, looked down behind him, and nearly let go: the missile was still there only because the wing and the tail plane were caught in the webbing; the main part of the net had ruptured and was hanging loose, being flapped to shreds. But at least the missile was right side up, its nose section was pointing at the plane.

Hooking his arms through the webbing, he crept down closer to it, the reek of the turbojets poisoning the wind that was trying harder than ever to steal him. Like any torpedo the warhead had to be in the big second section behind the guidance system, eight bolts it looked like, eight bolts to get off. He clung with one arm and both feet, dug into the big, cumbersome tool belt he'd buckled around his waist, fumbled out a wrench. The nuts were all the same size and loosened quickly; the problem came when he had to shift to the other side. If it hadn't been for his harness and the safety wire, which the loadmaster was keeping taut, he would have been blown into the back of the net like a football.

But he got them free, all except the front one on top, which he left till last. He hadn't even got it halfway off before the wind rushed under the section cover and chattered it up and down like the lid of a boiling saucepan. When he freed it, the heavy steel sheet was whipped back and bowled away, end over end, spanging off the propulsion unit and giving the missile another little nudge downward.

The bomb man hadn't thought it possible to feel roasting hot in a thirty-two-degree temperature, but the sweat broke out of him when he peeped inside the warhead: an aluminum barrel, an altimeter under thick, heavy glass, and everything locked down solid under a cover that would take a machine shop to pry loose.

The white blip, the Hercules, was really stationary on the display board and it was the map underneath it that was moving. Yet the effect was the same, and it appeared that the transport was overflying an area a few miles west of Sevenoaks as indeed it was. Moving in tandem with the yellow blip of the helicopter, it progressed slowly and serenely without a hint of the panic emergency. The Undersecretary had been on the phone with both his superiors, and the PM himself, but until one of them actually arrived he was still in charge of the situation, and the situation had become disastrous. The bomb man had been in the net five, six minutes, and not a word out of him yet.

Hurley wanted to ask again why the pilot couldn't just turn a little bit east a few degrees, anything to get him off that beeline he was making for the city, but he knew they'd only politely explain once more how you couldn't just ease a giant aircraft like the Hercules; everything it did it did in a big way. If they tried it they'd lose the missile for sure.

He picked at his lip, caught himself at it and stopped immediately, then rounded on the senior officer and tried to put some starch in his voice. "How long before he's on top of us?"

"At his present speed, ten minutes."

"Will he last that long?"

The officer was watching the blip; it would keep showing as long as the plane kept flying. "Hard to say. An unchecked wing fire's the worst thing you can have." He turned blank eyes on the Undersecretary. "The inner engine on a Hercules is only ten feet away from the underwing fuel tank."

The room went back to a taut, breathy silence; they'd seen the lightning and were waiting on the thunder.

Jakes hadn't spoken for a long time. Ever since Uher had shot down the Phantom he'd listened silently to the reports from the Tornado, the helicopter, and the transport and hadn't even commented on the demise of the Focke-Wulf. He'd just stayed where he was, right behind a console operator, watching the display board like a spectator at a chess match.

His silence was partly because the way things were happening, one disaster after another, there was nothing a man in a windowless room in London could say that would help anybody. But it was also because he kept asking himself how he could have let things get to this incredible stage. If he'd just given Pelham a bit more support a bit earlier on, done his job instead of letting Pelham do it for him, they wouldn't be living this nightmare right now. But then three minutes later the nightmare got worse.

The blips had reached Reston, barely twelve miles from where they stood, when the voice of the transport pilot burst out at them, higher and tighter sounding than before.

"Bit of a snag, Control. The bomb's in a big beer barrel. Altimeter definitely set for five hundred feet. But he can't get to it. The casing's riveted closed. It's impossible to defuse. Do you read me? Impossible to defuse where it is."

Jakes broke his silence, gabbled a question. "Can he get it loose? Can he get it out of the missile?"

"Hold on!"

There was a long, heavy wait, nothing to listen to but the static of an open radio, nowhere to look but at the map, and the blips, already over the suburbs.

"He's going to have a shot. Control. Can't promise anything. Only thing I can promise is this plane's going to fall out of the sky."

Jakes was already rapping out an order to the console man. "Call the chopper, quick!" He spun round to check with the senior officer but the man just gave him a fast go-ahead. He knew what Jakes was going to try. It was the only thing left for them to try.

It was standard practice to have an air-sea rescue helicopter standing by for a Channel operation but to use one inland in a support role had been Jakes's idea. He'd originally thought of employing a helicopter to grab the V-1 in the air, but there wasn't one fast enough to catch it. However, it had still seemed worthwhile to keep one around, the new Sea Kings were so strong they were like flying cranes, and if they got that missile into the net, a flying crane might be just what they needed. Jakes had allowed thirty miles for the transport to snag the missile, which was about what it took, so the Sea King, waiting over Pembury, had been nicely positioned to pick them up. It was just bad luck that it was right at the point at which the Focke-Wulf attacked the Hercules, because Uher had been correct when he'd thought he'd winged the helicopter. The Sea King's pilot had been horrified to find himself in the path of the fighter and knew he'd been hit when he'd felt his aircraft jar. But no red lights had popped on, and the winchman couldn't see any damage, so wherever it had been it couldn't have been important. The Sea King was an amazingly strong aircraft, designed to take punishment—even when they'd been badly hit in Vietnam many of them had kept right on flying and simply fluttered to the ground—and besides, the pilot had other things to worry about, especially when he got the call to try to grab that godawful bomb.

He gave it a good shot. With its twin turbos close to their maximum revs he brought the helicopter over the top of the transport, which was burning steadily, the flames eating up the wing, thick, oily smoke streaming back for miles.

The winchman did his best, but it was going to take too long; the cable was an inch thick with a snap hook on the end weighing twenty pounds, but the wind treated it as if it were a paper streamer. Every time he dropped it behind the transport's wing, the backwash whipped it away, it was just too light.

Crouched in his safety harness at the open side door, the winchman knew what he was fishing for; the pilot had told him everything, but it only had made the job harder. Through the patchy clouds he caught a glimpse of red lights in the sky fifteen hundred feet below and knew they had to belong to the TV tower at Crystal Palace.

Crystal Palace! Even if the Herc's wing went right at that moment the plane would still come down somewhere around Dulwich, and Dulwich was less than five miles from Piccadilly.

In the net under the aircraft the bomb man watched the cable hissing down again, and again blow away out of reach. There was nothing he could use to snare it, and nothing the hold crew could use either; they'd just have to get lucky. He checked the heavy hammer weighing him down at his belt—at least he could try to free the bomb in case.

There was no way he could loosen the pieces of wood chocked each side of the bomb except by belting at them, and there was no way he could do that without climbing up onto the missile. He didn't let himself think about it, he just did it—took hold of the open warhead compartment and hauled himself up, squeezed his legs around the sides of the missile and let his lifeline hold him. He fumbled out the hammer and started smashing one of the wooden chocks, the gonging sound audible even in that screaming bedlam of noise. He felt every blow ring through his body but didn't dare try to see how much he was jarring the missile; he didn't want to know. He concentrated on swinging the hammer against the shrieking wind and refused to contemplate the fact that he was in the classic, the ultimate, situation of a bomb disposal man: riding fair and squarely on the back of the tiger.

The wooden chock jerked loose at the same time the helicopter's cable almost took his head off; a sudden crosswind had lashed it against the net where its head had spun around a piece of webbing and trapped itself. The bomb man was used to small miracles—he'd been playing with high explosives for fifteen years and was still alive—so he didn't question this one. He tumbled off his mount and, clutching at what was left of the net, went after the cable.

He inched along the webbing battling the furious wind, reached the other side, unraveled the cable, and snapped its hook onto a ring on his tool belt.

He would never have made it back dragging it with one hand; as it was he moved like a man underwater, struggling slowly toward the spot he'd just left. It was a crazy sixty seconds; hooked up to two different aircraft, he could have been torn apart.

He lunged for the missile, skipped a heartbeat as the missile swayed underneath him, clawed his way back on top of it, and fought the lashing cable that was trying to jerk him into the sky. He had to use both hands to unclasp the spring bolt from his belt, strained to shift it twelve inches, and snapped the hook, in a trembling tug-of-war, onto the handgrip of the beer barrel.

He swung himself down, waving one arm in a wild, circling motion that got a quick response—he was winched up the net too fast to touch it, grabbed under the arms, and hauled in over the lip of the hold. He saw the bomb being ponderously lugged free of the missile, felt the transport rise with the new lightness, then he was grasping for support as the Hercules tipped forward.

The captain was surprised to be diving his plane under his own control; he'd been pretty sure, as had everybody on the flight deck, that the next dive they made would be a spiraling fall all the way to the ground.

He took the plane bumping down through the cloud layer, the increased rush of wind flattening out the flames on the wing, but the fire was burning too brightly to make much difference now. Nor did the light rain affect it when they burst through into a darkening evening one thousand feet over Brixton. A mile ahead the chimneys of Battersea Power House stood up like thick brick bars, and the captain moved to bank around them.

It was only a tiny shift in course, but underneath the plane the missile almost went, and probably would have had it still had the weight of the bomb on board.

The co-pilot was babbling into his mike as the navigator called out, "Nine miles."

The captain didn't dare increase his speed, so nine miles meant that if they wanted to walk away from this they had to stay aloft for four and a half minutes, and dump the missile in the meantime.

He knew where he was going to try it; as they crossed the river and swooped over Belgravia, he could see it ahead: the green swatch of Hyde Park and the dark curve of the Serpentine, the lake that split it in half.

"Stand by! Get ready to ditch that thing."

In the hold the Flight Officer stabbed fingers at the two winchmen, held up a hand, waited.

The captain leveled off, trying to ignore the bonfire on his right as he lined up on the widest part of the lake. At the angle of their approach their target would be about three hundred yards across.

"Stand by! . . ."

Five hundred feet below, the traffic swirled around Hyde Park Corner, emptying into Knightsbridge. The street was jammed with last-minute shoppers who heard a thundering whoosh and got a half-second glimpse of the aircraft pounding overhead.

To a man jogging in Hyde Park the long dark thing slung underneath the transport appeared to barely clear the trees of Rotten Row.

"Steady . . ." The pilot said it more for his own guidance than for the men in the hold.

"*Now!*"

The Flight Officer's arm swept down and the winchmen kicked at their cable brakes.

The missile dropped the moment the net flopped open, tumbling out, falling away end over end. It hit the water farther into the lake than the captain had intended, but it was still a perfect shot. The steel shell smacked down belly-up, leaped like a fish as it skipped on the surface, then plowed back into the water in a towering burst of spray.

A flock of startled geese went honking up into the sky, leaving the missile to drift for a moment, water pouring into the open warhead compartment, then, a dozen feet from the far bank, it sank slowly like a wrecked miniature submarine.

The Hercules soared up, freed not so much by the weight it had shed but by the reduced drag.

The navigator sang out a new course, but they were so low he could have given the captain the same directions as he would have a man on a bicycle: across the park, up the Edgware Road, through Paddington and Kilburn, on through Cricklewood and into Hendon. Impossible to miss, it's seven and one half miles straight ahead. Like a man climbing a mountain, the captain fixed his eyes on some landmarks below and just concentrated on reaching them one by one: Paddington Station, then the dark oval of Lord's Cricket Ground, then the open rise of Hamstead Heath.

Dead ahead he could see the airstrip at RAF Hendon, the runway lights burning. Just three miles now, one and one half minutes to touchdown. Allow sixty seconds for the runout, twenty seconds to get clear of the plane, call it three minutes. All they needed was three more minutes. And they almost got them.

The captain had wondered which would go first, the wing or the gas tank but, in fact, both went practically at the same time. There was just no way, after the kind of trip he'd had, that he could have landed the plane like a soap bubble . . . a touch too anxious, a bit too eager to get out of the sky, he brought it down heavily, thumping into the tarmac, and the wing, almost burned through at the interior engine stem, snapped like a stick of wood.

The pylon-mounted gas tank hit the tarmac first and went up instantly, a shattering, shooting red-and-white explosion.

The plane heeled over, the other wing slashing into the grass on the side of the strip, plowing up the earth in a bursting brown fountain. The wing tip buckled but the main spar held and braked the plane as it left the runway and was pulled around the wing in a curving arc. The tires blew, it rocked and leaped for another fifty yards, then broadsided into a heavy wire perimeter fence.

It was a stunning impact, the fence was flattened, but it saved the aircraft. The crew slipped and slithered through the listing plane, tumbled out onto the grass and into the Land Rover which came racing up. Two fire trucks followed it, already pumping foam.

"Bleedin' Hell," the bomb man said, looking back over his shoulder. "If I'd known I was in for a ride like that I would've held onto the bomb and gone with the chopper."

But he wouldn't have said that if he'd known what had happened to it.

The sudden weight and drag, which the helicopter had taken on close to its top speed, jerked the craft to one side, and the pilot had to compensate in a hurry. He slowed gradually and maintained his course so as not to set up a pendulum motion on the barrel, then signaled the winchman to raise it.

It came up slowly, the winch engine, not designed for such a load, complaining as it hauled it level with the side of the helicopter. The pilot tipped the craft to the left and the barrel swung through the double doors and crashed down onto the weight-supported floor. The winchman guyed it in place, and they had their prize.

But it had been at a price.

The shell from the Focke-Wulf had struck the craft at the stem of one of the massive rotor blades, and it was the rotors that had taken most of the tremendous stress of the sudden drag. And so fifteen minutes after he'd been blown out of the sky Uher got his last kill.

The blade was spun off, hurled away. The helicopter pitched and shook and, like a bird with a broken wing, began to flutter helplessly down toward the river less than a mile away from Victoria Station.

The room had seemed to let out one big collective breath when the barrel had been lifted clear of the missile. There was still the worry of the burning transport, but the overwhelming priority of stopping the bomb appeared to have been accomplished.

The final arrangements were well in hand: a bomb squad from Scotland Yard would be picked up by a helicopter in St. James's Park and whisked to a rendezvous with the Sea King fifty miles out over the estuary. They seemed to be home and dry until a frantic voice from the helicopter crashed in on them.

It was a staggering piece of news made even more horrific when the pilot reported his position. It was grotesque, the bomb was being delivered exactly on target almost as if they'd intercepted it expressly to help it find its mark.

Jakes snapped out questions, trying to keep spaces between his words. "What's your height?"

"Seventeen hundred. We're dropping at two hundred feet a minute."

"How fast can you fly her?"

The pilot sounded as if he were being choked. "Maybe sixty knots if I want to stay in the air."

The console operator was cooler than anybody. His fingers flew over a calculator, then hit buttons on his machine. The moving map vanished, replaced by a static one of greater London. A red ring popped onto it, the figure 6 flashing onto the digital display.

"Six miles," the senior officer said. "He can fly six miles in any direction before he's down to five hundred feet." He turned to the Undersecretary who knew he was being asked to choose where the bomb should explode.

He shied away from the ghastly thought, tried to postpone it by grasping at a straw. "The other helicopter . . ."

"I'm afraid not. Something that size and weight, it would take at least twenty minutes for a midair transfer." The faster pace of the officer's reply was a polite way of asking him for an immediate directive.

The Undersecretary hesitated for another moment, hoping to be saved by High Wycombe, but they were silent: it wasn't an Air Force decision.

He gazed at the map, at that wide red ring encircling most of London.

"Control!" The pilot's high voice filled the room. "Directly over Victoria Station now. Awaiting instructions."

Right over the station . . . that was only about a mile away from everything—the palace, the Houses of Parliament, Whitehall, Number 10—the whole seat of the government. Hurley wiped his wrist over his mouth; he had to get that bomb as far away as possible. He drew a visual line between Whitehall and Victoria, extended it in the opposite direction to the far rim of the red circle which, at that moment, popped off the screen then popped back on, its diameter shrunk by two miles.

"See if he can make the middle of Richmond Park."

When they heard the man say the words, which he barely got out, the room seemed to realize that it really was going to happen: a nuclear device was going to detonate a few miles from the center of the city and, incredibly, it had somehow just sneaked up on them. They were all familiar with the contingency plans in case of an all-out nuclear attack, but there were no plans covering a single bizarre threat like this, how could there be? The hard fact was the attack had been successful because it had been so tiny—too small to contain. It was too late to do any of the things they might have done, too late even for any kind of civil defense measures. All they could do was try to get used to the idea that there was going to be a new grouping of cities: Hiroshima, Nagasaki, London.

Of all the men in the room Jakes was the only one who wasn't thinking along these lines. He hadn't taken his eyes off the map, but he wasn't hypnotized by it like the others; he was searching it for something.

And he found it.

"Wait! The Post Office Tower. How high's the Post Office Tower?" He spun around. "It's got to be five hundred feet. And if it is it's worth a try."

An officer snatched up a phone, everybody else looked at Hurley who shook his head, confused. "The tower can't be more than a mile away. If it doesn't work where are we?"

"It won't work if we don't try it," Jakes said.

"But you can't guarantee it. You can't be sure it won't go off anyway."

"I'm pretty damn sure it will go off at Richmond though, because we'll be doing everything to help it." Jakes was out of order, speaking up the way he was, but he didn't care.

The pilot's panicky voice broke into their argument. "Thirteen hundred feet. Control. Request immediate instructions."

"Tell him to head for the tower," Jakes said, but Hurley had made his decision and didn't want to change it now.

"I can't take the risk. It's just too close to everything." He turned to the Air Vice Marshal. "Tell the pilot Richmond Park."

Jakes heard the order going out but still kept talking; they had a chance, they had to gamble. "We don't know anything about that bomb but it could be a hell of a big one. You heard the experts. What if it's a super bomb? Richmond's only five miles away. It could make five miles look like fifty yards."

An officer jerked his head up, a phone at his ear. "Sir," he called to Jakes, "the tower's five eighty feet to the base of the lattice mast."

Jakes saw the platform in his mind's eye, knew they'd never get a squad up there in time. "No good. How high's the restaurant?" The man spoke into the phone, answered almost right away. "Five twenty."

The Undersecretary looked dismayed; it would have been so much easier if the tower had been too low. Everybody was looking at him. He shook his head, kept on shaking it. "I can't risk a nuclear blast so close to Government."

In a rapid change Jakes spoke very slowly. "If this works there won't be a nuclear blast."

The prospect of that, of there being no blast, no deaths, no damage, no blame stopped Hurley, and he wavered. The senior officer saw it, and with a small, quiet movement closed his hand on a phone, the one he'd used to talk to the helicopter pilot.

It was a subtle gesture implying nothing and everything, but it was enough to sway the balance. "Very well," Hurley said, "we'll try it." The rest of his words, a pessimistic expression of hope, was lost in the whirl of instant action.

"Get me that bomb squad," Jakes called. "And get hold of the tower's security. Tell them to clear the restaurant. And tell them to do it now."

The tower, shooting up like a slim green skyrocket, would have been a standout building even in New York, but in London it was absolutely unique. It rose in a smooth cylindrical line for half its height, then was crazily interrupted by four open circular galleries, two of which supported clusters of giant horn aerials thrusting out like hi-fi speakers. Then it continued again in a smooth tube of green glass, bulged slightly for the revolving restaurant near the top, smoothed off again, and ended in a high platform topped by a gawky-looking radar scanner.

The helicopter pilot saw it plainly in the waning light a mile away to the north, but wasn't sure if they could make it—they would never have made Richmond in a million years. The problem was that instead of slowing their rate of descent, opening the throttles had increased it so that they were dropping faster than ever in a continuous slide.

The craft shook and vibrated worse than before, the imbalance of the rotors setting up a sick palsy that shuddered the helicopter throughout its whole frame. It was only a matter of time before a second blade went, then they'd fall like something tossed from a window.

The co-pilot was, of course, every bit as aware of their situation as his captain and, for once, so was the man on the winch.

He had the evidence all around him as well as in front of his eyes: the hand of the altimeter, under the glassed-in cover on the barrel, had stirred to life as they dropped to eleven hundred feet. He could see that it didn't have far to travel to hit the metal pin on the five, and it had already started its trip.

It was registering one thousand feet as they flew right over the top of Buckingham Palace, of which he had a grandstand view: the gardens, the inner parade ground, the tourists hanging around the gates even on Christmas Eve. The winchman was a Londoner, born and brought up in Camberwell, but he'd previously flown only over the river, never over the city itself, and he thought that it was a hell of a time to be taking his first tour. He recognized the crisscross paths of Green Park, then the long, wide stretch of Piccadilly. The altimeter hand was at nine hundred feet as they passed over the glass roof of the Burlington Arcade, and had dropped another one hundred as they overflew the packed stores of Regent Street.

Then Oxford Street appeared, at that moment probably the most densely populated mile of real estate in the world.

The altimeter pointer was on the 7, the tower less than half a mile away, when the pilot's voice blared in his headset.

"Get it out! I want fifty feet."

The pilot had left it to the last moment, knowing that the drag would be horrendous, and he was right. When he tipped the helicopter, and the bomb dropped out and dangled in the sky, the rotors made a shattering racket and shook the craft violently. The winchman clicked off fifty feet on the ratchet, locked it off, sang out.

The pilot had already begun his run. He opened the throttles, the twin jets screamed—he could hardly see because of the vibration. The shaking helicopter, still falling down its slope, rushed at the tower, the big silver barrel dragging underneath it.

He didn't know whether or not they were ready for him inside but if they weren't it was going to be too bad. He had the height for only one run, and this was it.

The police bomb squad, part of a section kept on a year-round, twenty-four-hour alert, was sitting in a station wagon at the northern end of the Mall just outside the park. Four men and a driver, they waited in a tight silence for the helicopter that was supposed to take them downriver. Then the radio buzzed. A moment later the car screeched away from the curb, shot under Admiralty Arch, and plunged into the traffic of Trafalgar Square, its siren braying cars out of the way. The square was jammed, but the traffic somehow squeezed over, moved, made a path for the car. It swerved into Charing Cross Road, ran two red lights, zoomed by all the book shops, and plunged across Oxford Street into Tottenham Court Road. It was plaited with people crossing back and forth to shop the stereo stores, and the police car had to honk and bully them out of the way as it went around traffic, cutting in and out of the oncoming lane.

The car heeled around the Howland Street corner, straightened, roared the half block to Fitzroy, skidded around several cars, stopped for the light, and almost flew the last fifty yards to the Post Office building.

The security force had the entrance cleared, an elevator waiting.

The squad bundled out onto the sidewalk, grabbed their tools, ran up the steps, and down the hall. The elevator whisked them up the tower in exactly thirty seconds.

The restaurant hadn't yet opened for dinner so there'd been nobody to get rid of apart from the staff, but it was still going to be a tough place for the bomb squad to work. Tables, gleaming with glass and silverware, were ranked in two rows against the huge glass windows, which completely circled the room. Outside, London stretched away as far as the eye could see, but the squad didn't have any time for gawking—the helicopter was rushing down at them, dragging the big aluminum barrel through the sky.

"Get down!" somebody yelled, and the four men dived for the central pillar.

The helicopter roared toward them. They could see what the pilot was going to try but it looked as if he'd left it too late. They thought the chopper was about to hit the tower when they saw the pitch of the rotor blades sweep up and the craft stop as if it had been jerked from behind.

The barrel kept coming.

Carried forward by its momentum, the barrel swung on the cable in a curving arc toward the green glass windows.

It was a fine piece of judgment, and a lucky piece, too, because the barrel could have hit one of the windows' vertical steel supports, but it didn't. With a tremendous boom it took out an entire window, raking the room with a salvo of shattered triple-glazed glass, flattened a table, kept going, and slammed into a heavy oak sideboard in a jangling crash of splintered wood and flying cutlery.

The policemen were running for it while there was still a fine powder of glass in the air, dashing across the room, grabbing for the cable hook snapped closed on the barrel's handgrip. The thrash of the helicopter's engines poured into the room as it appeared outside the ruined window fluttering there like a monster insect trying to get in. It drifted down out of sight, the cable flopping around in thick loops on the restaurant floor. The men pulled at the spring hook, kicked at it, but the barrel had jammed it tight, landing on it.

The helicopter kept dropping, was level with the aerial galleries now, dragging the cable down with it.

They gave up on the spring hook, caught the cable in a pair of two-man wire cutters, chomped its parrot jaws again and again till the cable parted and was free. It hissed out of the window, narrowly missing the rotors as the pilot held his failing craft together for one more minute and headed for the green patch of Fitzroy Square.

The four men grabbed hold of the barrel, strained against it, rolled it a few feet to get a look at the altimeter.

They knew it would have to be very close; they were a mere twenty feet above the height it was set for, and in an instrument that measured feet in tens of thousands, twenty wasn't much to be out.

But the pointer wasn't as near to the pin as they thought it might be. The crash of the barrel's landing had broken the altimeter, snapping the delicate springs that compressed the plates of the aneroid capsule inside. With the tension released, the plates had begun to expand again, and the needle was moving slowly in the opposite direction.

It was going to contact the pin from the other side.

It didn't matter about height anymore, the bomb was going to detonate.

The squad leader rapped out an order, an unnecessary one because his team was already in action. One of them snapped open a big, oblong toolbox, grabbed up a long electric lead, and threw it like a lasso to his partner who plugged it into the power outlet he'd found. The third man was lifting out the thing the lead was attached to and running back with it.

It looked like a small road drill, except it ended in a hollow pipe large enough to swallow a golf ball. Around this circular mouth was a double row of very fine bronze teeth tipped with tungsten. The squad leader placed the drill on the steel cover, just underneath the glass plate, leaned his weight on the handles, then hit the switch.

It ate into the steel with a high, descending scream, a spray of metallic dust spurting up. It was a fantastic machine, weighing thirty pounds, most of the weight belonging to the electric motor that drove the revolving bit at a colossal rate. The shriek of the drill came down a note as the circular bite deepened, but there was still a long way to go.

They tried not to watch the pointer, which had started down the right-hand face in a slow, smooth glide.

With the bit well and truly into the cover, the leader went to full power, the head blurred with speed, the teeth-grinding noise rose higher, the metal dust cascading up.

One of the men had a small can in his hands, which had a right-angled nozzle; he was shaking it up and down and wondering if he'd get a chance to use it—the leader was bearing down hard on the drill, the bit beginning to change color, steam beginning to rise as it was automatically cooled by jets of water. It was making headway, it was getting there, but so was the hand on the altimeter.

When it swept past the 3, they had to watch it, as if their combined stares could will it to stop. There was nothing else they could do except continue what they'd started, yet they just seemed to be standing there—even the drill operator was like a statue as he bore down with his whole body.

The bit was spinning so fast that it appeared to be stationary; the only thing in the entire room that was plainly moving was the pointer under the glass.

It was approaching the 4.

And the drill's scream seemed to be one of anguish.

When it happened, it was very sudden: the drill plunged through the cover like a bayonet thrust and screeched on the casing of the bomb itself. They tugged, pulled at the drill, which the intense heat had swollen, wrenched it up and out, the pointer about to touch the pin.

But it didn't hit it. It ran into a blob of graphite instead.

The man holding the little can had slipped the angled nozzle into the hole and beaten the pointer with one fast squeeze.

But he hadn't stopped it entirely, just slowed it—like a knife spreading thick butter, the pointer was moving the graphite out of the way.

The leader shot out a hand for the pair of long-nosed rubber tweezers that was slapped into it, slid them into the hole and up under the glass, closed them over the stem of the pointer, then twisted the tweezers.

The graphite oozed between them but he had the pointer firmly gripped, moved his hand around, twisted the tweezers, kept the pressure on.

The pointer snapped off.

He spent a full thirty seconds getting it past the pin, slid it out, wiped it down, then dropped it into a top pocket of his uniform. Very slowly, everybody straightened up and took their first deep breath for a long, long time.

The leader flicked something away from his eyebrows, looked at his men, looked past them at London through the windows.

"Smashing view from here, isn't it?" he said.

London, December 25, 1978

Jakes saw to it that Pelham and Rossi spent a minimum amount of time answering the questions of the French police, then sent a small plane for them. But they spent a lot longer answering questions when they got back; a panel of stern-faced men grilled them, then had them go through it twice more before they let them go. They got to bed very late, and slept very late next day—the reaction had caught up with them and they were exhausted. But they'd recovered somewhat by the time Jakes phoned, asking if he could see them for a few minutes. The rain had stopped, and the day seemed relatively mild, so Pelham suggested they meet somewhere outside. As Jakes lived in Bayswater, they agreed on Kensington Gardens.

They met him by the Round Pond; he was there before they were and they found him sitting on a bench.

"Merry Christmas," he said, getting up.

Pelham introduced him to Rossi, they swapped pleasantries, then they all sat down. There were only a handful of people around: a man sailing a scale-model boat on the pond, and two others a little farther away squinting up at the big box kites they were flying high overhead.

"You have to hand it to the English," Pelham said. "If you have a hobby, you have a hobby. Even on Christmas Day."

Jakes smiled. "We always have been famous for our enthusiasts." He looked at Rossi. "I read the transcript of your interview last night. Quite a job you two did."

Rossi gave a pretty little shrug. "I was just along for the ride."

"Not true," Pelham said. "She's going to be a great little burglar when she grows up."

That got him a sideways look, so he quickly spoke to Jakes.

239

"They told us what happened at this end. Some of my racetrack friends would call that a real squeaker."

"Some of mine would, too," Jakes answered.

"It wouldn't have been so close," Rossi suggested, "if you hadn't had such a run of bad luck."

Jakes didn't quite agree. "I've been thinking about that, and I realize that our bad luck was really only the result of their good luck, the three Germans."

"I don't follow," Pelham said.

"It's just that what they did, finding the site and firing those buzz bombs, was a remarkable feat, and anytime you can do something really exceptional it tends to generate a luck of its own."

Pelham considered it. "Maybe. Although Uher really made their luck for them. What about him, incidentally? What about everything, for that matter? How are you going to handle it?"

"We're going to keep it quiet for a while," Jakes replied. He glanced around him but there were still only the kite fliers and the man at the pond; nobody to overhear them. "We'd like to find out how they got their hands on a nuclear bomb and where it came from. The wires have been singing all night between this country and France and Germany, and at a very high level, as you might imagine. There are three countries involved and none of them wants this breaking till they have some solid answers. And perhaps not even then."

"But there must have been a lot of people who saw what happened," Rossi said. "At the Post Office Tower. And the plane that was on fire."

"And the jet that was shot down," Pelham added.

They waited on Jakes to answer: his eyes looked sandy and there were bags under them. He clearly hadn't had much sleep.

"It's not as difficult as it sounds. The Press Office came up with a fair enough story, a midair collision over South London. Two aircraft on different exercises. The Sea King strayed into the wrong airspace, nicked the transport, and lost a blade. It was heading for RAF Hendon when the dummy depth charge it was carrying hit the tower."

"And the transport? What's its story?"

"It was trying an experiment carrying a slung cargo. In this case a target drone. The old ones look a lot like a V-1. The collision started the fire, it was losing height so it jettisoned its cargo and managed to make Hendon."

"Do you think they'll buy it?" Pelham asked.

"Why not? Something similar really happened a few years ago." Rossi asked about the jet that had been shot down. "And Uher, too. You still have to explain them."

"The cloud layer hid the dogfights, so nobody saw them. And the Phantom that was shot down crashed on a routine patrol."

"So officially," Pelham said, "the RAF just had a bad day yesterday."

Jakes looked a little pained. "We have umpteen flights a day every day of the year all over England, plus Malta, Cyprus, and Hong Kong, and our safety record's still the best in the world."

"Then I guess you're allowed a couple of mishaps. Although you wouldn't have had any if Uher hadn't been loaded for bear," Pelham said.

Jakes allowed that that was true but it was still cold comfort.

"The fact remains that something sneaked through our fence. Normally we'd have to report that and take a roasting from the press, but not in this case. Not with a nuclear device involved."

"You don't want to give anybody else the idea, right?"

"Exactly. Nuclear terrorism, thank God, has remained just a horrible possibility. Commercial aircraft had been flying for forty years before anybody hijacked one. Then everybody hijacked one."

They were silent, thinking about it for a moment, watching the sailboat slide across the pond. Then Pelham asked something that had been on his mind. "Lauter, Uher, and Hoff we know about. But who was the guy in the hut?"

"Deiter Bruning. An aeronautical engineer and systems designer. He worked on the V-1s in the Luftwaffe."

Pelham looked uncomfortable about something and Jakes correctly guessed what it was. "He's okay, by the way. They both are. Mending nicely in a prison hospital near Amiens. Bruning had only superficial wounds, Lauter's leg is broken but it's nothing they can't fix."

Pelham let out a little breath. "I'm glad of that. I've never shot anybody before, and it's not a nice feeling."

"What will happen to them?" Rossi asked. "Those three men."

"Go to jail for armed robbery, Hoff and his two accomplices. With a bank guard dead they'll never see daylight again."

"So that will effectively hush them up," Pelham said.

Jakes frowned at that, ran a hand over the stubble on his chin. "I doubt they'll tell anybody anyway. They know they failed, of course. If they'd succeeded the entire northern sky would have lit up. According to a preliminary psychiatrist's report they're crushed by their failure, so the last thing they'd do is advertise it."

Pelham, remembering the shrine in Lauter's apartment, said, "They failed the Fuehrer again. They had their chance and blew it."

"Something like that, yes."

"What about Planckendorf?" Rossi asked.

"No proof against him, I'm afraid," Jakes said. "But I rather think the German authorities will invite him to join his friends in South America." He checked his watch, shuffled his feet. "There'll be some official thanks coming your way. Firm handshakes from important people is all it will amount to, I'm afraid, but I wanted to say thank you first."

"I want to thank you for not kicking me out at the start," Pelham said.

"I'm paid to look after the nuts, remember?" Jakes chuckled as he said it, ran a hand over his stubbled chin again. "I'd better go home and shave and make a hash of carving a turkey."

They got up with him, then he spoke again.

"You'll be reinstated, of course. Your job, I mean."

"Thanks," Pelham said, "but I'll be getting a new one."

Jakes told him he could take his time about that. "You have about five thousand pounds coming to you."

"Me? How so?"

"They found what was left of the money Hoff stole, at the farmhouse. German banks traditionally pay a 10 percent finder's fee for money that's recovered, and you found it."

"Well, how about that?" Pelham said, smiling at Rossi. "Yes, Virginia, there is a Santa Claus."

Jakes held out his hand, told them he'd be in touch in a few days' time, then they watched him walk up the path toward Bayswater, a very tired man.

Pelham took Rossi's arm and they started strolling around the pond.

"Did you mean that?" Rossi asked. "About getting a new job?"

"Yep." Pelham paused for a moment, considered something. "Around three this morning I woke up and found it was home-truth time. I figured out a few of the mistakes I've been making lately, like for the past five years."

Rossi waited for him to go on.

"Firstly, I'm crazy to work for a boss. I should be my own boss. That way I wouldn't keep getting fired all the time."

"That makes sense. What kind of job did you have in mind?"

"A partnership. You and me. It'd be strictly business by day, strictly pleasure at night."

"Us? But what would we do?"

"At night? I'll show you after dinner."

"Seriously . . ."

Pelham shrugged. "I don't know. But we've got five thousand pounds to find out."

"But I don't know much about business, Jimmy."

"Business is basically people, and you're marvelous with people. Why do you think we did okay on this little number we've just been through?"

"Because you stuck to your guns, and you wouldn't quit," Rossi said.

Pelham waved that away. "That was just my stubborn streak. The real reason is because you stopped me from screwing up. I don't mean solving those map numbers or speaking the lingo, I'm talking about the way you finessed us into Uher's apartment. And Lauter's. And the way you handled cabdrivers and travel agents. If we'd had to depend on my usual gung ho approach we wouldn't have even got close to that site."

Rossi, turning aside the praise, said, "Let's get back to this new business of ours. It would be here in London?"

"Sure."

"But I didn't think you got on with the English."

Pelham scratched the bridge of his nose; he looked a bit sheepish. "That's something else I figured out. I always thought I didn't get on over here because the folks were still sore about the Boston

Tea Party. But maybe it's not my accent that upsets people, maybe it's that ol' debil approach again. I mean, in New York, I'm just average aggressive, but in London they think I'm being rude." Pelham lifted his arm, and let it drop to his side. "Hell, I've been trying to take on fifty million Englishmen single-handed. Instead of trying to lick 'em, maybe I should think about joining 'em."

He looked at Rossi for a reaction, and saw a touch of doubt in her face.

"You don't think I can do it, huh?" Pelham nodded at something ahead of them. "See that guy over there? That's a forty-year-old man playing with a toy boat. The old Jimmy Pelham would have said something smart to him like 'Watch out for submarines,' then wondered why the guy ignored him."

"And what would the new Jimmy Pelham say?" Rossi asked softly.

"Let's find out."

Pelham went up to the man who was bending down at the edge of the pond retrieving a large, beautifully made boat.

"Good morning," Pelham said. "That's a handsome-looking craft. Gaff-rigged yawl, isn't it?"

The man looked up. "Gaff-rigged ketch, actually. My father bought in in 1920. You like boats?"

"I used to have one when I was a . . . when I was younger. A Marconi-rigged sloop."

"Ah, yes," the man said. "They can look very pretty on a down-wind leg."

"What's her name?" Pelham asked.

"*Londinium.* It's the old Roman name for London. An old name for an old boat, if you see what I mean. Here," the man said, "take her for a spin."

Pelham found himself holding a ten-pound boat that was dripping water all over his shoes. "Hey, wait a minute. I don't—er—"

He caught sight of Rossi watching him; there was something like amused challenge in her look.

Pelham took a deep breath. "That's very kind of you. I hope I'm not too rusty."

He knelt, adjusted the rudder, placed the boat in the water, and pushed it off.

Straightaway the boat heeled alarmingly, its sails flapping and soaking up water. It flirted with disaster for a long, long moment, then a sudden cross breeze snapped it upright, the sails filled and billowed, and the boat skimmed majestically onward. Its owner sighed with relief. "Near thing. For a moment I thought *Londinium* was going under."

Pelham, watching the boat scoot across the pond, looked beyond it to the far bank, and the soft green stretch of the park, and the stately oaks in the distance.

"So did I," he said.